COME HELL

OR

HIGHBALL

Also by Maia Chance

FAIRY TALE FATAL MYSTERIES

Snow White Red-Handed
Cinderella Six Feet Under

COME HELL

OR

HIGHBALL

Maia Chance

MINOTAUR BOOKS

New York

COME HELL OR HIGHBALL. Copyright © 2015 by Maia Chance. All rights reserved. Printed in the United States of America. For information, address St. Martin's Press, 175 Fifth Avenue, New York, N.Y. 10010.

www.minotaurbooks.com

The Library of Congress Cataloging-in-Publication Data is available upon request.

ISBN 978-1-250-06787-6 (hardcover)
ISBN 978-1-4668-7654-5 (e-book)

Our books may be purchased in bulk for promotional, educational, or business use. Please contact your local bookseller or the Macmillan Corporate and Premium Sales Department at (800) 221-7945, extension 5442, or by e-mail at MacmillanSpecialMarkets@macmillan.com.

First Edition: September 2015

10 9 8 7 6 5 4 3 2 1

For Zach and Jennifer—
my biggest supporters through thick and thin

I've always loved high style in low company.

—ANITA LOOS

COME HELL

OR

HIGHBALL

1

....

May 30, 1923

I n all fairness, my husband was the one who *should've* been murdered.

Each of the mourners, huddled beneath dripping umbrellas around his open grave, must've itched to kill him at one point or another. That was the sort of fellow he'd been. Ginky. Insufferable. Yet it was only a heart attack that sent Alfred Woodby slinking over the Great Divide in his hand-stitched wing tips. It was someone else entirely who would get blipped off.

"Bastard," I mumbled, and pitched a clod of damp earth down onto Alfie's casket.

My cook, Berta Lundgren, stout and stern beside me in her black rubberized raincoat, clutched the locket at her throat. "Not yet, Mrs. Woodby," she whispered in her homey Swedish accent.

"Sorry," I mouthed.

All eyes were upon me, glaring out in silence from beneath trickling hat brims.

The ham-shaped priest on the far side of the grave made an *ahem* and resumed the burial rites. "Unto Almighty God we commend the soul of our brother departed, and we commit his body to the ground. Earth to earth—"

Chisholm Woodby, Alfie's younger brother, tossed the second chunk of soil onto the casket. *Thunk.* Chisholm's smooth-shaven jaw was clenched. He had the same dark, suave good looks Alfie had had. But whereas Alfie's eyes had glittered with misdemeanors real and imagined, Chisholm's face had the moral pinch of a world-class prig.

Still, Chisholm surely must've dreamt from time to time of popping off Alfie, heir to the Woodby millions.

"—ashes to ashes—"

Then there were Alfie's pals—those, anyway, who'd managed to peel themselves out of bed early enough to attend a ten o'clock funeral. These were for the most part dissipated playboys, inheritors of vast family fortunes and mosquito-like intellects. Fizzy Van Hoogenband, as a choice example, still wore last night's glad rags. His bow tie was unraveled, lipstick sullied his collar, and he had droops like a basset hound's under his eyes. Fizzy showered a handful of earth onto the casket. The cigarette that dangled from his lips fell into the grave, too.

Mightn't one of Alfie's gin-and-jazz-club cronies longed to whack him over cards, girls, or dinner reservations at Philippe's?

"—dust to dust."

Which brought me to the girls. Alfie had had many weaknesses. His heart, evidently. Cashmere socks. Anything gold and engraved. And chorus girls. A gaggle was in attendance at the burial. I studied them surreptitiously. Vampy, bob-haired damsels shivering in cheap dresses, legs bare. Lots of vermilion lipstick. Most of them were peroxide blondes, but one of them—short and compact like a tightrope walker, wearing black satin and a fox fur—had bordello-red waves under her cloche hat. For a second, her eyes met mine. Then her gaze darted back to the casket below.

Broadway was probably swarming with chorus girls who had yenned to throttle Alfie.

"Mrs. Woodby," Berta whispered in my ear, "stop twitching, for goodness' sake. Anyone would think you needed to visit the *powder room*." She straightened her hat, patted her gray bun, and trained her eyes back onto the droning priest.

I flattened my lips, simulating grief. Who would buy it? The thing was, I'd been nineteen, only a girl, when my parents thrust me into a union with Alfie. My marriage had been a stroke of fortune for Father's Wall Street endeavors and a windfall for Mother's social calendar. But Alfie had been a horror of a husband. I'd survived my marriage with an unholy combination of highballs, detective novels, and chocolate layer cake.

Really, anyone would think that *I* should've killed Alfie.

Now I was a thirty-one-year-old Society Matron with life unspooling like blank ticker tape before me, an apartment on Park Avenue, a rambling oceanfront mansion, and oodles of bucks I hadn't the foggiest how to start spending.

"Lord have mercy upon us," the priest finished. He drew a hankie from somewhere inside his vestments and swabbed his rainspattered forehead.

St. Percival's Cemetery in Hare's Hollow, New York, is a charming spot to push up the daisies. Acres of rolling green grass, antique headstones, and graceful old trees overlook the little town, with a vista of Long Island Sound beyond. That morning, however, a low gray sky churned. As soon as the burial ended, everyone hoofed it toward the long row of parked motorcars.

"Darling!" someone shrilled just as Berta and I set out for my own motorcar.

Phooey.

I turned. Olive Arbuckle, Society Queen Bee, sidled toward me. She wore an eel-black dropped-waist dress and a black taffeta rain-coat. Years of tennis, sailboating, golf, and dressage had whittled Olive's figure down to that of a dried herring. Her girthy husband, Horace, trundled behind, holding an umbrella over her.

"Lola, you *poor* darling." Olive smooched the air on either side of my hat. "Such a shock, a dreadful shock for us all."

"So awfully sorry for your loss, Lola," Horace said. His mountain-ous bulk was clothed in fine Italian wool, and a fedora hid his balding head.

Horace Arbuckle was a food industrialist. As a young man, he'd inherited his father's two-bit canned goods business and nurtured it into a whopping success. Everyone, of course, is familiar with his bestselling item, Auntie Arbuckle's Pork and Beans.

"How are you feeling?" Olive asked me. "Keeping up your strength?" Her eyes flicked to my ankles.

Okay, I admit it. I wasn't blessed by Nature with a flapper's phy-sique. Without high heels, it is at times difficult to distinguish ex-actly where my legs end and my feet begin. And these new cylindrical fashions are a bit of a challenge, since I carry somewhat more freight on my luggage rack (so to speak) than is fashionable, and my bust-line would have been better appreciated in Anna Karenina's day.

Nonetheless, I do adore beautiful things. I thought I cut quite the figure of a chic widow that morning: drapey black raincoat that but-toned over one hip, black hat with a neat little brim, black T-strap heels. My Dutch-bobbed hair was glossy brown, and I wore just enough face paint to flatter my dark blue eyes.

Nobody needed to know that egg yolk hair treatments, gallons of Pond's cream, and an industrial-grade girdle made it all possible.

"I'm fine," I said to Olive. "Truly."

"And I see you have your—your housemaid in attendance?"

"Cook, actually," I said.

Berta drew up all five feet one inch of herself in magisterial silence.

"My family could not arrive in time for the funeral," I said.

"What a pity."

Not really. "Yes," I said. "They set off from Rome just as soon as they heard the news. I believe they'll arrive home sometime tomorrow." Mother, Father, and my sister, Lillian, were at present hurtling across the Atlantic aboard a Cunard ocean liner, returning from a three-month-long European shopping excursion. "And my brother, Andrew, is in the thick of studying for his final exams at Yale, so I told him to stay absolutely chained to his desk, or Father would be cross." I actually suspected that little Andy—the rotten apple of Mother's eye—was carousing with his fraternity buddies.

"Ah, well, at least the hired help are there for you," Olive said.

"Berta is my rock."

In fact, Berta had demanded that I drive her to the funeral. Somehow, Berta always managed to get her way with me. Probably something to do with her cinnamon rolls. My butler, Hibbers, had offered to deliver Berta to the cemetery in the estate's Ford depot hack but Berta had refused, saying the depot hack smelled of underarm.

No other member of my staff had come to the cemetery, blaming headaches and sniffles and the need to prepare the funeral luncheon. Alfie had not been adored.

"Horace and I cannot, I'm afraid, go to luncheon at your place today," Olive said. "Some dreary business thing has come up, you know. But we wished to extend an invitation to you, for this weekend. It'll be a simply *scrummy* gathering. Quite small, intimate, really, but"—her eyes glittered—"Bruno Luciano will be there."

Horace sighed.

"Bruno Luciano?" I asked. "Do you mean the motion picture actor?"

"Yes!" Olive squealed.

I tried to picture Bruno Luciano—Byronic matinee idol, star of *All About Town* and *Casanova*—playing tennis doubles with Olive and Horace.

"I met the head of a great big new motion picture production company," Olive said. "Pantheon Pictures—have you heard of it? Their studio is in Flushing, Queens, quite in the middle of the industry. Well, Mr. Zucker, the company head, was at the Cliffords' country place last weekend. We simply hit it off."

"Latched on like a leech," Horace said.

Olive was undeterred. "Mr. Zucker's girlfriend, Sadie Street, is to be the next big star. She's got a contract to be Bruno Luciano's leading lady in three new pictures. Only, they've been having a bit of a tiff."

My eyes were glazing over. "Who's having a tiff?"

"Bruno Luciano," Olive said. "And the starlet. Sadie Street. So, I said to Mr. Zucker, why, my country place is a simply *brilliant* spot for them to have a sort of, I don't know, a sort of reconciliation."

"Goddam reporters already crawling around the place," Horace said.

Berta clutched her locket at Horace's *goddam*.

"But, darling," Olive said to him, "*we* haven't got any secrets. It's true." She turned back to me, eyes aglow. "Reporters absolutely everywhere, for the motion picture weeklies *and* the papers. They somehow got wind of the reconciliation at our place and are angling for photographs of Bruno."

"On a first name basis already," Horace muttered.

Beyond them, I saw someone dart behind a large tomb. I was pretty sure it was the red-haired chorus girl.

Was she eavesdropping?

"There will be other friends there, too, of course," Olive said. "The Wrights have telephoned to confirm, and so has Lem Fitzpatrick. I thought, Lola darling, that even though you're in mourning, you could do with a little company."

Company, my foot. Olive was inviting me so she could gloat about her motion picture guests. Society Matrons, if you're unfamiliar with the breed, groom and train to compete in matches more snappish and bitchy than those of the Westminster Kennel Club. I would know: I've attended dog shows *and* society luncheons.

"You're absolutely the elephant's elbow to invite me, Olive, but I'm afraid I simply couldn't." I watched the red-haired girl creep out from behind the tomb and totter toward the parked motorcars. I looked back to Olive. "I must spend some time reflecting." Reflecting, with a highball in one hand and a novel in the other. "And Hibbers said he'd help me sort through Alfie's things."

At the mention of Hibbers, Olive's expression went brittle.

Hibbers, my butler, made tiny, crustless chicken sandwiches worthy of a buffet table in Elysium. His opinions on drapery fabrics were infallible, and his cocktails were the bee's knees. To top all, he was British. Hibbers was the envy of every Society Matron from the Gold Coast to Grand Central Station. And he was all mine.

"You're certain you couldn't pop by?" Olive feigned sadness.

"Positively certain," I said. I bade Olive and Horace good-bye, and Berta and I made our escape.

"That Arbuckle woman is a demon," Berta huffed.

"Don't you think that's a bit extreme?"

"Well, her husband *is* well fed."

"That's in spite of Olive's efforts. Horace once confided to me, after two mint juleps and a sidecar, that she keeps everything in the kitchen but the carrots and celery under lock and key."

Berta *tsked* her tongue.

We trotted along toward my Duesenberg Model A, which I'd left under a dripping oak tree. The Duesy was cream colored, with cinnamon brown wheel wells and whitewall tires.

Sure, a Society Matron like me should, by rights, be chauffeured about in something longer, lower, and blacker. But I insist upon driving myself. Duesenbergs, you know, are wickedly fast. The motorcar salesman said that they can reach 106 miles per hour on the highway. I was sold.

Although I couldn't, back then, imagine why I'd ever need to drive like a bat out of hell.

Through the misting rain, I spied a small, orange, puffy form bouncing behind the steering wheel. Faint yipping sounds pierced the air.

"Poor little Cedric," I said, picking up the pace.

Berta shuddered.

When I got behind the steering wheel, Cedric, my Pomeranian, leapt onto my lap and licked my face.

"Did you miss me, peanut?" I cooed.

Cedric wiggled.

Some people find solace in philosophy or religion. Others find solace in mashed potatoes or a bottle of gin. I find solace in my dog's fluff. (All right—maybe I find a *pinch* of solace in tipply, trashy novels, and chocolate, too.)

Berta hoisted herself up onto the passenger seat and slammed the door. As usual, she and Cedric ignored each other.

I was just jamming my toe on the starter box when a figure moved into my peripheral vision.

2

....

"M rs. Woodby?" the figure called. She was several paces from my
motorcar, but I recognized her: the red-haired girl who'd
been creeping around behind the tomb.

I rolled the window down.

"You're Mrs. Woodby, ain't you?" The girl stopped a pace away
from my motorcar. Her fashionable yet cheaply made black cloche
hat came down so far over her eyes, she had to tilt her chin to
look at me. Large, luminous brown eyes lined in thick black.
Shiny Cupid's bow lips. Imitation-alligator handbag with a missing glass eye.

"Yes, I'm Lola Woodby."

"Awful sorry about your hubby, Mrs. Woodby."

"I beg your pardon," I said. "What is your name?"

"Miss Simpkin—Ruby Simpkin."

"What is it, Miss Simpkin? Conscience flaring up? Thought you'd
say a kind word to the missus to clear up your guilt? Believe me,
there's no need for that. Alfie went through girls like—"

"No," Ruby said, her voice flat. "Nothing like that. Alfie—I mean, Mr. Woodby, was . . . Well, I guess I did know him. Like you say. But I saw you didn't shed a single tear at the funeral." She looked me straight in the eye. "You're glad he's pooped, ain't you?"

My jaw fell open. I heard Berta gasp.

"Well, I never!" I said.

Ruby leaned in. "I ain't saying you chilled him off, but I bet you wanted to. He carried on with near every bird at the Frivolities. Tossed me over after only two months. Two! I know I ain't as young as some of the other girls, but I still got—"

"Miss Simpkin," I said. "I was fully aware of my husband's various . . . gentlemanly pastimes. So if that is all you wished to tell me, then—" I reached around Cedric to the steering wheel.

"No, it ain't. I wanted to ask you a—a sorta favor." She pressed her lips together. "I heard you, back there, talking with the Arbuckles."

"You *were* eavesdropping, then."

"I heard them inviting you to their country house and all that."

"I declined the invitation."

"Well, supposing you changed your mind."

I lifted my eyebrows.

Ruby crept closer. I caught a whiff of discount perfume. "This is real sticky and hush-hush, see, but I need something." She looked past me, at Berta. "Who's she?"

"My cook."

"Funny, a grande dame like you motoring your cook around."

Grande dame? "You may say anything you like in front of Berta. She has been with me for seven years." Seven years and twenty pounds. "Go ahead, Miss Simpkin."

"Well, it's like this, see. I need something. From the Arbuckles' country house." She fiddled with her handbag's clasp.

"You want me to—what? Steal from my friends? For one of my

husband's chorus girl mistresses?" I laughed aloud from the sheer out-
rageousness of it. "That's what the Frivolities are, right? A sequins-
and-feathers revue?"

"Yeah." Ruby's shoulders slumped.

"What was it you thought I'd nick for you?" I asked. "Jewelry? A
priceless oil painting?"

"It ain't nothing like that. It's something that—it's mine. And I
want it back." She jutted her chin. "I woulda paid you, you know."

"I am not presently in need of funds."

"Fine. Looks like I'll have to get it myself." She spun around and
crunched away down the gravel drive.

"Floozy," Berta said.

We watched until Ruby reached the one remaining motorcar in
the cemetery besides mine, a junky Model T with a sagging rear
fender. She bent in front of the bonnet and cranked the engine to a
chug before settling into the driver's seat.

Was I crazy to pity her?

The Model T rattled away through the cemetery gates.

"Dear old Alfie did know how to pick them," I said, and stomped
on the Duesy's starter box.

I lurched into gear, rolled out of the cemetery, and took the coastal
highway toward home. It was only a few miles from the cemetery,
through lush woodland and waterlogged meadows, which now and
then afforded glimpses of the misty gray sound. Along the way, we
passed many grand gatehouses, stone walls, and ornate iron gates
that marked entrances to the palatial estates along this, the sump-
tuous Gold Coast.

My own house, which Alfie had named Folie Maison, snuggled
back in the trees, only its four brick chimneys visible from the road.

I braked at the wrought iron gates, and the gatekeeper scurried out of the little brick and half-timber lodge. He gave me a salute. "Mrs. Woodby," he said. He jogged over to unlatch the gates. He wore a black armband. Very proper. He *also* wore a sickly little smile, and he kept glancing at me out of the corner of his eye.

"Mr. Blunt seems . . . jumpy," I said to Berta.

"Perhaps because he consumes nothing but tinned kippers and chicory."

As we waited for Mr. Blunt to drag the gates open, my eyes strayed to the ivy-draped pillar upon which one gate was hinged. I blinked.

"Amberley?" I said. "*Amberley?* Berta, what has happened to the sign?" I pointed. Where there had been a sign reading FOLIE MAISON in gilt, there was now a sign that read AMBERLEY in square black letters.

Berta's eyes widened. "Good gracious, I do not know, Mrs. Woodby. Someone has changed the sign. How very odd."

"It was changed today. This morning, while we were at the funeral. I would've noticed it, otherwise. I motored through the gates twice yesterday."

Berta met my eyes. We both knew who had changed the sign.

I set my mouth and zipped the Duesy through the gates. My thoughts were twirling as I roared up the lane. Several other motorcars were parked in the circular driveway, and still more by the carriage house.

I screeched to a stop.

"Calm yourself, Mrs. Woodby," Berta said.

"Calm?" I shouted.

Folie Maison was an enormous house—a mansion, really—built to look like a Tudor cottage: brick, with brown and white half-timbering on the top half, and loads of chimneys and mullioned windows and steeply gabled wings. Ivy crept up the foundation stones.

I stormed up the wide front steps, Cedric pattering at my heels.

Just as I reached for the iron handle, the huge front door swung inward.

"Hibbers!" I said, tearing off my hat.

"Madam." Hibbers, my butler, was tall and distinguished, with not a wrinkle on his dark suit, nor a single hair out of place on his graying head. He really spruced up a doorway.

"Who has changed the sign at the front gates?" I asked. "It was Chisholm, wasn't it?—Mr. Woodby, I mean to say. Where is he?"

I was about to toss my hat into Hibbers's usually welcoming hands, when I noticed that he held his *own* hat in one hand. And a suitcase in the other.

Uh-oh.

"I regret to inform you, madam," he said, "that I must give notice." He placed his bowler hat on his head and slid around me.

I followed him. "You're quitting? But I've treated you so well! Now that Alfie's gone, there won't be such a mess to clean up. No more mad parties, I promise, and—"

"That is precisely the trouble, madam." Hibbers placed his suitcase on the rack of his black Chrysler, which was parked in the driveway.

"What do you mean?"

He buckled the luggage rack's straps.

"Do you want a raise?" I said. The thought of life without Hibbers and his little sandwiches, his angelically shaken cocktails, made my throat ache.

Hibbers slid behind the steering wheel and slammed the door. "You do not fully comprehend, madam," he said out the window. "I shan't work for that insect."

"Insect?" I said. But I knew who he meant. "You don't work for Chisholm. You work for me! And where are you going?"

He started the engine. "Dune House."

"*What?*" Dune House was Horace and Olive Arbuckle's estate, three miles down the road.

"Mrs. Arbuckle has, many times in the past, extended me offers of employment. I have decided at last to accept, as their butler, Mr. Hisakawa, was quite abruptly dismissed recently. Good afternoon, madam."

He swung the Chrysler around the drive with a spurt of white gravel, and rumbled away down the tree-lined drive.

I stared, dumbfounded, until the chrome bumper disappeared from view. Raindrops smacked my face. All my relief—and even, I confess, glee—over my newly minted widowhood was shriveling.

The front door was open. Subdued voices and the scent of coffee drifted out. A cold luncheon had been planned for the funeral guests, and then Chisholm and I were to meet the lawyer in the library for the reading of Alfie's last will and testament.

But it was starting to look like Chisholm had already gotten a sneak peek at the will.

How I pined for one of Hibbers's highballs. And how I hankered to short-sheet Chisholm's bed.

I swooped Cedric into my arms. He nuzzled my cheek.

"It'll be all right, peanut," I whispered to him. "I hope."

The good news, it turned out, was that Alfie hadn't actually written a will, so everything went to me. The bad news was, there wasn't a nickel to inherit.

I perched in a green leather chair in Folie Maison's library, opposite the lawyer. He was a grayish little fellow with a nasal voice. The last of the funeral guests had trickled away after gorging themselves on smoked salmon sandwiches and Berta's miniature napoleons.

"Nothing," I repeated to the lawyer. "How could I be flat broke when Alfie was so wealthy?"

"Although your late husband was the elder of the two Woodby children," the lawyer said, "your mother-in-law, Rose, controls most of the family fortune."

Rose was a tyrannical invalid who lived in secluded splendor in Palm Beach, Florida. She was far too delicate to have traveled up for Alfie's funeral. Besides, she'd never cared much for Alfie. She doted on Chisholm—who at that moment lurked near the fireplace.

"Father had the foresight to tie up Alfred's inheritance in trust before he went to his reward fifteen years ago," Chisholm said. "It was doled out to Alfred as a monthly allowance."

Like dog treats. It made perfect sense. Still, this was all news to me.

"Your late husband was . . . indiscriminate in his spending habits," the lawyer said. "Were you aware that he owned three yachts? Six racehorses?"

Chisholm emitted a desiccated chuckle. "Alfred's entire life was indiscriminate from start to finish, I'm afraid."

"Fine," I said, "then I'll sell the yachts and racehorses and everything else, and put the money in the bank. Duck soup."

The lawyer shook his head. "Selling off your late husband's assets will not even cover the tip of the iceberg in terms of his debts. There is a veritable legion of creditors clamoring for settlements. Tailors, decorators, motorcar dealers, costly restaurants, auction houses, hotels—even the casino in Monte Carlo has sent a rather nasty letter. There are also several substantial loans against his trust fund, which he took on to free up more cash. He was spending hugely beyond his income."

"Like sand through an hourglass," Chisholm said.

"Pity you didn't sign up to be a preacher," I said to him. I was parched, so I crossed the library to the cabinet where Alfie had kept a stash of booze.

"If only," Chisholm went on, "dear Alfred had had a moral compass to guide him across this vast wasteland we call Life, with which to—"

I opened the liquor cabinet. It was empty. I swung around. "You," I said, pointing a finger at Chisholm. "Where did you put the gin?"

"Down the bathtub drain from whence it came."

Chisholm belonged to the Gentlemen's Temperance Society, the Booze Is Bilge Club, and the Association of Medical Physicians Opposed to Tippling. Although he was the chief nerve specialist at Babbling Brook Hospital, I knew he had ambitions to enter politics. In short, his zeal for the Eighteenth Amendment was both sanctimonious *and* strategic.

"I am afraid, dear Lola," Chisholm said, "that I must ask you to vacate Amberley."

"Amberley?" I stomped my T-strap shoe on the carpet. "When did my house become Amberley? Sounds like one of your loony bins!"

"And it certainly is beginning to seem like one, dearest Lola," Chisholm said.

"Your husband, Mrs. Woodby, never owned this house," the lawyer said. "You merely occupied it. It has always belonged to Rose Woodby. And she has telephoned from Florida to say that, as you failed to produce an heir, she wishes for you to vacate the house and turn it over to Chisholm."

"What? Are we trapped inside a Jane Austen novel? This is America! Younger brothers can't pull out the rug from under wives like that!"

"They can, and do," the lawyer said.

"And about the heir," I said, "if you need one, Alfie probably has *dozens* of little heirs crawling around backstage on Forty-second Street."

"Get a handle on yourself, Lola," Chisholm said. "I would allow you to stay on, of course, but there is the problem of your immoral lifestyle. I have my reputation to think of, my career, and a single, indecent female under my roof—"

"Indecent?" I balled my fists. "Immoral? Your brother was the indecent, immoral one, not I!"

"I'll be acquiring a wife soon, and she shall produce offspring in time. Now, I *had* considered allowing you to stay on here—"

"What, as some kind of poor relation?"

"—but your habits are reprehensible. In fact, some of them are illegal."

"Everyone we know drinks."

"Everyone *you* know, perhaps. Then there are the lurid dime novels. I've seen them scattered on every surface. The covers alone!" He made a mock shiver.

"Some of that is real literature," I said. "Sherlock Holmes. He's *British*."

"So was Jack the Ripper. I am sorry, Lola, but I must ask you to pack your bags and leave. And *don't* take my mother's jewelry with you."

I faced the lawyer. "Could I stay at our Park Avenue place?"

"I'm afraid that the apartment and its contents must be sold immediately to settle the bulk of the debts," he said. "I understand repossession agents will enter the premises tomorrow."

"Your parents will be overjoyed to have you back home," Chisholm said.

I shot him a molten-lava glance.

Then, my memory jiggled and spit something out, like a gumball machine.

Of course. The key.

I looked back to the lawyer. "Are there any . . . any other places I might live?"

"You must know, Mrs. Woodby, that there are no other real estate holdings."

That's what *he* thought.

"Of course there aren't," I said.

3

I left Chisholm and the lawyer in the library and walked up Folie
Maison's—pardon me, *Amberley's*—grand staircase. From down
below came the sounds of the maids clearing away luncheon in the
dining room. By the time I reached the top of the stairs, Cedric had
appeared. Doubtless from either the kitchen or the dining room,
since he was diligent about helping the maids clean morsels from
floors.

We walked through corridors lined with polished wainscoting,
Persian runners, and British landscapes in gold-encrusted frames. All
of it belonged to Chisholm now.

"It's enough to make you lose your luncheon," I muttered to
Cedric.

We slipped through a door into Alfie's bedroom.

Alfie's bedroom adjoined mine, but the door between our rooms
had been shut—in every possible sense—for many years. The
room had been tidied, but it still smelled of debauchery: spicy co-
logne, Turkish cigarettes, smuggled brandy, and the scent of other

ladies' foundation powder. And since there had been, since Cedric's earliest puppyhood, bad blood between Alfie and Cedric, Alfie's furniture exhibited tiny teeth marks, and tiny shreds in the satin upholstery. There was more than one suspicious stain on the carpet.

I went to Alfie's mahogany highboy. I knew he'd kept important odds and ends in the top drawer. For instance, it was there that I'd discovered the first chorus girl's address, written in foolish, looped script on the back of Alfie's own calling card. That had been three months after our honeymoon.

Today, however, I was searching for something a tad more useful. I slid open the drawer, scanned the contents, and sighed in relief: there, amid cuff links, extra buttons, betting cards, and loose cigarettes, was a smallish brass door key.

I snatched it and hurried through to my own bedroom.

My bedroom was done up with yellow rose-blossom curtains, plush carpeting, and a matched set of English-style rosewood furniture. The latticed windows had a view of the sea, but my favorite spot was the sofa by the fireplace, where I had loved to read.

I smeared hot, furious tears across my cheeks. I could rough it for a spell. *I'd* grown up in Scragg Springs, Indiana, by golly, and Father hadn't always been rolling in greenbacks. Cedric, on the other hand, was used to the finer things in life. In fact, he insisted upon them.

I had an all-too-lucid vision of Chisholm tightening my straitjacket as I tried to explain to him Cedric's plight.

I refurbished my tear-blotched makeup in my vanity mirror. Then I started packing.

Ten minutes later, I was loaded down with two suitcases, three hatboxes, and a handbag. Cedric and I took the servants' staircase; I had no intention of bidding a formal adieu to the Prig.

I'd almost made it outside when Berta intercepted me.

"Mrs. Woodby, there you are," she said. "Might I have a word?" Her request was uttered in the most dignified old-world style, but she'd blocked my path to the door. She wore a floral shirtdress, but no apron.

Alarm bells jangled in my head.

"I'm in a bit of a hurry, Berta." I set down the luggage. "I guess you haven't heard. Chisholm is now the master of this household. I've been given the bum's rush."

Berta sniffed. "I have been informed of the turn of events, yes, but I shall not work for him. He wishes only health bread to eat in the mornings. Health bread does not have any *yeast* in it." She shook her head. "He wants no strudel, no biscuits, no pies. Nothing with butter or cream—"

"I know, I know," I said, wincing. Chisholm was not content to deprive himself in the beverage department; he adhered to abstemious eating habits, too.

"I gave him my notice."

"Good thinking." I started buttoning my coat. "You were always a wonderful cook, Berta." Maybe a little *too* wonderful—my coat buttons were straining at their threads. "Thank you. If I can write a reference for you, please telephone my mother. She will hunt me down eventually, I'm sure."

"I shall continue to work for you."

"I wish you could, Berta, but the problem is, I'm on the nut." I picked up my suitcases.

"'Nut,' Mrs. Woodby?"

"I'm broke."

"But surely you will not do for yourself. A lady of your position?" Berta clucked her tongue. "Do you even know how to boil an egg?"

"I'm not sure *what* my position is anymore." I really needed to stop feeling sorry for myself. That would lead to tears, and I couldn't foot the mascara bills.

"You will stay with your mother and father? Perhaps they need a new cook?"

"Stay with my family?" *That* notion was more hellish than health bread. "No!"

Berta seemed to loom over me, though she was over sixty years old and possessed the approximate dimensions of a garden gnome. "You owe me three months' pay. Mr. Woodby was not current with our salaries."

I gulped. "I didn't know. I'll do my best to—"

"I shall not work for Chisholm Woodby. I shall go with you, wherever you are going, and you shall employ me." Berta's mild round face went stony. "Or else pay me now."

"Very well." I sighed. "I'll just wait in my motorcar while you pack your—"

"No need." Berta produced her dumpy Edwardian hat and squashed it atop her bun. She picked up a shabby little suitcase and her raincoat that I hadn't noticed in the shadows of the hallway. "I already packed."

It was still drizzling when we motored across the Williamsburg Bridge and into the shining-wet glitter of Manhattan. My spirits were dwindling, and I was developing a charley horse in my gas-pedal foot. Cedric was snoozing on top of Berta's suitcase behind me. Berta had snored through the entire forty-mile trip, mouth wide, head thrown back.

When a taxicab driver honked at me for cutting him off, Berta snorted abruptly awake. "Where are we going?" She glared out the window. "This is not near your parents' apartment."

"We're not going to my parents' apartment—something I would've told you had you not fallen asleep in two seconds flat. We're going to Alfie's, um—" I licked my lips. "—love nest."

Berta fumbled for her locket.

I maneuvered around a snail-slow Buick. "Surely you aren't surprised. This is Alfie we're speaking of."

"I chose to ignore Mr. Woodby's shortcomings."

"So did I. But ignoring only works to a point." Tears bubbled up in my eyes. Oh, rats. What had become of me? All those years, stacked up behind me. Miserable, wasted years. And now . . . now what?

"Pardon me for asking, Mrs. Woodby, but . . . why did you stay?"

I thumped my fist on the car horn. "Did you see that? That pill in the Buick almost dinged me!"

"You knew Mr. Woodby had a love nest, for goodness' sake."

I snuffled back my tears. "I found out the address three years ago, quite unexpectedly, when there was a mix-up with our Wright's Department Store delivery. My standing order of jams and things had been replaced with a hamper full of chocolate caramels, beluga caviar, gumdrops, and Beech-Nut chewing gum. Chewing gum!"

Berta clucked.

"When I telephoned the store to complain," I said, "I learned that Alfie had an apartment in Washington Square. Nine Longfellow Street, apartment B." The address had lodged in my memory like a splinter.

"The scoundrel!" Berta said. "If, of course, you do not mind me saying so."

"Be my guest."

That discovery had been nine years into my joke of a marriage. I don't think I'd even been stung. Merely relieved, because a love nest meant that Alfie wouldn't take girls to our Park Avenue place. Later, when looking for an extra button in Alfie's highboy, I'd noticed the key. But I'd never actually been to the love nest. Not yet.

....

I found Longfellow Street. Quiet, narrow, lots of leafy trees, brown-stones all in rows. Respectable, but not Park Avenue.

Berta scowled. "Washington Square is where the bohemians live." She pronounced *bohemians* the same way one might say *plague of locusts*.

I motored slowly along, squinting up at the house numbers, until I spotted 9.

I parked the Duesy at the curb. We loaded our arms with luggage and trudged inside and up a dim, creaking stair. We stopped outside the door marked B.

A slice of yellow light shone beneath it.

"Alfie must've left the light on the last time he was here." Dandy. Another bill I wouldn't be able to pay.

I fished the key from my handbag, and Berta, Cedric, and I bundled through into a tiny foyer.

Cedric growled.

I stared through into what appeared to be the sitting room.

A man stared back.

He was bent over a side table. It looked like he'd been in the middle of rifling through a stack of newspapers and magazines.

My scream lodged in my throat. Luckily, Berta wasn't having the same kind of trouble. She let rip a bloodcurdler. Cedric bounced and yapped.

"Ahhh!" Berta screamed. "Police! Help! Police!"

The man straightened. He wore a dark rumpled suit and a gray fedora. His eyes were shaded by his hat brim, but I saw a firm chin and a sheen of gold-red stubble. "What do you think the police'll do?" he said. "You're breaking and entering. And would you make that dog shut up?"

I picked up Cedric and stepped in front of Berta. "Who the

heck are you? And I'm not breaking and entering. I—I own this place."

"Huh," he said. "Own it. Don't you mean rent? I found a copy of the lease under a sofa cushion."

"Right," I said. "Rent. I rent it."

"And you live here?" He swept a hand around the sitting room.

Only then did I take in the low-slung, white velvet furniture. The cream-and-black striped wallpaper. The taxidermied zebra head mounted on the wall. The several reprehensibly executed female nudes in gilt frames. The furry white rug—polar bear?—on the hearth.

"Interesting taste in decoration," the man said.

I had no business noticing him. His tallness, his bright agate-gray eyes, those farmhand's shoulders. I was a widow of less than a week, for Pete's sake. But his fedora was tilted down at an intriguing angle, and he had an Irish gangster's swagger. If a lady *didn't* notice him, she needed to schedule a trip to the eye doctor.

He quirked his lips. "Also kind of interesting that there aren't any ladies' clothes in the bedroom. Well, except for a few unmentionables that I'm not so sure are yours." His eyes slid down my frame. "They were kinda small."

I gritted my teeth. "I have, Mr.—"

"Oliver. Ralph Oliver."

"I have, Mr. Oliver, a good mind to smack you with my handbag, but seeing as it's genuine Florentine leather, I think it's rather too good for you."

Berta piped up. "I could smack him with my handbag, Mrs. Woodby. It is very durable."

"*Shush*," I whispered.

Ralph chuckled. "It wasn't an insult, Mrs. Woodby—"

"How do you know who I am?"

"—since not every fellow likes to cuddle up to broomsticks." He was looking at my hips again. "Some of us like a girl with a little volume."

I almost threw a hatbox at him. At the same time, I had a vision of him sweeping me into his arms—I'd glimpsed taut muscles under that rumpled suit. "What, precisely, are you doing in my husband's apartment, Mr. Oliver? It appears that you're searching for something. Looking for recompense for a debt, perhaps?"

"What do you mean? Woodby was low on sugar?"

"Don't pretend you don't know how my husband left me in the lurch." Phooey. I was tearing up.

Ralph shoved his hands in his trouser pockets. Why does weeping make men so nervy?

"Okay, okay. I'm a private detective," he said, and sighed.

"Like in a dime novel?"

"Sure. Like in a dime novel. Just looking into a small matter concerning your late husband."

"What kind of matter?"

"Not at liberty to say."

"Are there more debts? Wait, it's a kid, isn't it? No, wait—a long-lost nephew!"

"Nothing like that, Mrs. Woodby. And stop crying, all right?" He sauntered toward us, reaching inside his jacket.

"Gun!" Berta shrieked. "He's got a gun!"

Ralph held up his hands. "No gun. See? Only my card." He passed it to me, and then dodged around us to the front door.

"I saw a gun in there," Berta grumbled.

The door slammed. Ralph was gone.

I stared down at the card.

RALPH OLIVER

PRIVATE INVESTIGATOR

7 PLINY STREET, SECOND FLOOR

Berta stared at the card, too. "Mr. Woodby was in some sort of trouble," she said. "Why else would a private detective be here?"

"Alfie was always in some kind of trouble," I said. "Do you think there's any whiskey and ginger ale in this apartment?"

4

....

I woke the next morning facedown on Alfie's white velvet sofa. I was fully clothed, and my tongue felt *and* tasted like a delicatessen pickle.

But a heavenly scent drifted on the air, an olfactory Hallelujah Chorus of cinnamon, butter, and yeast dough.

I sat up. The left side of my bob clung to my cheek, and the other side flipped out. My eyes were scratchy from failing to remove my makeup last night, after two and a half gin and tonics in the kitchen. (There had been no whiskey or ginger ale in sight.) And Cedric was prancing around in the foyer, an urgent look in his eyes.

I almost called out, "Hibbers!" Then everything came flooding back.

I shrugged into Alfie's Burberry trench coat, pulled on some oversized galoshes, leashed Cedric, and clumped downstairs and out into the sparkling spring morning. Once Cedric was finished, we went back up to the kitchen.

The love nest's kitchen was a cramped, yellow-tiled space with white cupboards and drawers from floor to ceiling. An enamel cookstove-oven combination, a zinc sink, and a table took up most of the floor. Two windows overlooked a brick wall. A wood-encased radio sat on the windowsill. Berta had placed a bowl of water on the floor for Cedric. Cedric found it, and lapped. Droplets went flying.

Berta was pulling a tray of cinnamon rolls out of the oven. She saw my hair and face, and assumed a quietly appalled expression.

"Did you enjoy sleeping in a *real* bed?" I asked.

"No, not especially. I had no choice but to remove all of the bedding. Luckily, I had packed a small quilt in my suitcase."

I pictured her suitcase. How had she fit a quilt in there?

"That bedroom is outfitted like the fifth tier of hell," Berta said. "Mirrors on every surface. All that black satin." She shuddered. "And the lavatory is still worse. What sort of person would place a mirrored drinks cabinet by the bathtub?"

"That *could* come in handy. Is there any coffee?"

"In the percolator." Berta transferred rolls onto plates.

I found two coffee cups. True, they were painted with a Byzantine design of reclining nudes. But they'd do. "Did you go to the market this morning?" I asked, pouring coffee.

"Do you think Mr. Woodby kept flour and sugar in this den of sin?"

Berta's hair was braided into the Swedish bun she always wore. She wore a clean, pressed dress, too. How had she found time to iron a dress?

I passed her a coffee cup, being careful to turn the Byzantine design away.

She sat. "You do not serve me, Mrs. Woodby. I serve you."

"Seeing as I owe you three months' worth of wages and I have no idea how I'm going to pay for anything ever again, *I* ought to be serving *you*, Berta. And since I'm no longer your employer, please, call me Lola. We're equals."

"Hmph." Berta sipped coffee. "A Society Matron like you, without money?"

"Don't call me that." I sank into a chair.

"Why, it is like a chicken without its feathers."

"You mean I'm, what? Cold? Plucked?"

"Pathetic."

I stuffed a piece of cinnamon roll into my mouth. Maybe Berta was right. Here I was, holed up in my deceased spouse's lair of iniquity, smothering my anxiety with baked goods. No house, no money; I probably needed a plan. Because if I didn't figure out how to pull myself up by my bootstraps soon, I'd be living in my parents' house and having daily tea parties with whole flocks of Society Hens.

I swallowed. "I wasn't always, you know—"

"Wealthy?"

"Right. I grew up in a little town in the Middle West. It had only one paved street, running down the middle. The rest were dirt. I lived there until I was seventeen, which was when my family moved to New York and my father started working on Wall Street."

In 1910, the Duffys of Scragg Springs, Indiana, had become the DuFeys of New York, New York. My parents, Eula and Virgil, keep this fact hidden like a contagious rash. Along with the embarrassing details of Father's patent farm machinery dealings.

"If you were not always wealthy, then you might not be opposed to finding employment," Berta said.

"Well, yes. Once I think of what I'm cut out for."

"Did you attend school?"

"Public school in Scragg Springs, and then for one whole year here in New York I attended Miss Cotton's Academy for Young Ladies."

"Ah. Finishing school. Then you might teach piano or singing, or watercolor painting. Or flower arrangements."

"I wasn't really a . . . gold-star pupil at Miss Cotton's." I had almost been expelled. Twice. Once for sneaking a cigarette with my friend Daisy outside the servants' entrance, and once for shortening my hemline three inches. That, of course, was back when the distinction between my legs and ankles was crystal clear. "Music wasn't really my—"

"Tin ear, yes. I thought so."

"Wait a minute."

"No need to be ashamed."

Berta was taking this Equals thing and running with it. "I could make a pretty penny if I wanted to, you know."

"Oh?" Berta served herself another cinnamon roll. "I hope that you do not mean to become a lady of the night? You are too old for—"

"No!"

"What about the offer for employment you received yesterday?"

"What offer?"

"From Miss Simpkin. The red-haired harlot in the cemetery."

"Are you crazy, Berta? I can't steal from my friends!"

"She said she would pay you. Beggars cannot be choosers."

"Wait." I narrowed my eyes. "You want me to do the—the job for Ruby Simpkin so I can pay you your back wages. Is that it?"

"Of course. And so we can eat. And—" Berta looked around the kitchen. "—purchase some proper kitchen equipment."

"Kitchen equipment? What about clothes?" What about whiskey and ginger ale?

Berta sniffed. "There would be nothing improper about setting up a small, discreet business of . . . retrieving things."

I snorted. "A discreet retrieval agency?"

"Yes. My uncle Sven, in Sweden, he used such an agency once to find his missing bride."

"Did he find her?"

"Indeed, snug in the bed of his groomsman. Poor Uncle Sven

always smelled of fish—he was a fishmonger. The girl could not bear it. The important point is, although the bride refused to go home, Uncle Sven still had to pay the finding agent."

"Sounds like a detective agency to me."

"You would make a fine detective, Mrs. Woodby."

"Who, me?"

"I have noticed you are equipped with an especially fine eye for detail, as well as a cynical view of mankind."

Was that a compliment?

There was a thud on the front door. Berta and I both jumped. My coffee sloshed, and Berta dropped a piece of cinnamon roll on the floor. We stared at each other.

Another thud. Then, a key—*scritch, scritch*—in the latch.

Cedric was too busy eating fallen cinnamon roll to bark.

"That's *it*!" I jumped up. "If it's that rotten Irish detective again, why, I'll sock him one."

But it wasn't Ralph Oliver. It was a small natty fellow with a Charlie Chaplin mustache and surly lips.

"Who in Sam Hill are *you*?" His beady eyes flicked from my hurricane hair to my maraschino toenails.

I drew myself up. "I might ask the same of you. How did you find yourself in possession of a key to my abode?"

"Lady, I don't know what language you're speaking, but I own this joint. I'm the landlord, and Woodby ain't paid up in two months."

I deflated. "Landlord?"

"That's right. You one of Woodby's hotsy-totsy girls, huh?"

"I am his wife."

"Yeah, that's what they all say." He craned his neck. "Who's the pudgy dame?"

I turned. Berta loitered in the hallway that led to the kitchen. "My cook. But she doesn't speak English." I shot Berta a significant look.

"I don't know what's going on here," the landlord said, "and trust me, I don't even wanna know. Tell Woodby he's gotta pay up by next Friday, or I'm taking all his junk and throwing it in the street, and then I'm changing the locks. Ya follow?"

"Quite."

He scuttled off.

I turned to Berta.

"Discreet retrieval agency?" she said.

I rubbed my temples. "Just this once."

The Frivolities was a wildly popular revue that had been running for three years straight, seven days a week in the Unicorn Theater on Forty-second Street. I'd never been myself, since if I want to look at a scantily clad lady, all I need to do is take a gander in the bathroom mirror.

Driving in New York City is a recipe for a bad mood, so Berta and I took a taxi to the Unicorn at nine thirty that evening, well after the show had started. We found the stage door in a side alley.

Berta eyed the rubbish bins and prowling cats and clutched her handbag to her bosom.

I had a sort of creepy-crawly feeling myself. But nobody else was around, except the cats.

I tried the stage door. Locked. So I did what any dime-novel gumshoe would do, and rapped out "Shave and a Haircut." The door squeaked open. After bribing the weedy doorman—he seemed to take us for outraged wives come to wreak revenge on offending chorus girls—Berta and I made it inside.

"How much did you bribe him with?" Berta whispered.

"Five dollars."

"Five! These are business expenses, Mrs. Woodby."

"Lola," I corrected.

"You must learn to be more moderate."

Why was Berta speaking as though we were in this for the long haul?

Backstage was stuffy, and it reeked of smoke and greasepaint. Leggy girls costumed as feathery birds, angels, top hats, and Egyptians buzzed around.

Berta cheeped into her palm.

"It's all right," I whispered. "They're only doing their jobs."

"Their jobs? In Sweden, a young girl would be cast off forever if she wore such things."

"Are you sure you're from Sweden, and not the Middle Ages?"

A blonde in a silvery costume darted by.

"Excuse me," I said to her.

She stopped. "Yeah?" She snapped chewing gum and eyeballed my matronly black suit.

"Could you tell me where I might find Ruby Simpkin?"

"Whatcha want her for? You ain't that lady who said Ruby tricked her son into promising to—?"

"What? No. I—she asked me to meet her."

The blonde jerked a thumb down the corridor. "Number three."

Dressing room number three looked like it had been bombed. Chorus girls dashed to and fro, getting ready, by the looks of it, for a number in which they were sequined ducks. Sparkly costumes were flung over chairs and exploded from garment racks. Makeup counters were framed by hot yellow lightbulbs. The counters were strewn with lipsticks, powder puffs, eyebrow pencils, coffee cups, magazines, and brimming ashtrays.

I spotted a red head of hair at one of the makeup counters. We picked our way over.

Ruby was applying lollipop-red lipstick. She lifted her eyes to meet mine in the mirror. "Oh," she said. She screwed the lipstick down and popped its cap on. "You came. Both of you."

"Miss Simpkin," I said, "I—we, actually—have decided to take you up on your offer about the, um—"

"Hold on a minute," Ruby said. "I'm not in the next number, so wait'll the rest of the girls clear out."

A man yelled out in the corridor, " 'It's a Ducky-Duck World'! Places, girls, 'It's a Ducky-Duck World'!" All the chorus girls except Ruby stampeded out of the dressing room, leaving us alone.

"It's my hair," Ruby said. "Sam—he's the director—says it clashes with those lousy duck costumes." She wore a jester's costume, with a purple-and-yellow harlequin bodice, and purple high heels. "So. Changed your mind about my offer, huh?"

"Well, yes. I—"

"Let us first discuss the fee," Berta interrupted.

"Sure," Ruby said. "Three thousand smackers."

I blinked. "Three thousand—?"

"Clams. Bucks."

"Does she speak of dollars?" Berta whispered to me.

Ruby smirked. "That's right." She found a packet of Luckies and a lighter on the counter, and lit up. "Nothing up front. Find the item, then I'll pay."

"Deal," I said.

"Alfie leave you broke?"

"None of your business," I snapped. "Tell me what it is you want from the Arbuckles' country house."

When Ruby put the cigarette to her lips, her hand shook. She inhaled, and blew a long stream of smoke.

Berta wrinkled her nose and waved her hand in front of her face.

"It's a reel of film," Ruby said.

"Motion picture film?" I asked.

"Yeah."

"I don't even know what that looks like."

"Sorta like a big, flat metal spool of thread. Should be in a round case, a canister, you know, with a lid. To protect it."

"Why do the Arbuckles have a film reel?"

"Never mind why. Just get it back."

"Fine. What color is it?"

"Metal color, silly. Silver, I guess you'd say. It'll have a stamp on it, though. One of them little French flowery thingums you see on soaps in fancy hotels."

"A fleur-de-lis?"

"Guess so."

"What does it signify?"

"Signa-what?"

"The mark—what does it mean?"

Ruby puckered her lips, took another long drag. "Don't know," she finally said.

Liar.

"It's in Horace Arbuckle's safe," she said. "In his study. Just get it."

A film. A chorus girl. A filthy-rich fellow. My expression must've been knowing. I'd heard about what naughtiness the French put on film. Berta must've heard, too; her body seemed to vibrate.

"It ain't what you think," Ruby said.

I glanced over my shoulder to the dressing room doorway. It was empty. But if somebody were to overhear . . .

"I need the film back for career reasons," Ruby said. "I wanna be a motion picture star, see. I've been told I could make it big. But that film reel—oh, golly, that film, if the wrong people see it, would ruin my chances. It'll date me, see. They only want really young girls for the pictures, and I think you'll understand, Mrs. Woodby, when I say that—between the two of us—I've shaved off a year here and a year there."

"Why would I understand? I'm only thirty-one."

"Sure," Ruby said. "Maybe get yourself some new clothes, then. My grandma would think that suit you're wearing is real swell."

I sucked in a shaky breath.

Berta intervened. "Perhaps, Miss Simpkin, you are not proud of the content of the film?"

"Not really."

Berta sniffed. "I knew it. Lewdness."

"You got it all wrong, lady. It's simply bad . . . bad acting. I've taken acting classes since then, see."

"I *do* need to know why Horace Arbuckle has the film," I said.

"Why?"

"Because I need to know if I'm doing something morally reprehensible. Or illegal."

"The film is mine," Ruby said. "You won't be glomming it. You'll be restoring it to its—what do they say?—oh yeah, to its rightful owner. Arbuckle only has it because your bastard husband stole it from *me*."

"Alfie?"

"I knew he was broke. Well, I figured it out, anyway, once he stole that film from me a couple weeks ago, so as to sell it off to Horace. Alfie's the one who told me it's in Horace's safe."

"Alfie *sold* it to Horace?"

"That's right." Ruby, somewhere beneath her layers of Max Factor, was blushing.

I sighed. "I apologize on behalf of my husband." Being married to Alfie had been like owning the dog who soiled the neighbor's lawn: a life of contrition by proxy. "And Horace wanted to buy the film because—?"

"I said never mind what's on the film! Just get it for me, okay?" Tears pooled in Ruby's eyes, threatening a mudslide. "Get it before it's too late."

5

Berta and I made a beeline down the corridor, toward the Unicorn Theater's stage door exit.

"Piece of cake," I said. "Get the film reel, get out, and collect three thousand bucks. Think of what we could do with that money!"

"Are you not curious as to why a chorus girl is in possession of such a large sum?" Berta asked.

"Not really. Probably pawned off some diamonds from another lady's husband." I was only pretending to be glib; I knew that three thousand dollars was a fortune for the likes of Ruby. She had to be desperate.

"And Miss Simpkin was lying about why she wants the film," Berta said. "Does *that* not concern you?"

"How do you know she's lying?"

"First she said that the film would date her. Then she said that the problem was her poor acting on the film. She contradicted herself."

"Oh. Thanks, Dr. Watson."

"*Dr. Watson?*"

"From the Sherlock Holm—"

"I know quite well where it is from. But what makes *you* Sherlock and *me* Watson?"

We dodged around a man carrying a trumpet.

"Perhaps," Berta said, "there will be danger involved in this—how do the gangsters say?—*heist*."

"Why do you sound so gleeful about the prospect? Listen, it was your idea to take this job."

"How will you get into the safe?"

"Easy. I'll use my feminine wiles."

"Oh dear."

We rounded a corner and passed into a lounge area—I vaguely recalled the term *green room*—that swarmed with chorus girls and swirled with cigarette smoke. Through the haze, a pair of keen gray eyes was looking straight at me.

I stopped in my tracks, so abruptly that Berta crashed into me.

"Hi there, Mrs. Woodby," Ralph Oliver called. He slouched in a dumpy armchair, fedora pushed back to reveal thick, ginger-colored hair. A chorus girl perched on either arm of his chair. One had him by the lapel, and the other toyed with his hat brim.

Despite Ralph's armchair décor, however, he grinned at *me*, and in a way that made me unsure whether I'd rather kick his shins or unbutton his shirt.

I narrowed my eyes. "What are you doing here?"

"Could ask you the same thing."

"I believed you were investigating my husband."

"Looks like you're doing some investigating of your own."

"Don't you ever give a straight answer?"

"Not if I can help it."

"Come on," I said to Berta through clenched teeth. "We're going."

It wasn't until we were in a taxicab, trundling toward Washington Square, that it hit me: Mr. Oliver must've followed us to the theater.

Was he investigating *me*?

The next day was Friday. I awoke on the white velvet sofa with a crick in my neck.

Right after walking Cedric and eating breakfast—Berta had made apple strudel, scrambled eggs, and fresh-squeezed grapefruit juice—I telephoned Olive Arbuckle at Dune House.

"Oh, hello, darling," she said, "how are you feeling? Lonely?"

Actually, I felt reasonably spiff and spry. But I affected a mopey voice. "I was wondering if I might take you up on your offer to come up for the weekend, after all."

A pause. Then, "Of course!"

"Wonderful," I said. "I'm in the city now, but I'll motor up and be there in time for cocktails." I thought of Berta. The discreet retrieval agency *had* been her idea. She was going to have to come, too. "And Olive, darling," I said, "I'll have my maid with me."

"Your maid? Do you mean Penny?"

Penny *had* been my maid. Now she worked for Chisholm, poor thing. "No, no," I said. "Berta."

"I thought Berta was your cook. She was at the funeral, too. Does she go *everywhere* with you?"

"Toodle-oo!" I made a smoochy noise and cut the connection.

The afternoon turned out to be splendid for motoring, balmy and bright. Berta and Cedric napped the entire drive, leaving me alone with my thoughts. I whipped down the highway, spinning plans about the new life I could start with fifteen hundred dollars—Berta and I had agreed on a 50–50 split. I could take a secretarial course—wait. Too much sitting. I had my hips to consider. What about learning how to be a librarian? Nix that; I look terrible in cardigans.

By the time we rumbled through Hare's Hollow, the sunlight had gone golden, the shadows long.

The Foghorn, a rambling inn on Main Street, was more lively than usual. Motorcars clogged the curb out front. I frowned. It wasn't tourist season yet. What was all the hullaballoo?

When I drew up to Dune House's gates a few minutes later, my frown deepened. A throng of men in baggy suits milled around the gates. Some held notebooks and pencils. Others toted boxy black cameras, with camera cases strapped over their shoulders.

"Reporters," I said.

Berta started awake. She mumbled in Swedish as she straightened her hat.

I braked inches away from a fellow who was aiming his camera at my windshield. "I'd forgotten. Horace complained about the reporters."

The reporters went saggy-shouldered when they saw it was only Berta and me. One of them kicked the ground.

"And I thought I didn't look half bad in this hat," I said.

"They wish to see the motion picture stars," Berta said. "Bruno Luciano and Sadie Street."

"Oh, I know."

The gatekeeper scurried up to my window. When he saw who I was, he yelled at the reporters to get back. They ignored him.

"Go on ahead, Mrs. Woodby," the gatekeeper said. "They're like flies—gotta swat them away."

I crept the Duesy forward, and the crowd of reporters parted. I was almost through when a familiar voice said, "Well, well, well. Lola Duffy. What a *treat*."

Duffy? My heart skittered like a gramophone needle.

"Hello, Miss Shanks," I said. I gripped the steering wheel so tightly I heard my knuckles crack.

Ida Shanks heard them crack, too, and it made her smile.

I have a nemesis, and her name is Miss Ida Shanks. She is the society gossip columnist for the *New York Evening Observer*, and she has enjoyed a profitable career at, in part, my expense. Not a month has gone by without a wicked comment about me from this harpy, my identity disguised by only the flimsiest euphemistic veil. The trouble is, I'm on quicksand when it comes to Ida Shanks: she is one of the few people who knows that the DuFeys are really Duffys, and that before we made it to Park Avenue, our return address was 5 Polk Street, Scragg Springs, Indiana.

Ida knows these secrets, by the way, because *she's* from Scragg Springs, too.

Ida wore her usual getup: blue suit, moth-eaten fox fur, wilt-flowered hat, stockings that bagged around her sparrow's ankles, witchy boots. "Gadding about so soon after your dear departed helpmeet's demise?" she said.

"Gadding about?" I asked "Are we caught inside a P. G. Wodehouse novelette?"

"Who *is* this appalling creature?" Berta whispered to me.

"I have heard murmurs," Ida said, "that your hubby's legacy was not so ample as one might've thought. No comment, Mrs. Woodby?" She dug a notebook and pencil from her dented satchel, and started scribbling. "Fortune," she said, "has . . . flown . . . the . . . coop . . . for . . . formidable . . . society . . . doyenne. . . . Wait. Scratch that. No . . . ample . . . inheritance . . . for . . . ample . . . upper crust . . . matron. . . ."

The gates were flung wide by the gatekeeper. "Toodles, Miss Shanks," I snarled.

I was about to hit the gas pedal when the reporters erupted in a tizzy. Ida craned her neck.

Berta and I swiveled in our seats. A glossy black Rolls-Royce pulled up behind us. The reporters swarmed. The driver of the Rolls beeped the horn.

"The chauffeur honks at you, Mrs. Woodby," Berta said. "Get a move on."

"'Get a move on'?" I whizzed through the gates. "Tell me again, when did you take up speaking like a gangster?"

Berta compressed her lips.

We drove up the tree-lined drive. The Rolls was hot on my fender.

Dune House came into view. Four mammoth wings, slate roofs, and five towering chimneys mimicked an English baronial hall. An ornate iron railing ran along the roofline like a high lace collar. Stone gargoyles lurked at the edges of the gutters. Windowpanes sparkled in the early evening sunlight. Despite its aged style, Dune House was brand-spanking new and had been paid for, I suspected, mainly with proceeds from Auntie Arbuckle's Pork and Beans.

Several luxurious motorcars were parked in the white gravel drive, and more sat next to a stone garage large enough to house an army. I'd been to Dune House before, of course, and I knew that out back were tennis courts, a swimming pool, a hedge maze, stables, riding paths through the trees, and, about a quarter mile away, a stretch of beach fronting the sound.

I motored to a stop. The Rolls braked behind me. Two menservants, trussed up in double-breasted livery jackets, came down the walkway. I waited for one of them to open my door. Nothing happened. I spun around in my seat.

"Cheeky!" I said. The footmen were opening the Rolls-Royce's doors.

Berta turned around, too.

We goggled without shame.

"I've never seen a motion picture star," I said. "Not in person, I mean."

"Such a fuss," Berta said. Her eyes were glued to the Rolls.

A pair of slim girl's calves came into view. Then the whole girl emerged.

"Sadie Street, I'd guess," I said.

Sadie wasn't, I had gathered from Olive Arbuckle, exactly a film star. Yet. But she looked the part. She had a lovely face and lithe flapper's figure, dolphin-hipped and bosom-free, in a pale blue tube of a dress. Her flaxen bob came to curled points against her pale cheeks, under a blue hat.

"Oh, shut up, George," Sadie said, marching up the front walk. "I told you a thousand times, I'm awful tired of hearing about lighting and scripts and things!"

A man surfaced from the other side of the Rolls. He was short and dapper, wearing a three-piece suit. He had dark eyes and a trim gray beard. A pleasant face, yet long-suffering, like a schnauzer who needs to go for a walk.

Berta and I levered ourselves out of the Duesy. Berta went off to find the servants' entrance. Cedric and I went to the front door.

Hibbers was there to greet me.

"Oh, hello," I said to him. My voice had the hurt wobble of a jilted debutante.

"Mrs. Woodby," he said with a bow. He cast a regal smile down to Cedric. Cedric wiped his lips on Hibbers's trouser leg.

I stepped into the entrance hall. I was about to introduce myself to Sadie Street and George Zucker when Olive descended upon us. Then I was caught in a tsunami of shrill greetings, air kisses, and bony hugs.

Oh boy. Three seconds inside Dune House, and I was already daydreaming about an extra-thick slab of chocolate mousse cake.

"Where's the pie-faced simp?" Sadie Street said as soon as Olive finished the introductions.

"If you mean Bruno, he's sunning himself by the swimming pool, darling," Olive said. "Perhaps you ought to pop into your bathing costume, too, and join him. Nothing like a little fresh air and sunshine to—"

"Where's my room?" Sadie said. Then, to George, "I *told* you I couldn't bear it if everyone was going to push me to talk with Mr. Pipsqueak. And for God's sake, George, would you stop pawing at my arm?" She swished toward the stairs. "I suppose my room is upstairs somewhere?"

For a moment, Olive's face fell. But she plastered on a smile— remembering, probably, that Sadie was going to be a big star—and scurried after her.

"Nasty piece of fluff," George muttered.

Whew! What a way to talk about your main squeeze.

"Sadie and Bruno," George said to me as we followed Hibbers up the stairs, "—you've heard of Bruno Luciano?"

"Sure. Brightest new movie star of the year, the papers all say."

"Sadie and Bruno are under contract to co-star in three pictures together. Production gets under way on the first one, and whaddaya know? They decide two weeks ago, when we start filming *Jane Eyre*, that they can't stand the sight of each other."

"*Jane Eyre*?" I asked. "Sadie Street will play Jane?"

"She's pretty convincing once she's got the wig and everything on."

Mental memo: Skip that picture.

"The two of them have refused, flat out, to work together," George said. "Pantheon's investors are furious. I've got to get them to see eye to eye or we'll be in the hole."

"Couldn't you hire different actors?"

"No. They're under contract."

"Aren't they breaking the contract themselves, by refusing to work?"

George shook his head. "There are intricacies. Complications.

No. They gotta be reconciled. And firing Bruno is absolutely out of the question. Didn't you see *The King of Sheba* last fall?"

"The picture where Mr. Luciano was wearing a turban and all that kohl under his eyes?"

"Yep. That was the most profitable picture of 1922! We can't let him go. Some other production company will snap him up. Pantheon needs him."

"Well," I said, "maybe everything will get sorted this weekend."

"It's got to. The investors have given me a week to patch things up, or else it's curtains for Sadie."

"*Highball,*" I mouthed to Hibbers when he glanced in my direction.

6

As soon as Hibbers left me in my room—a lofty affair with Olde Englishe replica furniture—Cedric leapt from my arms and began sniffing about.

I went to the windows. Outside, the swimming pool glittered in the early evening sun, surrounded by topiary trees. Only one person was out there, lolling facedown on a teak lounge. A man, long and sun-bronzed, with a well-muscled physique and dark, curling hair, wearing small white bathing trunks. Bruno Luciano.

I was about to turn away from the window when a manservant stepped into view beside the pool. He carried a tray with a drink on it. Something about his swagger caught my eye.

The manservant bent down beside Bruno. Bruno said something without lifting his face. The manservant placed the drink on the table beside Bruno's lounge, and straightened.

Then he looked right up to my window.

Well, well. Mr. Ralph Oliver.

My fingernails clawed into the drapes.

Ralph tucked the tray under his arm, grinned up at me. And winked. I snapped the drapes shut.

Hibbers arrived with my highball minutes later.

"Thanks," I said after a bracing swallow. "Nectar of the gods."

"You are very kind, madam." He turned to go.

"Wait," I said. "Is there any new help here at Dune House? Besides you, I mean."

"Not as such, although Mrs. Arbuckle has hired a few extra servants for the weekend. From a temporary staffing agency. She did not wish for her motion picture guests to want for anything. Shall I take Cedric for a perambulation on the lawns, and then a light repast in the kitchen, madam?"

"Oh, that would be wonderful. I'll dig up his leash."

Moments later, Cedric frisked away with Hibbers without so much as a backward glance.

I sipped my highball and fumed while I dressed for dinner. Obviously, Ralph Oliver was here at Dune House because *I* was. But he'd beat me here. Which meant that he hadn't followed me. He'd known I was coming to Dune House in advance, so must have overheard my conversation with Ruby Simpkin last night at the Frivolities.

And *that* meant he was investigating something to do with Alfie selling that film reel to Horace Arbuckle. Or else, he was really investigating *me*.

Either way, *phooey*.

I wriggled and buckled myself into a long girdle. I pulled on black silk stockings, clipped them to my garters, and straightened my seams. I chose jet-beaded François Pinet high heels and a slinky black evening gown with a plunging neckline. I might not have a swizzle stick build, but with the right brassiere, my décolleté is probably worth writing home about. I caught myself wondering if Ralph Oliver would approve.

I gave myself a mental slap and polished off my highball. Then I patched up my mascara and lipstick, and headed downstairs.

I decided to make a detour past Horace's study. Maybe I could weasel in there, somehow pry open the safe, get the film reel, and be gone. On the way, I half hoped I'd bump into Mr. Oliver so I could give him a piece of my mind.

No dice; I didn't see a soul.

The study door stood about four inches open, and the room was lit up inside. I peeked in with one eye.

Zowie. I blinked. Was that really—? Yes. It was.

Horace Arbuckle was half-sprawled on his desk, in the throes of some kind of amorous tangle with a lady. She was crouched, and there were a lot of pink, fleshy limbs. Horace grunted, and I saw a lady's flushed face, framed in gray hair.

I ran away down the hallway so fast, I almost turned an ankle.

When I arrived in the drawing room, only Hibbers was there.

He glided past button-tufted furniture, palms potted in Ming, and tasteful bric-a-brac to deliver a highball to me. "Madam."

"Oh brother," I said. "I really oughtn't start on a second one yet." I took it, anyway. I needed something to erase the image of Horace Arbuckle Greco-Roman wrestling with that lady. "Where is everyone else?"

"The Arbuckle household, madam, runs on an exceptionally late schedule."

"I'll go outside and putter around a little, then. Thanks, Hibbers."

Outside on the flagstone terrace, the night air tasted of salt, and stars dappled the sky. The lawn was dark, except for rectangles of light shining down from the house's windows. Beyond the lawn stood a tall, shadowy hedge.

I gasped. Dark figures crept across the far edge of the lawn, along the base of the hedge. I squinted. Yes. Three figures. I heard a woman's voice. Heavy breathing. Was the woman barking . . . *commands?* The figures veered left and moved into a rectangle of light on the lawn.

Maybe I'd drunk one highball too many. Because what I *thought* I saw, galumphing toward me, were two roly-poly young boys driven along by a lady with some kind of stick.

The lady was twenty-odd years old, rail-thin, with a ferret's face pulled taut by a bun. The boys, of course, were Olive and Horace's progeny, Billy and Theo. They wore shorts, tennis shirts, and canvas tennis shoes that glowed in the half light. Yet their pudgy midriffs and doughy knees were a far cry from those of tennis players. Poor dears.

"Oh, hi, Mrs. Woodby," the elder boy, Billy, said, panting. He stopped at the base of the terrace steps.

"Hello, Billy," I said. "Out for a spot of exercise?"

"Billy!" the lady barked. "March!"

"Is that your . . . trainer?" I whispered to Billy.

"Nanny Potter," he said miserably. Then he was off, with Theo and Nanny Potter right behind.

"Fat little things," Olive said, sidling up to me.

I jumped.

Olive glistened, long and narrow, in a green beaded evening gown. She held a venomous-looking cocktail. "Take after their father. I do my absolute *utmost* to slim them, I swear, but it's hopeless. They always scrounge things up, somehow. If Cook serves them broth and boiled turnips for dinner, they turn around and hit up the chauffeur for chocolate bars. If Nanny Potter drives them for an extra lap in the evening, Cook tells me an entire bowl of custard has gone missing from the icebox." She sipped her drink. "I keep them locked up now."

My eyes widened. "Your children?"

"No, no. The icebox, and the pantry. Oh, do look. Eloise has finally come down. You know Eloise Wright, don't you?"

I turned.

And promptly choked on my drink. I was face-to-face with the lady I'd seen writhing with Horace in his study.

"Oh, hello," I said, extending my hand. "How lovely to meet you, Mrs. Wright."

In fact, I already knew Eloise Wright by reputation, since we swam in the same social circles. But I'd never actually seen her until that discomfiting instant in Horace's study.

Eloise was the very definition of a Society Matron: partridge plump, draped in a square acre of lilac chiffon, upswept steel-wool hair, tremulous diamond earrings, posture of a war general.

"Eloise is the Girdle Queen," Olive said to me after introductions. "Haven't you heard? She's grown quite famous."

"Oh, she exaggerates," Eloise said. "I've only got a little business, tucked away inside Gerald's Fifth Avenue store."

"Gerald is her husband, of course," Olive said. She gestured with her drink. Inside the drawing room, Horace Arbuckle (now, thank goodness, fully clothed) was speaking with a puny fellow in a too-big evening jacket. Gerald Wright had Coca-Cola bottle glasses, an amphibious face, and a bald spot. "*You* know, Lola. Gerald Wright. Of Wright's Department Stores."

"Of course," I said. "I simply adore Wright's." I *used* to adore it, anyway. I no longer had enough cabbage to shop there.

"Horace and Gerald are in business together," Olive said. "Horace sells a line of fancy tinned things—pâté and caviar and so on—in the food halls at the Wright's stores."

"And you sell girdles?" I asked.

"*Sell* really isn't the proper word. Of course, yes, I do sell them. But I consider myself more of an engineer. Foundation garments, dear, are as critical to a lady's turnout as foundations are critical to a house." Eloise surveyed my figure. "You are precisely the sort of lady who forms the bulk of my clientele."

Maybe it was because she'd used the word *bulk,* but if she called me Society Matron, I was going to scream.

"Elegant, well dressed," Eloise said, "but in need, due to the ravages of gravity and rich foods, of additional buttressing."

I unclenched my teeth and poured the remainder of my highball through.

"Come to the Foundations Department sometime, at the Wright's on Fifth Avenue," she said. "I'll see if there is anything I can do."

My self-esteem lay in rubble around my François Pinet shoes. And then, as luck would have it, two gorgeous men sauntered into the drawing room.

All right, *three* men sauntered in, if you counted George Zucker. But hangdog George was utterly eclipsed by the arrival of Bruno Luciano and some other tall, dark stranger.

"Sweet snugglepups," Olive said. "Suddenly it's rather like cocktail hour on Mount Olympus, isn't it?"

"If you like that sort of thing," Eloise said. She sipped her pink cocktail. I was pretty sure her eyes strayed to Horace.

There is simply no accounting for taste.

George stopped to chat with Horace and Gerald. Bruno and the other man joined us on the terrace, and Olive made the introductions.

Bruno Luciano had a rubber doll's perfection, and I wondered how much oil he'd used to gloss his suntan. His eyes were the same liquid brown that they appeared to be on the silver screen.

"Pleased to meet you, Mrs. Woodby," Bruno said, his voice high and piping.

No wonder Sadie Street had called him Mr. Pipsqueak.

Olive, beside me, was breathing in rasps. Bruno's voice didn't bother *her* a bit.

The other man was introduced as Mr. Ptolemy Fitzpatrick.

"Call me Lem," he said. His voice was gravelly, and his palm was rough. He was dashing in that half-hungover way, with stray locks of hair, five o'clock shadow, and purple half moons beneath scary dark eyes.

He was what you'd call a Wrong Number.

"Lem is another of Horace's business associates," Olive said.

"Tin cans," Lem said. "Arbuckle needs 'em, and I got 'em. I won't bore you ladies with the details. Hey, where's the gramophone, Mrs. Arbuckle?"

"Call me Olive. *Mrs.* sounds so . . . ancient."

"Can't have cocktails without jazz," Lem said. "Steer me toward the old horn, why dontcha?"

Lem set Duke Ellington spinning, and Hibbers dragged some furniture out of the way. Bruno and Olive started dancing, and then Horace swept Eloise out onto the carpet, too.

Gerald Wright slumped against the wall near the gramophone, watching Horace and his wife dancing cheek to cheek. His stare was angry-hot enough to steam up those thick glasses of his.

George Zucker edged up to me. "Dance, Mrs. Woodby?"

"I'm a widow," I said. But I gave him my hand, anyway.

"Have you ever suffered from unrequited love, Mrs. Woodby?" George asked.

"Can't say that I have."

"Well, you're lucky, then. It's hell. Sheer hell. Enough to make you want to—to *kill* someone."

"Good heavens. Don't do *that*, Mr. Zucker."

Despite his angst, George was a wonderful hoofer. We kicked and waggled, working up a sweat to sultry tunes riding on bouncy bass lines.

Then Sadie Street put in an appearance.

Between spins with George, I caught sight of her in the doorway, a lithe vision in yellow, her bob pomaded to a golden helmet. She glared at Bruno, who was in mid-whirl with Olive.

Then—I craned my neck as George spun me around again, narrowly missing a floor lamp—Bruno saw Sadie. His face went stiff. He released Olive from his arms, mid-dip. Olive crashed to the carpet, legs splayed and hair tufting.

Someone brought the gramophone to a nails-on-the-chalkboard stop.

Silence.

Horace went over to Olive.

"Help me, you big oaf!" Olive yelled. He complied.

Sadie and Bruno's eyes, meanwhile, were locked like two fighting roosters in the pit.

George was the first to speak. "Sadie, darling, how was your nap?"

Sadie ignored him. "Well, well," she said to Bruno. "Looks like Mr. Pipsqueak's in the middle of another one of his embarrassing screen tests."

"*My* embarrassing screen tests?" Bruno said.

"And how nice to see you've taken up dancing," Sadie said. "Again. Just like old times at Philippe's."

This question held some kind of weighty significance; Bruno's face turned mauve. "How *dare* you?"

"How dare *you?*" Sadie marched up to Bruno and slapped his cheek. It was quite the cinematic spectacle: a lock of Bruno's hair came loose across his forehead, and fury boiled in his lustrous eyes. Sadie glowered, chin tilted, her beauty glowing from within.

Wow. If Pantheon Pictures could catch this kind of thing on film, they'd have a humdinger on their hands.

Sadie swanned out of the drawing room.

Hibbers—he has impeccable timing—appeared with a tray of martinis. Everyone lunged for a drink. The gramophone blared up again.

7

I despise pimento-stuffed olives, yet I snatched one of the martinis from Hibbers's tray. No time to hang on for a highball. I took an icy swallow.

Through the French doors, I glimpsed motion on the lawn and heard a familiar yap.

Cedric.

I slipped out onto the terrace. Cedric was cavorting on the shadowy grass, his leash held by a tall man. I frowned. Yes, a tall man in servant's livery. With an annoying swagger. His back was to me, and he was whistling a ditty up into the sky.

"*Hey!*" I whispered.

He didn't turn.

I glanced over my shoulder, into the drawing room. Everyone was dancing and dipping their bills.

I turned back to Ralph. "Hey!"

Still, he didn't turn. What *was* that he was whistling—"Bugle Call Rag"? Or was it something from . . . a Puccini opera?

No, couldn't be.

I plucked the olive from my martini, aimed, and lobbed it through the darkness. It hit Ralph square in the bean.

He turned. When he saw me, his face lit with a slow smile. His eyes meandered south to take in my gown. On the way back up, they lingered on my front bumpers. "Hey, Mrs. Woodby. Nice dress."

"I have a good mind to throw my drink in your face for following me here."

"You wouldn't do that. You need that drink so's to get through the evening with this pack of goofs."

I wobbled (had my François Pinets always been so precarious?) down the terrace steps and across the grass. Cedric squiggled a greeting. I stooped to pat his head.

"Gonna bust my chops like that starlet did to Mr. Luciano?" Ralph said.

"You've been spying on us?" I straightened.

"Just walking the dog."

"Why are you following me?"

"Like I told you, I'm investigating a matter to do with your late husband."

"Does it have anything to do with . . . with a film reel, by any chance?"

His eyes glittered. "Film reel?"

Maybe he *hadn't* heard my conversation with Ruby Simpkin in her dressing room. Or maybe he was one swell actor.

"Never mind," I said. "Listen, Mr. Oliver, I don't believe for a second that you're investigating Alfie. I think you're investigating *me*."

His eyes landed on my mouth. "I'd *like* to be investigating you."

"I know you are, and I do *not* approve. Cease and desist."

Ralph chuckled. "Maybe you're used to pulling that high-and-mighty routine on other fellas, but it's not gonna work on me, all right?"

"For a man who's playing valet to a toy Pomeranian, you certainly have brass."

"You're broke, Mrs. Woodby. They don't know it yet—" He gestured with his chin to the drawing room. "—but I know. And I dug up some other real interesting things, too."

I licked my lips. "Oh?"

"Number five Polk Street, Scragg Springs, Indiana—ring a bell?"

"I can't say that it does."

I turned and reeled back across the lawn, onto the terrace, and inside.

Dinner consisted of broth, watercress salad (no dressing), steamed vegetables, parboiled codfish, and far too much tipply. I was still shaky from my encounter with Ralph Oliver, and I was speeding toward the four-cocktail mark. If I didn't get some substantial food into my engine, my tubes were going to be coursing 100 proof.

Once we hit the codfish, Gerald and Eloise wheeled out their marital misery.

"It's the goddam seconds," Gerald said.

"I beg your pardon?" Olive said, swilling a martini.

"All the corsets that my darling wife tosses aside when she comes up with a new design."

"It's called *innovation*, dear," Eloise said.

"It's called a big fat waste."

"No, no," Horace said. "Her girdles are scientific."

I suppose Horace *was* obliged to leap to Eloise's defense after their little tête-à-tête in the study earlier.

"What do you do with the seconds?" Lem asked. "Turn 'em into battleships?"

Eloise tilted her nose. "I no longer use steel boning in my designs. This is all very top secret, you understand—"

"*Innovation*," her husband said.

"—but I have begun to experiment with corsets—well, girdles, properly speaking—"

"What's the difference?" Lem asked.

Why was Lem so interested in ladies' unmentionables, anyway? He looked like the type who concerned himself only with peeling the things *off* a girl.

Horace shifted in his chair. "Should we really be speaking of ladies' undergarments?"

"Why not?" Olive snapped.

"The difference between a corset and a girdle," Eloise said, "is that a girdle stretches with the body, while a corset is stiff. Of recent date, manufacturers have begun to sew elastic panels into their corsets, rendering them, technically speaking, girdles. But I have invented something quite new, something extraordinary."

"Rubber girdles," Gerald said.

"*Gerald!*" Eloise whispered. She sighed. "I didn't mean to give the whole thing away. Why, anyone could take my invention and steal it. The patents are still pending."

Bruno yawned.

I prodded limp watercress with my fork. The conversation was having a soporific effect—or else I'd gone feeble with hunger—because I dropped my fork. I bent to pick it up.

Lem, I should mention, was sitting on my right, and Sadie was seated across from him. So I couldn't help but notice that Sadie had kicked off one of her shoes, and her toes were wrestling with one of Lem's sock-covered dogs.

I forgot about my fork and sat up.

Hibbers appeared at Olive's side, and whispered something in her ear.

"The little *piglet*." Olive stood. "I'm so sorry, but I must excuse myself. It seems young Theo somehow got his fat little mitts on an

entire batch of cinnamon rolls, devoured the lot, and has taken ill."
She swerved out of the dining room.

Cinnamon rolls? *Berta.* Maybe she'd made a double batch.

Dessert was trembling molded gelatin. I declined a helping. When
everyone migrated back to the drawing room, I excused myself for
bed.

But I didn't go upstairs. Instead, I stole back to Horace's study. This
time, it was dark inside. I tiptoed in.

I had made it as far as the desk when the overhead light
snapped on.

My heart lodged in my throat.

"There you are, Mrs. Woodby." Ralph stood in the doorway,
Cedric tucked under his arm like a football. "Looking for something?"

"Um. No. Just . . . lost."

"Sure you are. Well, I've come to deliver your mutt."

"Mutt?" I narrowed my eyes.

"So to speak." Ralph plopped Cedric on the floor.

"Come on, peanut," I called.

Cedric sat at Ralph's feet.

"He doesn't like being ordered around," Ralph said.

"He's *my* dog! Peanut, come to Mommy." I patted my knees.
"Come!"

Cedric didn't budge.

"He's kinda funny," Ralph said. "Responds better to praise and
cuddles. And kisses." He winked, and strutted off down the hallway.

I scooped Cedric up, flicked off the study light, and went upstairs.
I couldn't bally well break into a safe with Mr. Oliver slinking around
in the background.

The heist would have to wait till tomorrow.

....

When I entered my bedroom, the first thing I saw was Berta in a pool of lamplight. She was bundled in a pink quilted robe, reading in an armchair before a fire.

She glanced up from her book. "Oh, hello. My. You *do* look a bit worse for wear, Mrs. Woodby. On a whizzer, are we?"

"I only had three," I said. Or was it five?

A teapot in a knitted cozy sat on the table beside her. No cinnamon rolls—rats.

"Did you procure the film reel?" she asked.

"How could I?" I set Cedric loose. "There are people positively dotting the landscape. Never even had an opportunity to crowbar the safe open, or whatever it is I'm going to do."

"Yes. I have been thinking about that." Berta lifted her book so I could see the cover. It was one of my detective dime novels, *Hazard in Havana*, by Frank B. Jones, Jr. "Thad Parker gets into the evil scientist's safe by tricking him into opening it in front of him, and memorizing the combination."

"Hadn't thought of that. Good old Thad Parker." I kicked off my shoes and dumped myself into the other armchair by the fire. I told Berta about Ralph Oliver's new gig as a faux footman, Horace and Eloise's Amorous Olympics, and all the other outlandish details of the evening. I sighed. "By the way, is there any particular reason you're in my room, Berta? Wait—is it because the maid's room smells like underarm?"

"How did you know? It was terribly drafty, too. I did not think you would mind if I slept in your room. It is quite spacious."

"But there's only one bed."

"Yes, but the sofa looks *ever* so comfortable." She gave me a steely smile. "Doesn't it?"

8

By ten thirty the next morning, I was already whacking a tennis ball under an offensive sun. We were playing doubles, ladies versus gents. Olive was my partner. When Hibbers appeared with a pitcher of lemoned ice water at courtside, I crept away, croaking, "Powder room."

I was weak kneed, and my tennis dress was damp with perspiration. I hadn't packed any sports costumes during my flight from Amberley, so I'd been strong-armed into borrowing spare tennis and golf costumes that Olive kept on hand. At that moment, I wore a green-and-white jersey sack with gaping armholes.

Inside the house, the corridors were cool and dim. I went to the drawing room. I'd have fortifying quaff before returning to Olive's gladiator amphitheater of a tennis court.

The drinks table was in a corner behind a potted palm, so I didn't see the figure hoisting the whiskey bottle until I was inches away.

"I beg your pardon!" I pressed a hand to my heart.

The figure turned. A tiny, round, wrinkly face smiled up at me, framed with tight white curls and a high Victorian collar.

Why did she look so familiar?

"Oh, hello," the old lady said in a creaky granny voice. "I didn't see you there." She held up the whiskey bottle. "Drink?

"Drown me."

She poured three inches of whiskey into glasses and passed me one. We sipped in sneaky, companionable silence.

"That skinny she-devil running you ragged?" the old lady said.

"Golly. Yes. Tennis. Then it's the golf links after luncheon."

"Why he married her, I'll never know. That boy loves to eat! And she starves him within an inch of his life."

"Do you mean Horace?"

"Yes. I'm his aunt. Auntie Arbuckle." Her milk glass blue eyes twinkled. "No one told you about Auntie? Keep me locked away, they do. In the North Wing, away from the guests. Think I'll spill the beans." She tittered. "Oh! I *am* a riot—spill the beans!"

Perhaps she was touched in the head. Or sozzled.

She suddenly looked serious. "Like this whiskey?"

"Sure." I would've preferred it with a splash of ginger ale, naturally, but these were desperate times.

"Canadian," she said. "Down to my last bottle. You can taste the northern woods in it, and the peat smoke of Newfoundland."

"Really?" I sniffed my glass.

"No!" She hooted and slapped her knee with a wizened paw. "Got you good!"

Okay: she was crackers.

"The new butler won't get me any more Canadian hooch," she said. "Says he doesn't know how. You ever heard of a butler who can't get his hands on bootleg? Why, even before that danged Eighteenth Amendment passed, any butler worth his salt would get you a crate of liquor discounted, simply because he could. But Hibbers! Too hoity-toity for my taste." She took another healthy swallow. "Hisakawa—now, *he* was a butler. The fluid grace, the civility! And such exquisite serving manners. His mother was a geisha in the Orient, taught him how to pour things proper. Watching him pour this here Canadian whiskey was like watching honey pour out of an angel's—"

"Auntie!" Horace boomed, emerging from behind the potted palm. Sweat blotched his tennis sweater, and he was out of breath. "I see you've met Auntie Clara. Has she been on one of her rants again? Olive calls her Ranty Auntie."

Auntie said, "I was just about to tell this dear young lady here about how you and that scrawny shrew you married chucked poor Hisakawa out on his ear without so much as a day's notice." She turned to me. "Because of the recipe, dearie. The pork and beans recipe." She winked a crepey eyelid.

"Now, why would Mrs. Woodby want to hear about a private domestic matter like that? Supposing it was even true." Horace pulled me away from Auntie.

"Don't listen to him!" Auntie crowed after us. "He'll say I'm crazy, but I'm not!"

Now, I'm not a lady who enjoys been herded around like the most imbecile steer in a Texan herd. But since I'd been at Dune House for almost a day and was no closer to getting my hands on that film reel, I allowed Horace to lead me back outside, onto the terrace.

"Auntie Clara," Horace said, "she's . . . Well, her parents, if you must know, were first cousins. She isn't right in the conk. And ever since we changed the label of our pork and beans, she's been on the goddam warpath."

Through a whiskey haze, I conjured up the image of a can of Auntie Arbuckle's Pork and Beans. "That's why she looked so familiar! She's *the* Auntie Arbuckle. That's her picture on the can."

The pork and beans labels featured an image of Auntie's rosy face, complete with the cumulus curls, high collar, and sweet-as-pie smile.

"That's her," Horace said. "She's out of sorts about the whole business. She has been generously compensated, of course, and my home is her home as long as she is with us. I think it's a problem of, er, womanly pride."

I frowned.

"Vanity," he said. "She looks . . . *old* on the pork and beans can."

"She *is* old."

"Yes, but ladies always wish to look younger, don't they? At least, that's been my general impression."

Auntie Clara didn't seem the type to have her pantaloons in a twist about growing older. She'd been wearing an antebellum gown and ivory dentures, for crying out loud. And what was it she'd said about the butler, and a recipe?

"Horace," I said, "not to change the subject, but I've been meaning to have a talk with you. About something very, very important."

"Of course."

"Well, you see, now that Alfie's gone, I haven't got a fellow to consult about, um, business matters." *That* was a laugh; Alfie had had the business sense of a chickpea. "And you've got such a marvelous head for such things—you're so successful, so *important*."

Horace puffed up. "What seems to be of concern?"

"Not here. In your study, perhaps, before dinner?"

"Of course, my dear."

Olive came striding around the corner of the house. "*There* you two are." She thwacked the strings of a tennis racket against her palm. "We're playing another match! Chop-chop, Lola. Practice makes perfect!"

. . . .

"If you ask me," I said to Berta after luncheon, "this trip to the golf links is questionable. I mean, all those reporters have been held off at the gates till now, but the instant we go out to the country club, they'll swarm." I sat down on an ottoman in my bedroom and yanked on my borrowed golf socks.

"If you do not mind me saying so, Mrs. Woodby, it is those socks that are questionable," Berta said. She was cocooned in an armchair again. She took a sip of tea. "Sadly, there are certain people who should avoid argyle socks."

I tied my too-big, duotone saddle oxfords. "Listen. I don't know what *you* had for lunch—"

"Oh, merely a simple roast beef sandwich and potato salad. Nothing special."

"*What?* Roast beef?" My belly rumbled. Luncheon in the dining room had been like feeding time at the county fair: crunchy and green. "Well, *you* may be devouring medieval feasts with the staff, but the rest of us are on prison rations. So no snide comments, thanks awfully."

"You do not expect me to mind your dog this afternoon, do you?"

Cedric slept on the armchair next to Berta's, but his puffy back was turned against her.

"I asked Hibbers to come up and fetch him," I said. "He should be here any minute."

I went over to the mirrored wardrobe and studied my reflection. The on-loan white sports blouse and green sweater vest were all right—a bit stretched out in the paunch region. Likewise, the pleated golf skirt had a passable, though dumpy, fit. But the *socks.* They were a brash, green-and-brown argyle pattern that did nothing whatsoever for my ankle concern. "I look like an escapee from clown college. Not like somebody who's going to pull off a heist."

Berta picked up her book. "I was wondering when you were going to get round to that."

"We agreed to go into this thing fifty–fifty, if I remember correctly, but I'm starting to forget exactly what you're doing, besides wolfing down roast beef sandwiches and perusing novels. Oh yes, and baking treats to stuff into the mouths of Olive's children."

"I am tending to the back end of things."

"What back end?"

"I am conducting research." She tilted her book so I could see its cover. Another one of my Frank B. Jones, Jr., dime novels: *Shakedown in Shanghai*.

"I haven't gotten to read that one yet!"

"I shall tell you how it ends. Thad Parker is a most resourceful gumshoe. When he puts the gun to the smuggler's temple and—"

I poked my fingers in my ears. "Stop!"

A rap sounded on the door. I grabbed Cedric and yanked the door open.

Ralph Oliver stood in the doorway in his baggy servant's livery. "The butler sent me up to get the pooch." He looked me up and down, and lifted his eyebrows.

"Don't you *dare* comment," I said. I kissed Cedric, shoved him into Ralph's arms, and slammed the door.

"Oh, dear me," Berta murmured. "We *are* hungry, aren't we?"

As I'd predicted, as soon as our golfing party motored out of the Dune House gates, two reporters who'd been waiting in their jalopies revved their engines and followed us.

Auntie Clara hadn't been invited. Not that I could picture her with a putting iron. But it troubled me that there was some batty old dame stowed away in the house. It was rather *Jane Eyre*.

Hare's Hollow Country Club was a few miles up the highway. It was gated, of course, so the reporters who'd followed us were turned away by the two uniformed gatekeepers. But I had a feeling that the reporters would find a way in.

We motored past the edge of the golf course, with its velvet turf and oak trees, to the clubhouse. The clubhouse sprawled on a bluff, its large windows and wraparound white porches overlooking the sea. A flag whapped atop the cupola, and a row of expensive motor-cars squatted like shiny black beetles outside.

I parked, and joined the others. But it turned out that there was a lot of fiddling about to be done, finding golf clubs and caddies. I left them all to sort it out, and retreated to the shade of the club-house porch. I wasn't in a froth about getting started. Number one, I was famished. Number two, I was dressed like a vaudeville act. And number three? Oh yes: I loathe sports.

I was just sitting down in a wicker chair when someone said, "*Ahem.*"

I sighed. "Hello, Chisholm."

"*Lola,*" Chisholm said. "Good gracious, what on *earth* are you doing playing golf? You're supposed to be in mourning! Wearing *black*, I might add. Not—whatever that is you're wearing." *He* managed to make his houndstooth golf knickers, jacket, and cap seem bleak. "To be perfectly honest, I have fears for your sanity."

"You're supposed to be in mourning, too, you know. Anyway, I'm a grown woman, Chisholm. I shall do what I like." I leaned back in the wicker chair and crossed my legs.

Chisholm's eyes flicked over my argyle socks. He drew a shudder-ing breath and then glanced over his shoulder.

Four patriarch types—portly, bewhiskered, tweedy—stood sev-eral paces down the porch, conversing in thunderous voices. "Your doctor chums?" I said. "No, wait—they have the look of politicians. I get it. Hobnobbing with the bigwigs. I didn't know you were plan-

ning on running for office so soon. What a pity you've got embarrassing relations like me to keep under wraps. The strain is beginning
to show in your face."

"Oh, do shut up, Lola. Now, I expect a straight answer from you:
Where have you been the past two days? Your parents have been
frantic since their arrival home the day before yesterday."

"None of your business."

"If you're holed up at the Plaza or the Ritz, keep in mind that
you've no credit. If the hotel managers haven't figured that out yet,
they will in due time, and I for one have no intention of bailing
you—"

"I'm staying with friends."

"Friends?"

I wouldn't dream of telling Chisholm about Alfie's love nest; it
was the only place I had to hide from him and the rest of my family.
"I've been at Dune House. You know, the Arbuckles' place. With film
stars."

Chisholm's lip twitched. "Low company, indeed."

I stood. "Better low than uppity, Chisholm darling." I tromped
away down the porch, my too-big oxfords slapping like duck's feet.

Once our golf game was in full swing, I sent my caddie for a ham
sandwich from the clubhouse.

I'm not sure how I got roped into playing next to Bruno. I'll
admit, he *was* picture-perfect in his Fair Isle golf vest, tweed knickers, and cap. When he squinted after his ball sailing toward the
horizon, I saw a gorgeous Sir Walter Raleigh at the prow.

At the next hole, Sadie was just taking a few practice swings when
two trilby hats rose from behind a grassy rise, about six yards away
from her. Two boxy cameras emerged below the trilby hats.

"Look," I said to Bruno. "Photographers."

His head snapped up. "Where?"

I pointed. "I knew they'd find a way to sneak onto the links."

"Sneaky devils." Bruno strode over to Sadie.

I leaned on my golf club to watch the show. If only I had a box of Cracker Jack.

I was too far away to hear, but Bruno and Sadie got into some kind of spat, wildly gesticulating, nose to nose. The photographers jockeyed for angles, snapping away.

The caddie appeared with my ham sandwich. I tipped him extravagantly and hid the sandwich down the front of my sweater. I was ashamed to devour such a hearty snack in glamorous company, so I smacked my golf ball into a stand of tall reeds beside a pond and went after it.

I elbowed and crunched my way into the reeds. I tore the waxed paper from my sandwich and took a huge bite. The sandwich was half gone before I realized that there were other people in the reeds, several yards away, in earnest conversation.

I stopped chewing. If I wasn't mistaken, those were the voices of Lem Fitzpatrick and Eloise Wright. It almost sounded as if they were hammering out some kind of . . . business arrangement. I thought I heard Lem say *deal* and Eloise say *but it is only fair if. . . .*

Jeepers creepers. Why were Lem and Eloise doing business on the sly?

I gobbled up the rest of my sandwich, licked the mustard off my fingers, balled up the waxed paper, and stuffed it down my sweater. I pulled a spare golf ball from my pocket and marched victoriously out of the reeds.

9

After golf, I dragged myself upstairs to my room, looking forward to a hot bath and a cool highball.

I encountered Hibbers in the corridor.

"You mother has telephoned three times, madam."

"How does she know I'm—? Oh, wait. *Chisholm*. The sneaky prig!"

"Indeed, madam. Mrs. DuFey indicated that Mr. Woodby had alerted her to your presence at Dune House, after he encountered you at the country club."

"Tell her I'm not available."

"Very well, madam."

"By the way, Hibbers, do you know why the previous butler was fired? Hisakawa, I think his name was."

Hibbers straightened a picture frame. "I was led to believe that Mr. Hisakawa was let go in order to free up the position for me, madam. At the risk of sounding conceited."

"That's not what Auntie Arbuckle said. She suggested that Hisakawa was fired over something to do with the pork and beans recipe."

"If you refer to Miss Clara, madam, I would take her utterances with a substantial grain of salt. They say she was dropped on her head as an infant."

"I thought her parents were first cousins."

"Something to that effect, madam."

I took a steamy bath and dressed for dinner. I chose a black crepe dinner dress edged with gold lamé, and my favorite Pinet heels. Tasteful and chic. Not a speck of argyle in sight. I painted on my munitions, waved my bob with the curling iron, and went downstairs to meet Horace in his study.

He sat at his mahogany desk, back to the door, cradling a drink and staring at a wall of books.

"Hi, Horace," I said. "Why so glum?"

He swiveled. His face had a hunted-rhino look. "Lola. You look lovely. Come in. Nothing's the matter—oh, well, someone's made a whole mess of snickerdoodle cookies, and Billy and Theo got into them."

Snickerdoodles? Berta again.

"The boys ate themselves silly," Horace said. "Olive's up in the nursery helping Nanny Potter tend to them."

"Poor squirts," I said. "Although they do seem to be in . . . efficient hands with Nanny Potter."

"True, true." Horace's shoulders tensed.

Something about Nanny Potter bugged him. Oh, well. None of my beeswax.

I'd already made up my mind to go the Dumb Bunny route. I widened my eyes and said, "I wanted to see you about safes."

"Safes?"

"Like the one you've got there." I pointed. "I've gotten one for storing my valuables, see, now that Alfie's gone. But I simply can't figure out how to work the darn thing."

"It didn't come with an instruction manual?"

"Sure it did, but it might as well have been in Russian."

"All right, then. I'll give you a little demonstration."

Bingo.

Horace went over to his safe, which sat on a sideboard against a wall. I pulled up next to him.

"You turn the dial clockwise, see," he said, twiddling, "and then you stop the little arrow at the right number, and then turn it counterclockwise, and then clockwise again."

"Wait," I said. "Clockwise first?"

"Yes, of course."

"Gee. I still don't quite understand. Could you do a little demonstration, maybe?"

"Fine. Look. Like this." He twirled the dial.

"Twelve . . . three . . . seven," I said, to help myself commit the combination to memory.

"*Shh,*" Horace whispered.

Pop! The safe door bumped open. Horace slammed it shut again.

But not before I'd glimpsed something round, flat, and metal in there.

"Thanks, Horace!" I threw my arms around him and gave him a big squeeze. Mid-hug, my eyes flew to the open study door. I'd caught the briefest flash of motion as somebody retreated.

Somebody had been spying on us. Ralph Oliver, I'd bet.

But who cared? I knew the combination to Horace's safe! The film reel was inside! Thad Parker had nothing on me.

. . . .

The plan was to sneak into Horace's safe in the wee hours, and leave with Berta, Cedric, and the film reel at the crack of dawn. I careened through another boozy evening and made it back upstairs with only two highballs under my belt.

My bedroom was dark. I made out the sweet-potato shape of Berta on the bed. Cedric snuffled in his sleep.

I changed into my nightie and collapsed on the sofa with an extra pillow and blanket. I'd have a little shut-eye until it was safe to go down to the study.

But I couldn't sleep; I was too hungry. Salad and crab legs weren't cutting it. I tossed and turned for an hour, visions of snickerdoodles dancing in my head. I got up and switched on a lamp.

"Berta!" I prodded her. "Wake up. I'm starving."

She cracked an eye. "Do you expect me to prepare you something to eat at this ungodly hour? Turn off that dreadful light and go to sleep."

"Aren't you hungry?"

"No. I made dinner for all the staff and the children. Dessert, too."

"Oh, right. I heard about the snickerdoodle debacle. Come down with me to the kitchen. Please?" The truth was, I didn't want to be all by my lonesome if I got caught red-handed, stuffing my cake hole. At least if Berta were with me, I could claim she was sleepwalking.

"Oh, all right." Berta threw off the coverlet.

We belted ourselves into our robes and tiptoed downstairs.

We entered the service wing of the house through a door concealed in the dining room wainscoting. This wing housed the kitchen and pantries on the main floor, and the servants' quarters on the upper floors.

We passed the servants' staircase. We made it halfway down a hallway that led to the kitchen. Suddenly, a *bang!* rang out behind the kitchen door.

Berta clutched her locket. I smacked a palm over my mouth.

I'd been dragged along on enough pheasant hunts to know that sound. "That was a *gun*," I whispered.

"Of course it was!"

"Should we . . . go see?"

"You *have* got bats in the belfry. Mr. Chisholm was right."

"He said that?"

"If that was a gun, we could be in danger."

We stared down the long, dim hallway at the kitchen door.

"If that was a gun," I said, "someone might be hurt." Bile burned my throat. I forced myself forward.

Berta followed.

We reached the kitchen door. I nudged it open.

Moonlight poured through the kitchen windows. The tile floors gleamed, and the white cabinetry and steel cookstove shone. All was clean, silvery, and peaceful.

Except for the person-shaped mound on the floor. And the dark fluid pooling on the tiles beside it.

"It's Horace!" I dashed forward. "He's been shot!"

As soon as I knelt beside him, I knew he was a goner. His eyes were wide, and his bulky body seemed to take up less space than it had in life. Blood seeped across his pajama stripes. An unbitten snickerdoodle lay near his hand.

Berta mouthed a silent prayer.

"Go get help!" I said. "Call the police—there's a telephone in the entry hall."

"The murderer is here," she said in a hoarse whisper. "This man was killed not one minute ago. I do not go anywhere by myself."

Voices hummed out in the hallway. The door flew open, and Hibbers stood in the doorway in white pajamas. The pale faces of several of the household staff—I saw the cook and a parlor maid—rubbernecked around his shoulders.

"Oh dear Lord," Hibbers said. "I shall telephone the police at once."

I had, over the course of the last thirty-odd hours, drunk as much liquor as I usually drank in two weeks. Yet suddenly, I had the same clarity of thought that Thad Parker might've enjoyed during a daring rescue in the back streets of Buenos Aires. As soon as the police arrived on the scene, I'd lose my chance to get the film reel.

No one noticed as I backed away from the melee in the kitchen and headed to Horace's study.

My legs quaked as I went. A murderer was afoot. Yet my desperation to get the reel—and three thousand smackeroos—was more potent than fear.

I shut myself into the study and cracked the drapes. I bent close to the safe and spun the dial.

12 . . . 3 . . . 7. Click.

I pulled the safe door open.

Empty.

10

....

I cornered Berta outside the dining room, where the servants were congregating. Hibbers had gone to rouse the rest of the household.

"*Gone?*" Berta whispered.

"Afraid so." I glanced around to make sure no one was listening. "Horace must've moved the reel for some reason."

"No." Berta's mouth was grim. "Someone stole it. Think, Mrs. Woodby."

"I *am!*"

"You saw the film, snug in the safe—"

"I didn't say *snug*. You make everything sound like it's taking place inside an elf's cottage."

Berta drew herself up. "No, I do not. Focus, Mrs. Woodby. You have the shock. Do you wish for me to slap you?"

"No! And gee whiz, don't look so disappointed."

"Listen. Mr. Arbuckle is shot to death and the film reel disappears, both in the same evening? Too much of a coincidence for my blood. The killer—loose, roaming the halls of this house!—stole the reel. Mark my words."

"You've been reading too many Frank B. Jones, Jr., novels."

"The reel is dangerous. We do not know what terrible secrets it contains." Berta lowered her voice even more. "If the killer knows that we are looking for the reel—bang! They kill us, too, Mrs. Woodby. I am afraid."

"I'd bet my bottom dollar it was Olive who shot him. She probably saw that snickerdoodle heading for his chops and finally snapped."

"Mrs. Woodby! Are you not sorry about that poor man?"

"Of course I am." In fact, I felt really wobbly and on the verge of giggling. Maybe Berta was right; maybe I was in shock. "We've got to face it, Berta. We've failed." I couldn't bring myself to say aloud that I was little bit afraid, too. "Forget the film reel and the dough. It's off to work in the luncheonette for both of us."

The police from Hare's Hollow arrived, and then everyone took turns giving statements in the drawing room. George, Sadie, Eloise, Lem, and Bruno, all of them hollow-eyed and stunned, hid their brandy in coffee cups. Not that the cops would care about bootleg at a time like this.

Olive was still in the nursery with her boys and the nurserymaid. I imagined she'd be distraught, but not terribly so. Her marriage to Horace hadn't been exactly a love match. And now she was going to be independently, fabulously in the clover. I was heartsick for young Theo and Billy, though.

And where was Ralph Oliver? It was pretty darn iffy how he'd evaporated on the night of a murder. Not to mention on the night the reel was stolen.

I approached Hibbers as he poured fresh brandies in the dining

room. He had somehow found the time to change into his butler's
livery and pomade his hair.

"Hibbers," I whispered, "could I ask a favor of you?"

"Madam?"

"You can't mention it to the police."

Hibbers furrowed his brows.

"Hey!" I said. "You don't think I—?"

"By no means."

"Only checking. Listen, would you let me know if you happen to
see a film reel in the house?"

"Film reel, madam?"

I explained what it looked like.

"Very well." Hibbers went back to pouring brandy.

"Mrs. Woodby," Police Inspector Digton said when I was up for the
third degree, "you're a widow of only a week or so yourself." He was
about forty, with a boneless build and a push broom mustache. He
wore a linty suit the color of weak tea.

"True." I tried to look dignified. Tough when you're wearing a
pink chiffon robe. I sat on a sofa, and Digton paced around like a
fellow who's desperate to go to the lav. "No connection."

Digton's bushy brows shot up. "I don't get your meaning."

"Oh. Well. It sounded as though you were trying to make me confess to being a compulsive killer of rich husbands."

"But Alfred Woodby wasn't rich."

"Could we stick to the topic?"

"Sure. How about that the nurserymaid, Vera Potter, told me you
were seen seducing Horace Arbuckle in his study about six hours
before he was shot?"

"Seducing? Zowie, are you ever mistaken." That's who had been
spying on Horace and me, then. Nanny Potter.

"Yeah?" Digton glanced down to the V of my robe, which had gone a little loose.

I pinched it shut.

"Seems to me," Digton said, "you're a lady who knows how to get what she wants."

"What's that supposed to mean?"

"Seems to me, a lady who's used to having things her way might get a little, say, *hot-headed* when her plans are loused up."

"Plans?" Had this monkey-man learned about my plan to crack into Horace's safe? Berta was the only one who knew. After she'd been questioned earlier, she told me that she'd kept her lips zipped about the film reel, and about Alfie's love nest, too. "What plans?"

"Your plans to have Horace Arbuckle for yourself."

I laughed. "Horace? For myself? Don't get me wrong, I liked the fellow. But we were only friends."

"That so?"

"Listen here," I said. "I don't know if you're trying to trick me into some kind of confession—a false confession, I might add—but why don't we cut to the chase: If you've got evidence of anything, then go ahead, cuff me." I thrust out my wrists.

Digton shoved his hands in his pockets.

"Maybe," I said, "some lunatic sneaked into the house, shot Horace, and took off again."

"Playing sleuth, huh? Matter of fact, the house was locked up tight, and there were no signs of intrusion. Nope, it was what we call an inside job. The killer never went outside."

"You mean . . . ?"

"Yeah. It was one of you lot."

"But I found Horace in the kitchen, and I'd come down the servants' hallway—"

"There's another way out. Dodge into the pantry, and there's another door leading out into that same servants' corridor. Ever used a gun, Mrs. Woodby?"

"I beg your pardon?"

"Arbuckle's killer was a crack shot. Got him plumb in the heart." Digton made a gun with thumb and forefinger. "Bang! In one go, and in the dark. Knew what he—or she—was doing, all right. So. How's your aim?"

"I've gone pheasant hunting, but I've never even come close to hitting anything." Not that I'd been trying. "Is there a reason you've adopted an especially accusatory tone with me, Inspector? Any person in this house could've shot Horace. I'm simply the unlucky one who found the body."

"Rustling up a midnight snack, I'm told?" His gaze settled on my chiffon-encased thighs.

"A girl's got to keep her strength up."

"The butler told me that all the household staff were just behind him when he came down to investigate the gunshot. None of them would've had time to run back upstairs to the servants' quarters. Which means that the murderer is one of you houseguests. Or the wife. Narrows it down real nice. And you know what, Mrs. Woodby? I have to say, I think it was *you*."

I stopped breathing for a second. "I'm not so sure I like the direction you're headed, Digton." I stood. "I think I'll cut this session short. If you'd like to put me on the rack at a later date, I'll have my lawyer present."

"Have it your way, Mrs. Woodby. Where will you be staying? Not, I guess, your old house down the road?"

"The Algonquin Hotel," I lied.

"You can't hide from the law," Digton called after me as I swooshed out.

....

Of course, I couldn't sleep a wink after all that. At the crack of dawn, Berta and I took turns in the bathroom. We dressed, stuffed our suitcases, and made a break for it.

We'd made it as far as the stairs when a maid stopped us. I was wanted on the telephone.

I didn't have a good feeling about it.

I took the call by the main staircase, even though the entry hall was in commotion. Berta and I weren't the only ones who'd had the idea to flee Dune House posthaste. The front door stood open, and motorcars, people, and luggage jumbled up the drive.

I lifted the telephone's mouthpiece and put the receiver to my ear.

"Lola?" my mother shrilled. "Is that you? I hear rattling!"

"Hello, Mother."

"My sainted aunt! What are you doing at that house party? Daphne St. Aubin telephoned and told me Horace Arbuckle's been murdered! Didn't I teach you *anything* about decorum?"

I almost kicked the wall, but decided my shoe wasn't up to the strain. "How was Europe?"

"You're forever trying to put me off the scent, Lola. How I ever raised such a dodgy daughter, I shall never understand. I raised you to be a lady, and your husband's body hasn't even gone cold before you're off to one of your wild parties! And you didn't have the decency to let me know where you'd gone off to—it took Chisholm telling me he'd seen you at the golf links. Golf! Chisholm, by the way, is dreadfully concerned about your behavior."

Chisholm? My *behavior*? If he knew I was now an accused murderess, he'd probably spout steam from his hair follicles.

"I suppose," Mother said, "you're motoring yourself about in that masculine contraption, too?"

"Shall I come for a visit?" I asked, mock chipper.

"Immediately, Lola."

I was thirty-one years old. Why did Mother think she could order me around like a collie? "I'll call on you later today."

"But—"

I hung up.

"Lola!" Olive was beside me. "Oh, Lola, it's too, too dreadful. You weren't going to leave without saying good-bye, were you?"

"Um," I said. "Of course not. Olive, I am awfully sorry about—"

"No, no. I shall be fine." Olive looked fatigued, but her kohl was crisp. No tears, then. "The police are still here, you know. They're absolutely ransacking the house for clues. I do hope they find some. The very idea of a murderer loafing about is simply *not* to be tolerated."

"And Billy and Theo?" I asked "How are they?"

"Oh, still green about the gills from those cookies. Nanny Potter is *such* a marvel with them, though. I'd be lost without her."

"Is there anything I can do?"

"What? Oh no. No, I expect I'll be fine." Olive's eyes were fastened on something beyond me. I turned.

Out in the driveway, Bruno was stepping into a limousine. George Zucker waylaid him and they had a brief exchange. George looked pleading. Bruno seemed irritated.

Probably haggling about that film studio contract again.

I looked back to Olive. Her face was glowy.

Could Olive have shot Horace in order to free herself up for Bruno Luciano? How diabolical. And how *preposterous*.

When Bruno's limousine rolled away, Olive went inside without even saying good-bye to me.

I found Berta on the front walk. We watched George and Sadie bundle themselves into the Rolls-Royce. Eloise Wright, resplendent in a mink coat, whisked around Cedric and shot him a vile look.

"I guess Mrs. Wright doesn't like dogs," I said.

"There is no shame in that," Berta said.

"And for a lady whose lover—"

"Mrs. Woodby! *Language*."

"—has just been bopped off, she doesn't appear especially distraught."

Two menservants strapped luggage to racks, Hibbers overseeing it all.

Nanny Potter jogged into view from the side of the house, with Billy and Theo straggling like goslings in her wake. Poor fellows. What would become of them? Olive would probably pack them off to some chilly New England boarding school.

They jogged past the motorcars and out of sight again.

"I wonder what ever happened to that rotten Mr. Oliver," I said.

"He took himself off to the Foghorn in town yesterday evening," Berta said, "with the other extra hands Mrs. Arbuckle hired. No room for them in the house."

"I suppose he couldn't have been the murderer, then, or the one who stole the reel." How disappointing.

The Rolls-Royce and the Daimler drove off. Berta and I headed toward my Duesy.

"Leaving so soon?" Hibbers called.

I'm positive Thad Parker's getaways are much more slick.

"No need to stick around like a wad of chewing gum on the sidewalk," I said. "You look like you have something to say, Hibbers. Or maybe you had hot sauce on your eggs this morning? I told you to stop doing that, or you'll wind up a dyspeptic."

"Madam is most amusing." Hibbers came closer. "You requested that I inform you if I were alerted to the presence of a certain . . . item."

"You found the reel?"

Berta elbowed me. "Shush!"

I leaned in toward Hibbers. "Hand it over, pretty please."

"I did not *find* it precisely. It is more that I briefly . . . noticed it."

"Where?"

"In an open traveling bag, madam, but two minutes ago."

"Whose bag?"

"That is the predicament, madam. Miss Street and Mrs. Wright possess identical Hermès Frères weekend bags of fawn-colored calf-skin. Both bags sat in the drive, amid the other items of luggage, in preparation for loading their motorcars. I happened to glance into one—its top had not been fastened—and I spied what appeared to be a flat, round metal canister, approximately the size of a dinner plate."

"Silver colored?"

"Yes, madam. With, I believe, markings of some sort stamped on the top."

"That's the reel! Which lady's bag was it?"

"I cannot say."

"What do you mean?"

"I regret to say that when your canine took the opportunity to employ my pant leg as a napkin, I was momentarily distracted. During the time it took for me to disentangle myself from Cedric's jowls, both bags had been loaded into the motorcars."

Phooey.

"Thank you, Hibbers. One more thing—is it true what Inspector Digton said, that you vouched for the innocence of all the household staff?"

"Indeed, madam." He hovered.

"If you're expecting some jingle," I said, "I afraid I'm completely bust."

"Jingle, madam? Good heavens, no."

Berta, Cedric, and I heaped into the Duesy. Before I pulled away, I gave Dune House one last glance.

A small white face stared down from a high window. My heart lurched. Wait. It was only Auntie Arbuckle. She lifted her fingers to twiddle a farewell.

"Spooky little critter," I muttered, and peeled out of the driveway.

11

....

Berta and I motored halfway to New York and stopped at a roadside hash house for coffee and a bite to eat. If I claimed that such establishments were foreign to me, I'd be lying. Even in my Society Matron days, I'd now and again skulk into a cheap restaurant for a fry-up.

Once coffee was coursing through our veins, we talked over Horace's murder in low tones.

"Inspector Digton thinks it was me." I forked up some fried egg. "Goodness!"

"He thinks that Horace jilted me for another woman—Eloise Wright, I guess—and I was driven to murderous madness. Let's just hope he finds a better suspect soon."

"Inspector Digton was ever so kind to *me*," Berta said. "I even promised to mail him my shortbread recipe. True, he *is* rather stupid. He does not know about the film reel, either."

Oh yes. Berta and I had both lied to the police. Mustn't forget that.

"I can't help thinking it was Olive," I said. "She's gaga over Bruno Luciano, and now she's a wealthy widow."

"She is also at least a decade older than Mr. Luciano. Surely she has some sense of propriety."

"I wouldn't count on it."

"There *was* the key."

"What key?"

"Did Inspector Digton not tell you? The killer may have lured Mr. Arbuckle to the kitchen by placing a pantry key somewhere in his reach. A key, you see, was discovered on his . . . person. It was even labeled 'pantry.' The killer knew he could not resist having access to all that forbidden food. All they needed to do was give him access to the key, and then lie in wait."

"That's awful!"

"Mr. Arbuckle made straight for my snickerdoodles, I could not help but notice." Berta sipped her coffee.

"Don't look so smug."

"Leaving him the key is, perhaps, something only a wife would think up."

"A mistress would know about Horace's weaknesses, too."

"Mrs. Wright, you mean."

"Yes." I described Eloise's whispered conference with Lem Fitzpatrick at the golf links. "She's a sneak, mark my words. But, you know, everyone knew that the food was kept under lock and key. In fact, the way Olive was doling out the raw veg, *everyone* was probably peckish enough to kill." I took a huge bite of sausage with tomato catsup. "You know, if either Olive or Eloise had known Horace purchased a film starring Ruby—a saucy film, if that's what it is—they might've been jealous enough to kill."

"But to kill Mr. *Arbuckle?*" Berta touched her locket. "He was a nice man."

Not for the first time, I wondered what Berta's locket meant to her, and if there was a picture inside. She called herself *Mrs.*, but then where was Mr. Lundgren now? Berta was a forbidding lady, and I was too chicken to ask.

"I know what you mean," I said. "Horace was the last one of the bunch I'd expect to be bumped off." He'd always seemed to be, well, simply *there*, moseying in the margins, making big bucks, never complaining about his ballerina's rations. "Aside from his dalliance with Eloise Wright, he'd seemed to be a decent husband and father. It's a crying shame, especially since Digton's going to go barking up all the wrong trees." I pushed down my fear with more bites of sausage. "You know what I think, Berta? I think we ought to figure out who killed Horace ourselves."

Berta's eyes grew round. "That would be dangerous. And foolish."

"You still want to get ahold of the reel, don't you?"

"That is a financial necessity."

"Okay, well, if Horace's death is tangled up with the reel—and I'm not saying it is, but it *could* be—then looking for the film means looking for the murderer."

"Mrs. Woodby, it is one thing to search for a missing item, and quite another to attempt to unmask a killer."

"But if we're looking for the reel, will the murderer care about that distinction? Nope."

"This is *not* what I intended when we decided to retrieve the reel for Miss Simpkin."

"Well, *I* didn't exactly intend to be an accused murderess who's just maybe the *real* murderer's next victim, either."

Berta and I stared at each other for a long, long moment. We were going to do it. We were going to try to solve a murder.

Which meant I was unquestionably nuts, just like the Prig said.

. . . .

Once Berta and I were on the road again, I broke the silence. "To my way of thinking, it's obvious that we've got to locate Sadie Street and Eloise Wright. One of them has the reel in her bag." I half hoped Berta would call the whole sleuthing thing off.

But no.

"The little trollop has the reel," Berta said.

"Sadie?"

"Yes. I am not, of course, a lady who gambles. But if I were, my money would be on her."

"So then you think she's the murderer, too?"

"Why not? Her eyes are as cold as ice."

"But the way Hibbers told it, the reel could just as easily have been in Eloise Wright's bag."

"Why would that one have a film reel? A society matron—"

I pressed harder on the gas pedal.

"—a rich husband in the ever-so-dull department store business. The other one, the trollop, is an actress. Film reels are her bread and butter. Perhaps she is on the film alongside Ruby Simpkin."

A sudden thought hit me. I floored the gas pedal. We zoomed around a bend. Berta shrieked and clutched the dashboard. Cedric skittered on the rear seat.

"Come to think of it," I said, "Sadie *did* mention something about embarrassing screen tests the night before last."

"Aha! That is it. The budding starlet has something captured on the film that she would rather forget. Something she perhaps *killed* to forget."

"It'll be a cinch," I said. "We'll learn where Sadie Street lives, and pay her a little visit."

When we arrived at the Longfellow Street love nest, I went straight to the telephone and asked the operator to connect me with the

Hare's Hollow police department. When I was put through, first the secretary and then Inspector Digton scoffed at my request for Sadie Street's home address.

"Now, why would I give that to *you?*" Inspector Digton made a donkeylike guffaw.

I pulled the earpiece away. When I put it back to my ear, Digton was still hee-hawing.

"Thanks anyway," I said, and rang off.

Next, I had the operator connect me to the Pantheon Pictures studio in Flushing, Queens. It was Sunday, so I crossed my fingers that I'd get an answer.

"Yeah?" a woman barked down the line.

"Would you please give me Sadie Street's address?"

"You gotta be kidding me, lady."

"Wait! Don't hang up. I need to speak to her. It's urgent."

"Do you wanna know how many calls I've gotten for her, and for Luciano and Zucker, from you pests today? Holy cow! I got better things to do." She cut the connection.

You pests, she'd said. She'd probably meant reporters.

Motion picture stars *and* murder. What a sensation. That gave me an idea.

I asked the operator to put me through to the offices of the *New York Evening Observer*.

"Hello, Duffy," Ida Shanks said when I got her on the line. She was a hard worker to be there on a Sunday, I'd grant her that. "To what do I owe the pleasure of your call? Don't tell me you plan to give me an exclusive on your full confession of murder."

"Really, Miss Shanks," I said. "We've known each other since we were five years old. You know very well I wouldn't murder anybody."

"Dear me—doth the matron protest too much? And I do seem to recall a violent incident during which you pushed me from the seesaw and pulled my pigtails."

"That wasn't me! I've *told* you. That was Pansy Fennig. Anyway, I thought you might know Sadie Street's address. That's right up your alley, isn't it?"

Ida cackled. "Now, why would I do *you* any favors?"

"Why not?"

"I haven't got her address."

"Why do I think you're lying?"

"Think whatever you want, Duffy dear." Ida hung up.

12

At four o'clock that afternoon, I dressed in my most matronly suit, a silk blouse, Ferragamos, and pearls, and made good on my promise to visit my mother. I took a taxi uptown and alighted at 993 Park Avenue. This was a ritzy brick apartment building with Italianate embellishments of creamy stone. It was fewer than ten years old, but it was already established as a Very Good Address.

I said hello to the uniformed doorman and took the elevator to the twelfth floor.

Father (with Mother's militant counsel) had wrung Wall Street dry like a rag mop, so they'd been able to purchase the apartment next door to their first one, knock out some walls, and make quite a swanky spread of it. I rang the doorbell—gold leaf and rococo—and the butler cracked the door. He was a rangy, dark-skinned fellow with gray hair, flawless livery, and a condescending manner that I was pretty sure Mother had drilled into him.

"Good afternoon, Mrs. Woodby," he said. "Your mother has been expecting you."

"Hello, Chauncey."

Chauncey wasn't his real name, of course. His real name was Fred, but Mother had decided that Chauncey sounded more butleresque.

He led me toward Mother's sitting room.

The entry foyer had black-and-white marble floors, ornate moldings, and a ponderous chandelier calculated to bring on a migraine. I was used to those things, as well as the authentic Louis XIV furniture that looked fake. New to me, however, were the huge wooden crates everywhere. It looked as though a circus train had disgorged its contents into the apartment.

Chauncey acted like nothing was amiss, even as he picked around loose packing straw.

We reached the sitting room.

"Lola!" my mother screamed. She hurtled herself forward in her chair, but apparently ran out of sufficient steam to actually stand up. She was what you'd call a statuesque woman, with gray-streaked, upswept dark hair and a face that was still pretty, despite the calculating glint in her eye.

"Hello, Mother. Looks like you've bought up all of Europe's movable bits—that *is* what's in those packing crates, I guess?"

"She's redecorating," my sister, Lillian, said. "Again."

"Hello, Lillian. Where's Father?"

"His club," Mother said. "He said he needed to recuperate—from *what*, I cannot fathom."

Mother and Lillian reclined in blue brocade chairs beside a tea table. The room was overheated and smelled of old lady–ish perfume. Orchids burst from Chinese pots; satin drapes burst in swags around tall windows.

"Lola, come here this instant," Mother said. "Why, you look like something the cat dragged in, with those dark circles under your eyes."

"Because of the murder, Mother," Lillian said. "Don't forget that."

I kissed Mother's powdery cheek.

"How *could* I forget?" Mother said. "Lola, *must* you insinuate your-self in such unbecoming scenarios? First Alfie has a heart attack, then that Arbuckle affair so soon afterwards? We have Lillian to think of."

I sat, and started in on a lemon cream wafer from the tea table.

"That's right," Lillian said to me. She appeared too feeble to raise her pre-Raphaelite curls from the chair back. She was pleas-antly round, with that sort of marshmallow-white skin that burns in November and a face like a blue-eyed angel. Looks, of course, are deceiving. "I suppose you didn't think of *me* for a second be-fore you waltzed off to get involved in boozy murders with low company."

Low company. Now, why did that phrase ring a bell?

"We have Lillian's matrimonial prospects to keep in mind," Mother said.

Mother hallucinates, I have no doubt, about ordering bridal china for Lillian Carnegie or Lillian Rockefeller.

"It's not *my* fault that Lillian's debut was met with lackluster ap-plause last winter," I said.

"You're rotten!" Lillian said.

"Only checking to see if you still had a pulse," I said.

"Girls!"

"By the way," Lillian said to me, "what *are* you wearing?"

"Widow's weeds, darling."

Mother said, "I'm not certain that that length of skirt is advis-able with your ankles, Lola."

"You ought to be in a party dress," Lillian said. "You're finally rid of Alfie."

"Lillian!" Mother said.

"Mother, you said the same thing yourself just a few days ago, on the ship. Said he was a flat tire and an embarrassment and it was good riddance all around." Lillian gave me a nasty smile. "Too bad he spent all the money."

My jaws froze mid-chew.

"That's right," Lillian said. "Chisholm told us absolutely *every-thing*."

I looked at Mother. "Alfie a flat tire and an embarrassment? That's yesterday's news, of course, but I didn't know you felt that way."

"Aren't you sad?" Lillian asked.

"Why should I be? He was a hideous husband."

"But now you're poor."

"I'll manage."

"How *can* you speak in such a laissez-faire fashion?" Mother said, pronouncing *faire* like *fay-yuh*. She had been taking private French lessons. I suspected her tutor was a native of the Bronx. "Lola, you are to assume an attitude of correct decorum this instant. I arrived home after an exhausting journey—the Italians do *not* know how to cook, oh the things we were forced to consume—to learn that everything has gone to the underworld in a handbasket."

"The underworld?" I massaged my forehead.

"Do not goad me, child. Your husband is dead—"

"I told you as much in the telegram."

"—Chisholm Woodby has taken up residence in Amberley, and now Olive Arbuckle's husband has been murdered."

"You think that's all my fault? And back up a bit. Amberley? How did you know my—*the*—house's name has been changed?"

Mother and Lillian exchanged a sly glance.

"*What?*" I asked. "What's going on?"

"It is time you knew, Lola," Mother said. "For the duration of our Continental tour, Lillian has . . ."

The lemon wafer turned to sand on my tongue.

"Chisholm and I," Lillian said in her Miss Priss voice, "have been corresponding. We have an understanding."

"An *understanding*? You've—you're letting that prig, that absolute *prig*, romance you? Right under my nose, without even telling me? He's my brother-in-law!"

Lillian pruned her lips.

"It is not as though we intentionally hid anything from you, Lola," Mother said. "Only days before we set sail in March, Mr. Woodby requested my permission to write to Lillian, and hear of her impressions of Europe."

An awful thought struck me like a thunderbolt: If Lillian married Chisholm, Folie Maison, or Amberley, or whatever you called it—*my house*—would be hers. She'd probably redecorate the entire place in shades of puce.

"Oh, I wished to ask you, Lola," Mother said, "have you had the pleasure of making Mr. Raymond Hathorne's acquaintance? He is in the soda pop business. Such a delightful, interesting man—"

"Interesting?" Lillian said. "Mother, he was as dull as arithmetic."

"No, no, he was *très charmant*—"

Mental note: Ask Mother exactly how much she's paying that French tutor of hers.

"—when we met him at the captain's table during our voyage home. I was ever so impressed with his—"

"Bank account?" Lillian said.

"Lillian! No. With his character."

Was it possible that Mother was already attempting to reel in another big fish for me?

"I have no interest in meeting new gentlemen," I said. The briefest image of Ralph Oliver flickered in my mind's eye.

"Of *course* not. You are in mourning, and a proper duration of time must pass. But on the other hand—" Mother toyed with her bracelet. "—it never hurts to sow seeds, dear. And I got the distinct impression that Mr. Hathorne is not only on the wife hunt, but also not completely opposed to . . . *unconventional* sorts of ladies."

"*You're* unconventional, Lola," Lillian said. "Unconventional figure, unconventional face, unconventional habits, unconventional—"

"Oh dear me, look at the time," I said. I could've sent a few barbs in Lillian's direction, but she's so green. Life will knock the wind out of her sails eventually. One hopes. I grabbed a fistful of lemon cream wafers. "I really must be going." I made tracks across the carpet.

"But you haven't told me where you are living," Mother said. "At a hotel?"

"Yes. The Ritz."

"How can you afford it?" Lillian asked

"Lola," Mother said, "you can always come home."

When pigs fly.

Berta had made ham and pea soup in my absence. The apartment was fragrant, even homey—assuming you averted your eyes from the leopard-skin pillows and the naughty art books.

"Good heavens," Berta said when I came into the kitchen. "You look as though you have encountered a specter."

"Worse. My family."

"Oh dear me. I thought you were out shopping."

Berta knew all about Mother and Lillian. But when I told her about Lillian and Chisholm's courtship, her jaw fell.

"Come," she said. "Have some soup. I have already walked the dog."

"You walked Cedric?" I sat at the table. "I didn't know you were on speaking terms with him."

"Hmph."

Berta ladled soup over the scandalous picture in the bottom of the bowl. I dug in. Berta did the same. Cedric watched us from his cushion in the corner. A square, crackerlike object lay untouched in the bowl beside him.

"I purchased a box of Spratt's Puppy Biscuits at the market," Berta said, "but he refuses to go near them."

"Well, of course not. He wasn't raised in a barn."

"He is spoiled."

"He's pedigreed. There *is* a difference, you know."

"He will need to mend his ways, or he will starve. At any rate, I have been thinking."

"Uh-oh."

"We should visit the harlot again and ask her to tell us more about the film reel. Since we are not having good fortune in finding Sadie Street's address, we must, as Thad Parker says, sniff out a new trail."

I supposed *harlot* meant Ruby Simpkin. "All right," I said.

We arrived backstage at the Frivolities around nine o'clock. I was dog-tired, and hoped we wouldn't see Ralph Oliver under a heap of chorus girls again. Mr. Oliver had nothing to do, of course, with the fresh coat of lipstick I'd applied, or the way I'd slipped into a frothy peach Coco Chanel dress. A lady's got to keep her morale up. Not for the fellows. For herself.

Once again, we found Ruby perched at her mirror in the dressing room.

She twisted to face us. The muscles around her mascara-clumped eyes looked tight. "I was hoping you two would show. I read about, you know—" She leaned in. "—*Arbuckle*. Dead. In the evening paper. I didn't know how to reach you, see, and I was hoping you got the film before the shamuses started crawling around his house."

I swallowed. "We didn't find it," I said.

"*What?*" Ruby wailed.

A couple of chorus girls looked over.

Ruby lowered her voice. "What do you mean, didn't find it? Where the heck is it?"

"Well, we *found* it. But we didn't get it." I explained how I'd seen the film reel in the safe, and how it had disappeared at some point during the evening.

Ruby lit a cigarette.

"But we have a lead," Berta said.

Lead? Berta was certainly picking up Thad Parker's lingo like a sponge.

"What sorta lead?" Ruby asked.

Berta told her about the two calfskin weekend bags, and how Hibbers had seen the film reel in one of them. "Do you know either Sadie Street or Eloise Wright?"

"No," Ruby said.

I was pretty confident she was telling the truth.

"It might help things along if you told us what's on the film," I said. "Then we might be able to deduce whether it was Sadie or Eloise who stole it."

"Tell you what's on it? No way."

"But whatever is on that film was, maybe, enough to make someone commit murder."

"Listen, you agreed to get my film reel, and instead you've gone and lost track of it! It could be anywhere. *Anyone* could be looking at it." Ruby seemed small and terrified in her skimpy costume. "I'll give you more dough," she said. "Five thousand."

Berta opened her mouth; I shot her a firm glance.

"No," I said, "we'll stick to the original deal. Simply tell us what's on the film, for Pete's sake."

"If I told you that, *you'd* be in hot water, too. Just like me."

"What do you mean?"

Ruby spun back to the mirror and started brushing on more rouge.

"Just find it, okay? And if you ask me about what's on it one more time, I'm putting the fritz on the whole deal." She was acting tough, but her voice shook. "Now, scram. I gotta get ready for the next number."

I jotted down the telephone number of Alfie's love nest on a scrap of paper from my handbag. I placed it next to Ruby's rouge box. "Ring me up if you change your mind," I said.

13

"Whatever is on the film is incriminating not only to Ruby," I said to Berta once we were outside. "It's somehow incriminating to *anyone* who knows what's on it."

We walked down Forty-second Street. Theatergoers bustled along—ladies in furs and lipstick, fellows in dark suits and fedoras—chattering and pushing. Marquees with white lightbulbs lit up the air, and garish billboards advertising plays and revues studded the sides of buildings. In the street, horns beeped and cabbies yelled. The stale, tangy odor of the subway wafted up through sidewalk grates.

"I told you that harlot was lying about why she wanted the film reel," Berta said. "I had fancied it was one of those saucy French films. But it must be, instead, something quite different."

I dodged around a couple of soused sailors. "I've got it—maybe it's a crime or something. Caught on film."

"That is possible. If the criminal's identity was evident on the film, then whoever saw the film would therefore be in danger."

"Not to mention whoever is *looking* for the film would be in danger." I shivered despite the springlike evening air. "Berta, we aren't Thad Parkers by any stretch of the imagination. We're only a couple of ladies who need to pay the rent."

"Self-doubt doesn't suit you, Mrs. Woodby. It is terribly aging."

"Gee, thanks."

"And we *are* as clever as Thad Parker. True, Thad is in possession of a gun at all times. . . ." Berta tightened her grip on her handbag.

"That's just it." The crowd pushing along the sidewalk felt hostile. I lowered my voice. "The murderer could be *right here*, and we'd be none the wiser. I suppose we've got our wits, though, haven't we?"

"Indeed, we have. What is more, we have a sense of purpose, which is a quality that Thad Parker is at times sadly lacking."

We *did* have purpose in spades—if keeping yourself in an apartment and out of prison sufficed.

I slept until noon the next day. I struggled upright on the sofa, my back feeling like a rusted steel trap, and looked around the sitting room. "Cedric?" His little doggy bladder couldn't have lasted this long.

"In the kitchen," Berta called.

I wrapped myself in Alfie's paisley robe and staggered through.

"I walked Cedric already," Berta said. She was munching a raisin bun at the table. "You appeared to need the extra sleep, seeing as you were sleeping with your mouth so wide, I feared flies would buzz in."

Cedric sat at Berta's feet, staring up at her with steadfast attention. Well, not at *her* so much as at her raisin bun.

"Have you been feeding Cedric table scraps?" I asked.

"Good gracious, no."

I poured a cup of coffee for myself from the percolator. When I sat down, I noticed several magazines, one newspaper, and *London Lowdown*, the latest from Frank B. Jones, Jr., on the tabletop.

"I visited the newsstand and the bookshop when I took Cedric out," Berta said.

"So I see."

"These publications cost me nearly one dollar, all told. I added the exact amount in here." She waved a small notebook, upon which she'd printed *Business Expenses*. "We must do things properly."

"Are Thad Parker's further adventures really a business expense?"

"His insights are most illuminating."

"Okay. And maybe it's because I haven't had enough coffee, but I don't quite see what those magazines have got to do with business."

"Research." Berta held one up. It was an issue of *Motion Pictures Weekly*. The cover featured a photograph of some film star with Vase-lined eyelids and a wavy bob. The lettering read TEN CENTS, AGNES AYRES, WILL THE MOVIES SOON COST TWO DOLLARS? and WHAT MAT-RIMONIAL LOVE MEANS BY FRANCINE KERGSTALL. "Utter rubbish," Berta said. "Page after page of harlots displaying their anatomies."

I'd had a few sips of coffee by now, and understanding began to glimmer. "You don't think they'd actually print Sadie Street's home address in one of those pulp packets, do you? Why, she'd be swarmed by fans if they did. Not to mention reporters."

Berta's eyes flashed. "Perhaps we shall uncover a lead. Unless you have a better idea?"

I sighed. "Fine. Hand one over."

Berta slid over a copy of *Movie Love*, along with a raisin bun and the butter dish.

I devoured one raisin bun after another and thumbed through the magazines, inspecting them for any mention of Sadie Street. "No address," I said, "but she is quite the most talked-about girl at the moment. I had no idea. These columnists make her out to be a kind of wholesome, girl-next-door sort. Doesn't really line up with what I made of her."

"Nor I."

There were columns about new pictures, glamour photographs, and articles that relayed stars' beauty secrets, slimming diets, and romantic ruminations. Quite a bundle of pieces on Bruno Luciano, too. He had burst onto the scene only in the last year. It seemed the Latin Lothario enjoyed his beefsteak medium-rare, had his suits shipped from London, was devoted to Colgate's Rapid-Shave Cream (as long as they paid him to say it, I supposed), and slept only on silk sheets.

Yep. That sounded about right.

"Listen to this," I said. "This says that the head of Pantheon Pictures, George Zucker, discovered Sadie Street when she was working at the perfume counter of Wright's Department Store on Fifth Avenue. Says she was a sweet, humble shopgirl, working to pay for her sick little brother's operation, when George Zucker saw her angel face, gave her his card, and invited her to his film studio in Queens for a screen test."

"Wright's Department Store?" Berta frowned over the top edge of her newspaper. "The store of Eloise Wright's husband?"

"Yes. The plot thickens."

Berta was reading the *New York Evening Observer*. HIGH SOCIETY MURDER was emblazoned across the front page, with the subtitle MOTION PICTURE STARS QUESTIONED IN PORK AND BEANS KING'S DEATH.

"Perhaps now is not the proper moment to show you this, Mrs. Woodby," Berta said.

"Don't tell me it's Ida Shanks's column."

Berta pushed over the newspaper, folded open to the society page.

I bit the bullet (well, I actually bit into my fourth buttered raisin bun) and scanned the column. Ah, lovely, my mention came first: "Which monumental society matron"—Ida, bony-hipped as a mule, never could resist a dig at my figure—"has forgone mourning to partake in scandalous parties that end in murder?"

"That one has an axe to grind," Berta said.

"It's because we grew up together, in Scragg Springs. Attended the same schoolhouse, even, up until my family moved away to New York. Imagine my surprise when I ran into her again here in New York, with a herd of society reporters outside some gala or other. It was awkward, let me tell you. I'd come along in the world. She had, too, I suppose. I mean, she's got a newspaper job, and she attended a ladies' college in Illinois or someplace."

"Envious," Berta said. "Exactly like a girl in my village in Sweden—"

Not another one of these tales.

"—named Lotta. Scrawny little creature. Envious of my figure. All the lads liked me, liked my baking. Lotta could not bake, and she *looked* like she could not bake. Arms like drainpipes."

I carried my plate and cup to the sink. "Shall we go up Fifth Avenue and stop in at the perfume counter at Wright's Department Store? Maybe someone there can tell us where to find Sadie. And while we're at it, we could go and hunt down Eloise in the Foundations Department."

"Fine. But no shopping. We must keep our finances under control."

"Shopping? Who, me?" I said.

An hour later, our taxicab rattled to a stop on Fifth Avenue. I'd left the Deusy parked on Longfellow Street to avoid circling about for a parking spot. I paid the driver while Berta scribbled the fare amount in her business expenses notebook.

Wright's Department Store was several floors high, built of white stone, with lots of arched windows and brown-striped awnings. We pushed through one of the brass revolving doors.

Inside, the first floor was taken up by the food hall and the cosmetics department. The store was jammed. Voices echoed against vaulted ceilings, shoes clattered on marble floors, and if you squinted, the place looked like a swaying ocean of hats.

Wright's food hall peddled Belgian chocolates, caviar in tiny glass jars, tinned foie gras, funny little pickled things (these were meant to go with cocktails, but everyone pretended, ever since booze was outlawed, that they were hors d'oeuvres), biscuits in ornate tins, fragrant teas and coffees, and candies pretty enough to wear as jewelry.

"Hold your horses, would you?" I said, nudging Berta. I stopped in front of a wall of gorgeously wrapped chocolates.

But Berta hadn't felt my nudge, and she was swallowed up in the crowd.

I hesitated. It would be tough finding her again in this throng. On the other hand, I hadn't had good chocolate in at least a week.

"Torn?" a male voice said in my ear.

I turned to see Ralph Oliver's crinkle-cornered gray eyes. "Following me again?" I said. "I'd think it would grow wearisome."

"Not at all. It's one adventure after another with you, Mrs. Woodby. I was just starting to think you were getting a little boring—"

"How *dare* you?"

"—when Arbuckle went and got himself killed."

"That had nothing to do with me."

"Course not. But you were there."

"So were you."

"Not exactly. I was snug as a bug at the Foghorn in Hare's Hollow."

"Judging by the twinkle in your eye, I rather suspect you were dancing and drinking at an illegal gin mill."

"Maybe. My point is, I have an alibi. But *you*—you discovered the body. Can't you stay out of mischief, Mrs. Woodby?"

"If I stayed home and knitted socks all day, then you'd be out of a job."

"Naw. I told you. I'm investigating your dear departed hubby."

"Rubbish. You're investigating *me*." I added in my head, *And I'm worried you're working for a murderer.* I turned away from him and pretended to be absorbed in the chocolates display. The funny thing was, chocolate seemed a whole lot less interesting when Ralph Oliver was around.

He stood there, watching me. I assumed a starchy expression and read chocolate labels.

Out of the corner of my eye, I could tell he was grinning. I made an exasperated sigh. "Was there something I could help you with, Mr. Oliver?"

His eyes lingered on my lips. "Probably."

"Oh, go away, would you?"

He bumped up his fedora to scratch his temple. "Sure like your chocolate, don't you?"

My cheeks grew warm. "Well, I—"

"Don't get me wrong. Sweets for the sweet. Besides, I like my ladies . . ."

I prayed he wouldn't say *pleasantly plump.* Or *healthy.* Because then I would have to slap him.

"I like 'em satisfied," he said. His gaze sank into mine.

I swallowed. Why had it grown so danged *hot* in the store?

"What're you doing here, Mrs. Woodby?" He selected a large bar of milk chocolate with hazelnuts from the shelf.

"Shopping. Obviously."

"That all?" He took down another bar, nougat, and another, plain dark.

"What are you suggesting?"

Ralph paid the shopgirl with a mangled bill from his wallet. "I'm not suggesting anything. Merely piecing it all together, see. And to me, it looks a lot like you and your Swedish sidekick are up to something. Trying to solve Horace Arbuckle's murder? I dunno. I just don't think it's wise for ladies to get mixed up in these kinds of affairs. There are things you don't know."

"What things?"

"Dangerous things." He pushed the chocolate bars into my hands. "There. Got you an assortment." He tipped his fedora and stalked off, his shabby-suited form merging into the crowd.

14

After ten minutes of searching, I found Berta at the perfume counter.

"Where have you been, Mrs. Woodby?" she said. Her voice was muffled by the hankie she held over her nose.

I gulped down the square of chocolate I'd been chewing, crumpled the foil over the end of the bar, and stuffed it in my handbag. "Nowhere."

Berta tipped her head toward the shopgirls behind the counter. "I suppose these are the ones we should ask questions of."

One of the girls was wrapping a box in brown-and-white houndstooth paper. She was wispy, with a dark bob and pug-dog eyes. The other girl, kneeling behind the counter and rummaging in a drawer, had a gerbil-colored updo and a pudgy build. They both wore houndstooth Wright's smocks.

Berta and I waited until their customer left.

"Excuse me," I said to the wispy girl, "is this the counter where Sadie Street used to work?"

She rolled her eyes. The other girl boinged up beside her.

"If I had a nickel for every time I've been asked that," the wispy girl said.

"A nickel?" the gerbil-haired one said. "Why, we'd be drinking tea with Mrs. Rockefeller if we had a *penny* for every time." She turned to me. "Look, lady. We're trying to do business here. This ain't some tourist attraction."

Wispy elbowed Gerbil Hair. *"Isn't,"* she whispered.

"That's what I *said*," Gerbil Hair whispered back. She glared at me. "Now, if you're interested in some perfume, I can help you with that." She swept her hand along the counter. "We got your Lilac Aphrodite, your Musky Maiden, your Pompeia, and your Sphinx. Here we have the Elizabeth Arden Babani line—Ambre de Delhi, Ligeia, and Ming." She tapped fingers on the countertop. "So what'll it be?"

Berta removed the hankie from her face. "I shall buy a bottle—your smallest bottle—if you tell us about Sadie Street." She shot me a glance: *business expense.*

"Why're people so crazy about Sadie Street?" Wispy said. "She was nothing special."

"So this *is* where she worked," I said.

Gerbil Hair wedged herself in front of Wispy. "You got to buy something first. We work on commission."

"Oh, all right." I dug through the chocolate bars in my handbag, pulled out my coin purse, and found a fin.

Berta's eyebrows lifted. Five dollars was obviously more than she'd had in mind. But this was Wright's, not the five-and-dime. I placed the bill on the countertop. "What'll this get me?"

"A miniature Roger and Gallet Le Jade." Gerbil Hair stuffed the money in the till. "Okay, what do you want to know about the wondrous Sadie?"

"Were you here when she was discovered by the motion picture executive?" I asked.

"Nope," Gerbil Hair said. "Never saw the fish."

"Neither did I," Wispy said. "None of us girls ever saw him here."

"Do you even know what he looks like?" I said.

"Course," Gerbil Hair said. "His photograph's in the motion picture weeklies all the time. George Zucker. He's a big cheese."

"Do you know where Sadie lives?" I asked.

"What are you, some kinda fanatic?"

"Um," I said.

"We are private detectives," Berta said through her hankie.

Both girls blinked.

"Oh!" Gerbil Hair said. "Because of that murder! Saw it in the papers on my way to work. Is Sadie the murderer, you think?" She looked cheery.

"Sadie didn't really work here long," Wispy said. "Maybe three days."

"When was this?"

"Back in . . . let's see. January. I remember, because it was right after the Christmas rush, and all us girls thought it was funny that the management hired a new girl in the slowest month of the year. But like I said, she was only here a couple days."

"Yeah," Gerbil Hair said, "but them couple days was still long enough for the reporters to sneak in and snap her picture while she posed, all prissylike, at the counter. Acting like she was a hardworking girl. But we knew better, didn't we?" She elbowed Wispy.

Wispy elbowed her back. "We *said* we wasn't gonna *talk* about that," she muttered. She gave us a counterfeit smile. "Anything else, ladies?"

"You have not given us our perfume," Berta said.

"Didn't think you actually wanted it." Gerbil Hair stomped off to fetch the bottle.

We had Wispy alone. I leaned in close. "What was that she was saying, about knowing better about Sadie being a hardworking girl and all that?"

Wispy chewed her lip. Her eyes slid over to Gerbil Hair, who had her head buried in a cupboard. "All right. I'll tell you."

I saw Ralph Oliver, not three yards away, lounging against a marble pillar with his arms folded and his fedora tipped at that exasperating angle. He was looking right at Wispy, all ears.

The absolute *gink*.

But Gerbil Hair would be back in a second. I had no choice but to let Ralph listen in.

"Go ahead," I said, throwing Ralph a dirty look.

He made kissy lips at me.

"Don't tell a soul," Wispy breathed. "I went to one of those backroom bars, see. Blue Heaven, up in Harlem. Just the once, on a lark with my brother and his friend. This was before Sadie came here. In December, I think it was. And I saw her there."

"That's all?" I said. "Lots of people go to speakeasies."

"Sure, that's true. But Sadie wasn't there drinking. She was up onstage. Singing jazz."

"You're sure it was her?"

Gerbil Hair returned with the perfume. She wrapped it up in houndstooth tissue, and Berta and I headed toward the front of the store. Berta didn't notice Ralph as we passed him. I gave him a freezing look. He winked.

A few seconds later, I glanced over my shoulder to see Ralph sauntering away in the other direction.

As soon as Ralph's back was turned, I grabbed Berta's arm and pulled her toward the elevators.

"Where are we going?" she asked.

"Did you forget about Eloise Wright? She's still just as much of a possibility for having stolen the reel as Sadie is." We stepped onto the elevator. "Foundations Department," I said to the red-uniformed elevator boy.

He appeared to be wrestling with the inclination to smirk as he pushed the button for the fifth floor.

The Foundations Department was bathed in soft light. Soothing music wafted from somewhere. The carpet was like a soufflé. All, of course, to distract ladies from the reality that they were purchasing a garment made of steel and elastic panels to squash themselves into shape.

Eloise wasn't in. "She'll be here tomorrow," the saleslady behind the brassiere counter told us. "Would you like to make an appointment for a girdle fitting?" She peered over the tops of her oblong glasses at Berta and me—actually, at our middles.

"No, thanks." I turned toward the elevators and ignored Berta's appalled gasps as we passed a rack of lacy negligees.

I couldn't leave Wright's without buying caviar for Cedric in the food hall.

"That is *not* a business expense, Mrs. Woodby," Berta said.

"But Cedric hasn't so much as sniffed those Spratt's Puppy Biscuits."

"You indulge him."

"He'll waste away!"

I set the jar of caviar on the counter, and my last five-dollar bill next to it. "It's not beluga, anyway—only salmon."

"Where I come from," Berta said, "the dogs eat the offal and fish innards they find in alleyways."

The cashier gave me my change. I crammed the caviar into my

handbag, next to the chocolate bars. "Well, then. Cedric's not so very far off the mark, is he?"

It started raining around dinnertime. Berta and I ate bowls of left-over pea soup, spinach salad with vinaigrette, and fresh-baked buttery rolls. Cedric had caviar. A little later, we dressed to go to Blue Heaven.

"It's a speakeasy, Berta," I said when we convened in the foyer. "Not an ice cream social." She wore a dress printed with daisies and old-timey boots that gave me bunions just looking at them.

"You do not like my dress?" Berta pulled on her rubberized raincoat. "I do not care."

Next to her, I looked like a vamp escaped from the inferno: red lipstick, beaded purple dress with a plummeting V neckline, seamed black stockings, spiky shoes, mink-collared coat. The coat was kind of scrunched from being in my suitcase, but I figured that in this dress, no one would be looking at my coat.

We hustled out the door.

It took a couple of tries before we found a taxi driver willing to admit that he knew where Blue Heaven was. He drove us to an out-of-the-way street in Harlem. A few folks strode down the wet sidewalk, eyes cast down. A ramshackle brick building overshadowed us. Its windows were boarded up.

"Through there," the taxi driver said out the window. He jerked his thumb toward a dark alleyway.

Berta and I lingered on the curb.

"You're certain?" I asked.

"Listen, lady, I'm gonna charge extra if you keep me hanging around all night."

"Business expenses," Berta whispered.

I thanked the driver, and the taxi splashed away.

I hadn't been to Blue Heaven before, but I'd been to lots of speak-easies. So when I saw a door in the alley with a small sliding panel, I knew I was looking at a speakeasy entrance.

I knocked on the door.

The sliding panel whapped open. Two eyes appeared. "Yeah?"

"We are here to attend the festivities," Berta said.

"He wants the password," I whispered to her. Then, to the guard I said, "Um, hocus-pocus?"

He didn't flicker an eyelash.

"Gin rickey?"

"Open sesame," Berta said. "It is always open sesame."

"Not this time it ain't, mama."

"How about Louis Armstrong?" I asked.

"Don't think so." He started sliding the little door closed.

"Oh, very well," Berta said.

The sliding door stopped, halfway shut.

Berta bent over and drew up the hem of her dress to reveal a por-tion of her woolen-stockinged, bowling-pin calf.

"Berta!" I said.

The man chuckled. "Lady, I can tell you ain't one to go around flashing your gams at the drop of a hat. I can see you're desperate. Besides, we need some variety down there. All them flappers is start-ing to look the same." He slammed the little window shut and opened the door.

We were in.

We walked along an ill-lit corridor and down a rickety stair-case.

"Are you certain this is quite safe, Mrs. Woodby?" Berta asked.

"I'm pretty sure it's not." I pushed open the door at the bottom of the stairs.

We entered a raucous, crowded, low-ceilinged cavern that reeked of cigarettes, spilled gin, and sweat. A bar stood off to one side. Slick-haired men in suits buzzed around flappers in short, sparkly dresses. Bartenders rattled shakers, ice clinked, girls shrieked with laughter. Mismatched tables and chairs were packed with more people bobbing their heads to the music, smoking, and chattering. A dance floor, twisting with perspiration-glossed bodies, filled the space in front of the stage, where a jazz band wailed out a tune.

Berta and I would've looked like a couple of nervous nanny goats, standing there by the door, if anyone had paid us a bit of notice. But no one did.

No one, that is, except Ralph Oliver.

He sat at a table by himself, hunched over a drink in a teacup, and staring at me from beneath a furrowed brow.

My belly did a flip.

"Ah," Berta said over the ruckus. "So that is why you are tarted up so. You knew the Irish detective would be here."

The possibility *had* crossed my mind. "I'm not tarted up. And how was I to know he'd be here?"

"Perhaps because he was eavesdropping upon our conversation with the perfume girls this afternoon?" Berta toddled toward Ralph's table.

I followed her. "You saw him?"

"I am not blind. Thad Parker says that a private detective has eyes on the back of his head."

"You do know that Thad Parker's not a real person, right?"

By the time we reached Ralph's table, he was grinning.

I tossed my beaded clutch on the table and dropped into the chair kitty-corner to his. "Care to fill me in on the joke?" I shimmied out of my coat.

"Oh, nothing. You're kinda cute, that's all."

I gave him a withering look and flagged down the waiter, a short black fellow in a red waistcoat. "Highball, please. On the double."

"I shall have an orange blossom," Berta said. "With more blossom than orange, if you please."

"That's got gin in it," I said to her.

"Do you think you invented drinking, Mrs. Woodby?" Berta said.

15

After the waiter left, Ralph scooted his chair around the corner of the table so he was right next to me.

He wore evening clothes. They were threadbare, but the black and white made him look *just* a touch too handsome for such close quarters. His ginger hair was slicked up and over with brilliantine. His forehead was a little weathered, like he'd spent time working outside. By the looks of those sturdy shoulders, I'd have said in farming or construction. And on his right temple was a two-inch-long, deep, white scar.

He caught me studying it. "Shrapnel," he said over the hubbub. "France."

That was all he needed to say. The Great War had mangled half the young men you saw on the street. Those, that is, who'd been lucky enough to make it back home.

"Is that scar why you've always got your hat tipped down?" I asked.

"Nope. The tipped hat's for the ladies."

Ralph Oliver was nothing but a bee in my bonnet. But who *was* he, exactly? At Wright's, I'd worried he was working for the murderer, but now I almost wondered if he was working for Uncle Sam. And why, oh *why*, did I find the sight of his big square hand fiddling with that chipped teacup so mesmerizing?

"Where are you from, Mr. Oliver?" I asked.

"That's not something I like to say."

"Why not?"

"How come you don't like to say you're from Scragg Springs?" I frowned.

"Come on, kid. Lighten up." He gently chucked my chin.

I felt a bit melty. Good golly. I hadn't even started drinking yet.

"By the way," Ralph said, "you look gorgeous tonight."

Melty? Heck, I was practically a puddle on the floor.

He leaned his forearm on the table and turned to look at me more closely. "I've gotta say, I'm a little surprised you turned up at this joint."

"Well, Mr. Oliver," Berta called from across the table, "we are not surprised to find *you* here. You follow us like the little lamb after Mary."

"It's a bad habit you've got, Mr. Oliver," I said.

Ralph leaned in still closer. "Oh, I've got worse habits than that."

"I shudder to think." Actually, I felt kind of feverish.

"Listen, you two," Ralph said, slouching back in his chair. "I came here tonight because I worried that if you were crazy enough to show up—which I guess you are—you could be getting yourselves behind the eight ball."

"Oh, come off it," I said.

"This is an illegal establishment. There is, course, always the possibility of police raids. I can just imagine what the society page in the paper would have to say about you being collared in a raid, Mrs. Woodby."

"You read the society page? Not . . . the column by Miss Ida Shanks?"

"I read a lot, Mrs. Woodby."

The waiter arrived with our drinks. I grabbed my highball and took a gulp.

"The possibility of police raids aside," Ralph went on, "there's the dirty little fact that this place, like every underground jazz and booze joint in town, is run by gangsters. Including one real prominent gangster I think you know."

"I don't consort with gangsters," I said. "I've never met one in my life!"

"No? What about that one?" I followed his glance. So did Berta.

Lem Fitzpatrick sat a few tables down.

Lem held court amid a bunch of men who could've posed as gangsters for the funny pages: pomade-smooth hair, pinstripe suits, stubbly jaws. White spats flashed under the table.

"Lem said he was in the tin can business," I said.

"Oh, he's in business, all right, but it's not tin cans," Ralph said. "Fitzpatrick runs half the speakeasies in New York, and he's got his finger in lots of other pies, too. He's a gangster. One of the kingpins, actually, although he's just coming up in the world after his older brother Luke went for a swim in the East River last year."

"Are you sure about all of this?"

"Never met him personally—aside from seeing him up at the Arbuckles' place, that is—but I know him by reputation." Ralph took a swallow from his teacup. "Lucky for Fitzpatrick, he's not quite famous yet. And that Hare's Hollow police inspector, Digton, wouldn't recognize a gangster if he tripped over one."

"As you are obviously aware, Mr. Oliver, the reason Berta and I came here tonight was because we're trying to find Sadie Street, and we were told she used to sing here."

"Right," Ralph said. "I heard the shopgirl at the store this afternoon."

"Well, the funny thing is, when we were all up at Dune House, Lem and Sadie acted like they were meeting for the very first time."

"Why would they do otherwise?" Berta said. "According to the motion picture magazines, Sadie has a wholesome public image. She would not wish for anyone to know that she used to sing jazz at a sordid club."

"There's more," I said. I told them how I'd seen Lem and Sadie playing footsie under the Arbuckles' dinner table.

"Huh," Ralph said. "So not only did Sadie know Fitzpatrick from this club, but the two of them are an item."

"Yes," I said. "But why hide it?"

"Because," Berta said, "girls next door do not tumble with gangsters."

That made sense.

"What I'd like to know," Ralph said, "is why Fitzpatrick pretended to be in the tin can business at Dune House. I mean, did Arbuckle know he was really a gangster?"

Berta and I exchanged a glance.

"Listen, Mr. Oliver," I said. "Berta and I don't wish to get involved in Horace's murder."

"Oh no? Then what're you two doing here, looking for Sadie?"

"Business," Berta said. She waved her empty teacup at the waiter.

"Did you already polish off that drink?" I whispered to her.

She pretended not to hear me.

"What kind of business?" Ralph asked.

"Never you mind," I said.

The waiter took Berta's order for a fresh orange blossom.

I stared over at Lem Fitzpatrick. He had same moody, haunted look I'd noticed at Dune House, and that same nasty curl to his lip.

Lem caught me looking.

Rats.

His eyes narrowed, and he stood.

The fellow next to him stood, too. He was puny and bowlegged, with a beat-up face and a squashed nose. His diminutive pin-striped suit was exquisitely cut.

Girls gawked at Lem as he snaked through the tables toward us; men glanced at him with covert dread. The bowlegged guy followed.

I swallowed half my drink.

"Jiminy Christmas," Ralph muttered.

"Well, well, well. If it isn't New York's most scandalous widow," Lem said, hitching up a chair beside me. The bowlegged man sat down next to Berta.

"Read about you in the papers today," Lem said to me. He looked at Ralph. "Say, why do you look so familiar?"

"The name's Smith," Ralph said. "John Smith." He rose halfway and shook Lem's hand.

"Sure," Lem said, settling into the chair. "About half the fellers in this place are named John Smith. Funny, ain't it? This here is Jimmy the Ant. Say hello, Jimmy."

Jimmy smiled. He was missing some teeth, and I suspected one of his eyes was glass.

"Jimmy was the all-borough featherweight champ six years straight. What we always say is, don't fiddle with Jimmy or he'll fiddle with your face."

Jimmy said, "Heh-heh-heh." His voice was surprisingly gruff, given his petite stature. He winked his good eye at Berta.

Berta's eyes bugged.

Lem looked me up and down. "Nice dress."

"Thanks."

"Well," Lem said, "guess my secret's out."

I batted my mascara-globbed lashes. "What secret?"

"That I'm not a—what did I say up at Arbuckle's place?—oh yeah. I'm not a tin can salesman." Lem lurched toward me; I shrank toward Ralph. "What're you doing here, cookie? Following me or something?"

"Now, listen here, buddy," Ralph said.

"It's okay," I whispered to Ralph. I batted my lashes again at Lem.

"I seen that trick before, cookie," Lem said. "Blinking your big eyes like Krazy Kat, playing dumb. Not gonna work." A muscle on his cheek twitched.

You probably can't be a gangster kingpin without succumbing to a certain amount of deranged paranoia.

The atmosphere at the table was thick, but Lem was already on to me. Might as well pump him for as much information as I could.

"It's true," I said. "The beans are spilled. I'm looking for the film reel."

Berta made a tiny, indignant blat.

Not a flicker of understanding crossed Lem's features. "Film reel? Don't know about no film reel."

"She is, as they say, out on the roof," Berta said. "She does not make a bit of sense after she has been at the highballs." The waiter appeared with Berta's second orange blossom. She grabbed it right out of his hand and polished it off. She stood. "Mrs. Woodby, shall we—?"

"Dance?" Jimmy the Ant said. He jumped to his feet, and his chair crashed behind him. He grabbed Berta's hand.

Berta's mouth was an O of outrage. On the other hand, she'd downed two orange blossoms, so Jimmy was able to pull her out onto the dance floor.

The musicians launched into a sassy rendition of "The Sheik of Araby."

"Yeah, dancing sounds like a swell plan," Ralph said, and he pulled me out onto the dance floor, too.

"Rule number one," Ralph said, pulling me close to his chest, "don't show your hand." He twirled me around, then drew me close again. "Especially not to a gangster."

"Who are you, Professor Gumshoe?"

"I could be a *real* good teacher." His gray eyes glowed. "Of lots of things."

Oh boy.

Ralph was as good a dancer as a fellow could be before a girl started asking pertinent questions. He was at home in his body. And his eyes were all over me.

I'd had one highball. Only one. But I started to wonder in a dazed sort of way, as I shook my hips and swayed my bare shoulders to the devilish, divine jazz, if I'd made a fatal error in my mathematical calculations. This was a speakeasy. The booze was extra, *extra* strong.

But the thing about extra-strong booze is that it makes you not give a hippo's toot about your fatal errors. That was sort of the whole point of the stuff.

So I swam with Ralph in the glittery, steamy mess of bodies. My ears were full of skidding trombone; my mouth tasted like salt and whiskey.

And when Ralph, with his laughing eyes and serious mouth, got really close during the slow numbers, I can't say that I made much of an effort to act demure.

However, I *wasn't* too far gone to burst out laughing when I spied Berta gyrating on the dance floor with bandy-legged Jimmy the Ant. Berta must've lurched across her cocktail limit, too.

. . . .

"Hey," Ralph whispered when the music died down. The musicians were taking a break. "Let's go backstage. We can ask the musicians if they know where to find Sadie. After all, she worked with them, right? I heard this is the regular band here."

"What if Lem sees?"

"We'll just say we're looking for the powder room. Isn't that what you ladies always say when you go snooping?"

"Wait a minute. *We're* looking for the powder room? What's all this *we* business?"

Ralph pulled me toward a curtained door next to the stage. "Only trying to help out. I'd hate to see you not get what you came for."

It didn't line up quite right. Still, talking to the musicians was a great idea.

Backstage was a set of cramped little rooms with pipes crisscrossing the ceiling. We looked through an open doorway. The musicians, all of them brown-skinned men of assorted ages, lounged on chairs or stood around smoking. They were in their shirtsleeves, sweating from their performance. Shining brass instruments lay on a table, or inside cases on the floor.

"Hey!" one of them yelled. It was the trumpeter, paunchy and middle-aged. "What're you two doing back here? Musicians only."

Uh-oh. "I'm looking for Sadie Street," I said.

The musicians exchanged glances.

"You mean Sadie *Minsky?*" the trumpet player said.

"Um, I guess so. She must've changed her name. To become an actress."

"Well, there's your answer." That was the sinewy piano player. He puffed at a smoke. "The canary took off to be in the pictures. That's the last we saw of her. A shame, too, those beautiful pipes of hers wasted in them picture shows where there's nothing but crummy rags for sound."

"Do you know where she lives?" I asked. "Or where she used to live, back when she sang here?"

Again, the musicians exchanged a round of glances. The pianist stubbed out his cigarette. "Girl, you'd best be minding your own business about Sadie Minsky, if you know what's good for you. And I know what's good for me, so I ain't going to talk about her anymore." He turned his shoulder to me and started speaking to the trombone player in a private tone.

"Thanks," I said.

They ignored me.

Ralph and I hurried back to the dance floor.

"Minsky!" I whispered.

"Don't look now," Ralph said, "but Fitzpatrick is coming our way." He patted my low back. "Listen, kid, I think you'd better call it a night. Go grab your Swedish sidekick, and I'll get you a taxi."

Once Berta and I were careening in a taxicab through the midnight streets, I told her about Sadie's real last name.

"Are you even listening?" I asked.

Berta sat ramrod straight. Her handbag was propped on knees sandwiched together so tightly, you'd have thought she was a nun in the confessional booth.

"Thinking about Jimmy?" I asked.

"What?" she yelled.

"You made quite the conquest."

"I did nothing of the sort." Berta's face softened. "Although, Jimmy is not so low a character as one would suppose a gangster to be. He grew up on a farm. In Missouri."

"Oh, okay, does the farm cancel out the gangster bit?"

She tsked her tongue and turned to stare out the window.

I leaned my head back on the seat. I was woozy, and disheartened about the film reel. And extremely annoyed that I couldn't erase the feeling of Ralph's big, warm palms on my body.

It wasn't until I was nearly asleep, snuggled up with Cedric on Alfie's sofa, that the most important question came into focus: Why the heck was Ralph helping us look for Sadie Street?

16

I was stuffed like a Thanksgiving turkey with cinnamon rolls when Berta and I waddled through the doors of Wright's on Fifth Avenue the next morning.

"I can't keep on like this," I said. We walked toward the elevators. "I'm going to split my seams. Look at this dress! It's supposed to *drape*, for Pete's sake. Not hug." We got on the elevator.

"You ought not complain," Berta said. "Fellows like a homey girl."

"'Homey girl'?" I couldn't decide if that was better or worse than Society Matron.

The elevator boy said, "Which floor, madam?"

And when had I gone from being a *miss* to a *madam*?

"Foundations Department," I muttered.

He hid his smirk.

"Pronto, young man," Berta barked. "And have you tried witch hazel for your spots? It worked miracles for my cousin Edvard."

The elevator boy's smirk dissolved, and he hit the button marked 5.

"Remember what we agreed upon," I whispered to Berta after we stepped off the elevator. "I'm going to come right out and demand the film reel from Eloise, and we'll see where that takes us."

We'd talked it over at breakfast. After last night's impromptu questioning of Lem Fitzpatrick at Blue Heaven, we'd decided we needed to stay on the same page. However, that flea of a landlord was due back in three days, so we'd agreed that blustering might speed things up. And now that we knew Lem Fitzpatrick was a gangster, Eloise's little business conference with him at the golf links had taken on a decidedly suspicious cast.

We approached the saleslady at the girdle and corset counter. Her stout figure was frozen into the shape of one of those Russian stacking dolls. Her hair was a waved silver helmet. "May I be of assistance?" she asked.

"I was hoping to speak to Mrs. Wright," I said.

"Oh? Do you have a private fitting scheduled?" She opened up a pink suede book. "Name, please?"

"I don't have an appointment," I said. Darn it. I should've made one yesterday.

She slapped the book shut. "Then I am afraid—"

"*I* have an appointment," Berta said.

The saleslady opened the book again. "Name?"

Berta craned her neck, trying to read the appointment book upside down. "Mrs. Beeker."

The saleslady's fingertip stopped beside a name. "I have a Mrs. Bleeker. Not a Beeker."

"Silly girl on the telephone took it down wrong," Berta said. "They always do."

"Very well. Follow me."

We wove through long-line brassieres, garter belts, and dressing gowns, went down a hallway, and stopped at a pink door. The saleslady knocked.

"Enter," a voice called.

Eloise Wright sat behind a desk in a large pink chair—a throne, really.

The room was decorated with pink flocked wallpaper and swagged curtains, and one wall was taken up with built-in pink wardrobes. Cardboard boxes towered in the corner. The boxes were stamped with a picture of a crown and the words GIRDLE QUEEN.

Well, that explained the throne, then.

Eloise dismissed the saleslady. Then she turned to me. "Mrs. Woodby, what a surprise. I was under the impression that a—" She glanced through her reading glasses at a paper on her desk. "—a Mrs. Bleeker was here to see me?"

"Never mind that," I said.

"And who—" She looked at Berta. "—is this?"

"My assistant."

"And which of you is in need of a fitting?" Eloise looked first at Berta's midriff, tightly cased as always in her old-fashioned steel-boned corset, and then at my cinnamon roll middle. "Of course. Mrs. Woodby. Yes, I recall we spoke briefly of your . . . little problem at the Arbuckles' country place."

Little problem? "I actually came here," I said, "to—"

The telephone on Eloise's desk jangled. She picked up the earpiece and leaned close to the transmitter. "Yes?" She frowned, and glanced at the mountain of cardboard boxes. "As a matter of fact, yes, I have found a way to dispose of them, but—what? Oh, all right." She hung up. "I beg your pardon. It's my seconds." She gestured toward the boxes. "That's but a fraction of them, and there are always more coming from the factory. They'll be the absolute death of me. I'm afraid I must pop over to the freight elevators—I'll be back in a jiffy." She hurried out.

As soon as Eloise was gone, Berta poked through one of the cardboard boxes. "Girdles," she said.

"Her husband was complaining about the factory seconds at Dune House. Said they were a waste of money. There must be hundreds of them in those boxes."

Berta stared meaningfully at Eloise's desk, and then at me.

"What?" I asked.

"*I am not going to do it.*"

"Oh, fine." I went around to the other side of Eloise's desk. The top was cluttered with papers, all of them typed. Only one paper had handwriting: a small, lined scrap that said *17 Wharfside*.

I started opening the desk drawers, one by one.

"Anything?" Berta asked, peeking out the door.

"Lots of things." I crouched down and slid open the last drawer. It held a rubbery white mound. "But no—Berta?" I'd heard her peep.

Someone made a tactful cough.

Slowly, I shut the drawer and stood.

Berta stood there, looking mortified. Next to a red-cheeked Eloise.

"Might I inquire what you are doing in my drawers?" Eloise asked.

It probably wasn't the best time for a joke about underpants. "I, um—"

"She is here to demand the return of the stolen film reel," Berta said.

"The what?" Eloise's bosom heaved.

"The reel that you nicked from Horace," I said.

Eloise's face was blank.

I could bring her tryst with Horace into the mix. Maybe *that* would make her fess up. "I saw you with Horace Arbuckle the night before he died."

"Saw me with him? Well, of course you did. We were *all* with him last weekend. What are you doing? Poking your nose into the murder investigation? And would you mind getting away from my desk?

I am attempting to conduct business here. I don't want your bored little housewife's game to disorder my operations."

I took my place beside Berta. Eloise, meanwhile, marched around and resumed her seat on the pink throne.

"Now, then." Eloise folded her hands on top of the blotter. "Tell me again what it is you wish to confront me about?"

Why did I get the feeling she was trying to hide that scrap of paper that said *17 Wharfside?*

"Well, for starters, I saw you with Horace," I said. "In his study. Somewhat, um, in the altogether."

Eloise's face had been a perfectly powdered and lipsticked mask of puzzlement. Now, understanding (and what looked a lot like mirth) washed over it. "Oh! Dear me. You saw that, did you?"

"Did you tell the police about your liaison?" I asked.

"I assure you, Mrs. Woodby, I had no *liaison* with Horace Arbuckle. What did you think? That I shot him in some lover's crime of passion? Oh my. Horace didn't really inspire those sorts of sentiments. Unless you—?"

"Me?" I said. "And *Horace?* No!"

"One never knows. Horace and I merely . . . how shall I put this? I suppose I *must* tell you, or you'll go waltzing off to the police with your grievous misunderstanding, and then we'll be in that much more of a muddle. As you know, Horace was a stout man. Far more stout than his wife wished. He approached me with a matter of the utmost delicacy. He asked for my help."

I lifted an eyebrow. "No matter what you call it, it's still—"

"No, no. You see, I was fitting Horace for a girdle."

My mouth fell open.

"A prototype of my own design," Eloise said. "I have developed a new sort of girdle—patent pending, mind you—that is made of one hundred percent surgical rubber." She opened a desk drawer and took out the quivery white mass I'd noticed before. She held it up.

So *that's* what that was: a rubber girdle, a big flexible tube with little holes punched all over.

"The holes allow the skin to breathe," Eloise said. "Unlike traditional corsets and even the newer girdles with elastic panels, this girdle allows for a natural range of motion, all while keeping the problematic figure well contained." She looked at my middle again.

I inched my handbag over to cover it up.

"Because of the natural motion made possible," Eloise said, "my rubberized girdles are appropriate for gentlemen's use. No telltale rigid posture or inhibited movements, you see."

"Are you telling me that Olive Arbuckle drove Horace to use a man-girdle?" I asked.

"Well, yes. Although the gents' item is called a Chappie, not a girdle. Patent pending, of course." Eloise stood and picked up a pink measuring tape that lay coiled on her desk. As she did so, she placed the girdle on the scrap of paper she'd been hiding with her hands.

What could be so top secret about that address?

"Allow me to fit you for a complimentary girdle," Eloise said to me. "And then we'll forget this entire misunderstanding, all right?" She came at me with the measuring tape.

Twenty minutes later, Eloise Wright ushered us out of her office. I had a parcel of two different rubber girdles to try. Berta had her dignity.

After Eloise shut the door behind us, I accidentally dropped my parcel, and I stooped to pick it up.

I heard Eloise's muffled voice from behind the door.

"Who is she talking to?" I whispered to Berta.

"*Telephone*," Berta mouthed.

We looked up and down the hallway. Empty. I laid my ear against the door.

". . . *so we have a bit of a problem,*" Eloise said. "*A meddler. Yes. Mmm. Indeed. Something must be done.*" The earpiece rattled as she hung up.

"Meddler?" I said to Berta once we were outside. I crammed a square of the hazelnut chocolate Ralph had given me into my mouth. I was jittery.

"It does not seem to be an unfair assessment," Berta said. "You were snooping through her desk."

"Only because you told me to!"

Berta smoothed the collar of her raincoat. "The cops term such a ploy, I believe, 'Mutt and Jeff.'"

"But why do *I* have to be the bad cop?" We set off down the bustling sidewalk, toward the subway station. Taxis were no longer in the budget.

Berta said, "I am now convinced that—as I believe I said all along—Sadie Street has the film reel. Mrs. Wright appeared to be genuine in her confusion when we mentioned it to her."

"Which means Sadie Street is the murderer."

"Probably. It is possible that she learned to shoot a gun for a motion picture role, now that I think of it."

"That's a notion." I told Berta about the scrap of paper with the address.

"Seventeen Wharfside? Well, Mrs. Wright is a businesswoman. Doubtless she ships girdles to other places."

"But why act so secretive about it?" I broke off another square of chocolate. "She's up to something. I feel it in my bones. And that Lem Fitzpatrick gives me the heebie-jeebies, too. What a sneaky bunch the Arbuckles invited last weekend."

"I do agree. But neither Eloise nor Lem seem to have anything to do with the missing film reel."

Something still niggled in the back of my mind, but I said, "You're right. Let's focus all of our efforts on locating Sadie Street."

"By the by, shall we attend Mr. Arbuckle's funeral? There is a slight chance that Sadie Street will be there."

"You know, I haven't seen a word about a funeral in the papers." I burrowed the chocolate bar in my handbag. "I must ring up Olive and ask her about that."

17

When we returned to the love nest, I got on the telephone and had the operator put me through to Dune House.

Olive's voice held a note of hysteria. "Thank heavens you telephoned, Lola. I simply don't know *where* to turn."

"Why, what is it, Olive? Are you well? And the children?"

"The boys are well. They'll be going up to stay in Bar Harbor with my sister early tomorrow—and Nanny Potter will go, too. As a matter of fact, it was Nanny Potter's suggestion. She has been quite a trembling mess of nerves ever since Horace, well, *you* know. Having the boys gone will suit me just fine, because with all the film people arriving tonight and tomorrow, they'd be underfoot something awful."

"Film people?"

"Oh yes! Haven't you heard? Pantheon Pictures will be filming portions of their *Jane Eyre* picture right here at Dune House. George—Mr. Zucker, you know—said Dune House looks exactly like whatever that house is in the novel—oh yes. Thornfield Hall.

Horace, of course, was absolutely dead set against the idea. But now, well . . ."

Right. With Horace out of the way, Olive could indulge in her fascination with motion picture people to her heart's content. What if that film reel had nothing to do with Horace's death, after all? What if this was simply another dreary instance of one spouse bopping off the other? Did Olive have it in her? I hated to think it, but, yes, I fancied she did—if only because she hadn't eaten a decent meal since 1912.

"Will Bruno Luciano be there to film?" I asked. "And Sadie Street?"

"Why, of course. They are the stars of the picture. They're still feuding, George told me."

"You don't happen to know where Sadie Street lives here in the city, do you?"

"Why would you wish to know that, Lola?"

"Um. My mother wishes to send her an invitation. To a tea."

"Oh, I see. No, I don't know where she lives, and frankly, I don't care. Horrid little thing. I do hope she won't attend the funeral. Causes *such* a scene whenever she lays eyes on Bruno."

"I was meaning to ask you about Horace's funeral," I said. "I didn't see an announcement in the paper."

There was a pause. When Olive spoke again, it was in a frantic-sounding whisper. "That's just it. The funeral will be private. I don't trust a soul—not a soul. Well, I trust *you*, Lola. But Horace was *murdered*. It's awfully unnerving, don't you see?"

"Yes, of course. Do you feel unsafe?"

"It's, well . . . I suspect someone was blackmailing Horace."

"What? How do you know?"

"I went through all his bank books and papers and things, you see. There were the accounts I knew about—I always kept a close eye on everything, because Horace could be forgetful. Well, I found a checkbook corresponding to an account I didn't know about, at Sterling National—which isn't the same bank that our other accounts are in, First Federal. I went into the city yesterday, to Sterling National, and I closed the account and demanded a complete list of transactions. The account was only about nine months old—he opened it in August—and he had written several checks over the course of this time to the amount of nearly one hundred thousand dollars."

"That's a fortune! Checks to whom?"

"There was no record of that."

"But how do you know it was blackmail?"

"Lola, think about it. Horace is dead. Dead! It was blackmail, I tell you, and his blackmailer murdered him."

"Why would a blackmailer murder him? Wouldn't that be a case of—what do they call it?—biting the hand that feeds you?"

"Oh, Lola, you and your dogs! Perhaps the blackmail scheme got, I don't know, jiggered up somehow. All I know is, Horace is dead, and he was paying out a pile to some unknown."

After I promised to attend Horace's funeral in Hare's Hollow the next day and said good-bye to Olive, I found Berta in the kitchen. She was stirring a pot on the stove. I told her all that Olive had said.

"Perhaps he was being blackmailed on account of the film reel," she said.

"But it doesn't add up. He started writing checks in August, but Ruby said that Horace didn't have the reel in his possession until a few weeks ago."

We were just sitting down to lunch when there was a knock on the apartment door.

I fully expected it to be the landlord, or a repo man, or maybe an irate chorus girl with a pea in the pod. But it was Ralph.

Cedric pounced on Ralph like they were long-lost pals.

"Hi there, fella," Ralph said, crouching down to pet him.

My skin got toasty with the memory of his big hands on *me*, at Blue Heaven last night. I made my expression cool.

Ralph stood. "Hey, Mrs. Woodby. What's with the librarian face? Thought we had a real nice time dancing last night."

"Can I help you, Mr. Oliver?"

"Was it something I said?"

"I don't wish for you to get the idea that I'm *that* sort of girl. That you can show up on my doorstep simply because we danced together a bit." *Dance* didn't entirely capture what we'd done at the club. Something about jazz made everything extra spicy.

"Okay, I get it," Ralph said. "Bank's closed. I'll admit, before I met you, I would've guessed Woodby's wife was, well, more like Woodby himself. Not, you know—" He scratched his eyebrow. "—too delicate. But then I met you. And you're a real lady, Mrs. Woodby."

There I went, getting all melty again.

"I only came here because I found out something I think you might find interesting," he said.

"Oh, all right. Come in." I opened the door. "But shake a leg. The last thing I need is for the landlord to decide I'm the kind of lady who entertains gentleman callers."

After I latched the door, I surreptitiously kicked the parcel containing my new rubber girdles into the corner of the foyer. "I'd like to know exactly what's going on here," I said to Ralph in low tones. "Are you spying on me for Horace Arbuckle's murderer?"

Ralph frowned, and I saw the smart in his eyes. "No."

I believed him. "What about for the Bureau of Investigation or something?"

"I told you, Mrs. Woodby. I'm a private investigator. I work alone. And I'm not going to do anything that'll hurt you in any way. Got it?"

I swallowed. I didn't know what to say, so I led Ralph back into the kitchen.

"Smells delicious, Mrs. Lundgren," Ralph said. "Tomato soup? My favorite aunt used to make tomato soup."

Berta glowed, and pulled out a chair for him.

He sat. And stole my napkin and spoon. "I dug up something about Lem Fitzpatrick," he said.

Cedric leapt onto Ralph's lap. Little turncoat.

I fetched another napkin and spoon for myself. "Oh?"

"Seems that one of the pies Fitzpatrick had his finger in was a chain of motion picture theaters here in New York City."

"He owned theaters?"

"Yeah."

"But he doesn't anymore?"

"Nope. This past December, he sold the lot of them to Pantheon Pictures."

"Pantheon is Mr. Zucker's studio," Berta said. She placed a bowl of steaming soup in front of Ralph. "And the one that Bruno Luciano and Sadie Street work for."

"Right," Ralph said.

I'd heard about the hot competition between film studios. When they bought up theaters, they were able to control the distribution of their pictures. It was Big Business.

I sat down, and Berta set a bowl of soup before me, too.

"You know," I said after a couple spoonfuls, "Sadie Street gave up singing at Blue Heaven and started up with the motion pictures in January. One month after Fitzpatrick sold his theaters to Pantheon."

"Wonder if there's a connection," Ralph said.

Berta seated herself. She gave me a stern look.

"What?" I asked.

"We agreed to *focus our efforts*," she whispered.

"Oh. Right." I looked at Ralph. "We're trying to, um—"

"Focus your efforts." He slurped soup. "I get it."

"How nice to have a man about to feed," Berta said.

I ate as much as a man, and with full as much appreciation. "Since you're so good at digging things up," I said to Ralph, "could you find something out for me?"

"Maybe."

"I want to know which film company uses a fleur-de-lis as its trademark."

"Not Pantheon Pictures, I can tell you that much. Theirs is a kind of thunderbolt. I'll look into it. I know a junk dealer. My buddy Prince. He's an encyclopedia for that kind of thing." Ralph gave me a penetrating look. "Hope this reel you're looking for doesn't have anything to do with Arbuckle. Because that'd be a risky road to go down."

"Can't think what you mean." I stared down into my soup.

"Another question, Mrs. Woodby: I don't suppose you'd join me for a matinee showing of *Thor the Thunder God* after lunch?"

Was he asking me for a . . . *date?* "No," I said. I ignored the pitter-patter of my heart.

"That's all the thanks I get for my help?"

"Mrs. Woodby," Berta whispered, "be *nice* to the young man."

"I *am* nice," I said out of the corner of my mouth.

"A bit spoiled," Berta said. She took a prim sip of soup.

"Spoiled?" I turned to Ralph. "Spoiled!"

He shrugged. "Maybe a little."

"I've been sleeping on a sofa!"

"She takes ages in the bathtub," Berta said to Ralph.

"We've got work to do," I said. "I can't bally well go gallivanting off to picture shows when we haven't managed to track down Sadie Street."

"Have you looked up Sadie Minsky in the telephone directory?" Ralph asked.

"Um. No." Geewillikins. Why hadn't *I* thought of that? I dashed to the telephone table in the hallway and fetched the New York City directory. I plunked it on the kitchen table and flipped to the *MINs*.

No soap. I tossed the directory aside and went back to my soup.

"Perhaps you are—what do they say?—under too much nervous strain?" Berta said to me. "Perhaps an afternoon off would be beneficial."

I had the sneaking suspicion Berta wanted to curl up with *London Lowdown*, starring Thad Parker.

"Fine," I said. "I'll go to the pictures. Satisfied?"

I finished my soup, hurried to the foyer, and grabbed my Wright's parcel. Then I sneaked into the bathroom and wrestled myself into one of the new rubber girdles. It really was much more comfortable than the type I usually wore. I felt like I could practice Chinese acrobatics in it. Or at the very least, take a nap.

18

....

R alph and I rode the subway to the Zenith Movie Palace on the corner of Forty-seventh and Broadway. Guess he didn't have enough scratch for taxicabs, either.

He purchased our tickets at the window, and we went inside.

I hadn't been to the Zenith in years. It was a gorgeous sweep of a theater, with a golden arch over the screen, a domed ceiling painted with angels and clouds, plushy seats, and red velvet curtains. The theater was packed. Hundreds of voices hummed; hundreds of hats bobbled.

The lights went down and the organ yowled up. We ducked into a couple of empty seats near the back.

Good. No need for chitchat. That was a relief, because being out and about with Ralph was making me nervous. It felt nice being together, our shoulders now and then grazing. And that was the problem—it felt too nice. In fact, I couldn't recall having ever found a fellow half so interesting in my entire life.

But I was a new widow. This simply wouldn't do.

Thor the Thunder God turned out to be dull. The blond actor in the title role would've been better cast in a tooth powder advertisement, and the Nordic forests in the background looked suspiciously like Southern California. I found my gaze drifting to Ralph's hand on his knee, or to his rugged profile, washed with silver light from the movie screen.

"Bored?" he whispered, leaning toward me. I caught a glimpse of a gun in a holster, strapped beneath his jacket. I also saw a notebook tucked in his jacket's inner pocket.

"What's this?" I reached over and plucked out the notebook.

He lightly seized my wrist. "Work."

"Anything about me in there?"

He grabbed the notebook with his other hand and shoved it back inside his jacket. "Sure."

"What sort of things? You'd better tell me, or I'll make you talk."

"Yeah?" His voice was husky, and his eyes were inches from mine. "I'd like to see you try."

"Wouldya keep it down?" someone said behind us.

I slid my hand around the back of Ralph's neck. "All right, then. I'll make you talk."

"Hey," Ralph mumbled, "I thought you said you weren't that kind of girl."

"Oh, would you stop yammering?"

The kiss would've knocked my socks off, had I been wearing any. I hadn't canoodled with a fellow in several years. I was a little rusty. But Ralph hadn't been fibbing when he'd said he was a good teacher, and he was doing an impressive job of helping me pick up where I'd left off.

Until I felt my rubber girdle give way.

I tried to ignore the tugging and rolling sensations under my dress;

Ralph's mouth was far more interesting. But then he slid a hand down the bumps and dips of my figure, and I guess he felt one bump too many.

He patted around my hips, where the girdle had rolled onto itself like a window shade. "What's this?" He pinched at it, pulled, made it stretch through the fabric of my dress.

"Stop it!" I slapped his hand away.

"We're trying to watch the show!" someone said.

"No, really, what've you got under there, Mrs. Woodby? A life preserver?"

"It's not funny," I said stiffly. "And don't call me Mrs. Woodby."

"Yeah. Guess it *would* be a little too formal at this point. Lola."

I suffered through the rest of *Thor the Thunder God* in humbled silence, and then went to the ladies' room to unroll my girdle. Ralph insisted on escorting me home, but needless to say, conversation was stilted.

In a way, the girdle malfunction had saved me. I really oughtn't be smooching fellows at picture shows. Especially not fellows who were investigating me. How come I kept forgetting that germane point about Ralph Oliver?

"Well, thanks for the picture show," I said, standing on the steps of 9 Longfellow Street. I turned to go inside.

"There you are!" Berta yelled out the second-floor window. "For goodness' sake, was it a double feature? You have been absent for an eternity. I have stumbled upon a most exciting development." She slammed the window shut.

I looked down at Ralph. He grinned. "Fine," I said. "Come on up."

Berta was in her boots, hat, and raincoat in the foyer when we opened the front door. She waved a copy of *Movie Love* at us. "We have just enough time to get there."

"Get where?" I asked.

"To the Pantheon Pictures studio in Queens. They are holding an open casting call for character types and extras today, but they shall close the doors at five o'clock—and *Movie Love* indicates that they are most strict about the doors closing."

"I don't quite catch your meaning," I said.

"Sadie, Mrs. Woodby," Berta said. "*Sadie*. If we are able to get inside the studio, we might find her."

"But surely she won't have the film reel with her there at the studio. Wouldn't she be more likely to hide it at home?"

Ralph said, "I think what Mrs. Lundgren is getting at is that once we lay eyes on Sadie, we can follow her home."

We?

"Precisely," Berta said.

The three of us—plus Cedric, too—clattered down into the street and piled into the Duesy.

Pantheon's address was listed in Berta's copy of *Movie Love*. I drove while Ralph, in the backseat with Cedric, tussled with the New York City street map I always kept in my glove box. Berta's contribution was to fingernail the dashboard for dear life every time we turned a corner.

After forty minutes, two wrong turns, and a dash of burning rubber, we stopped in front of a huge concrete building in an industrial section of Flushing, Queens.

I'd read that film companies were starting to decamp to Southern California, where the sunlight made filming outdoors easier and the tax laws were softer. But a lot of companies were still here in the great sprawl of New York. After all, much of their talent still worked on Broadway and needed to shuttle back and forth between gigs.

I switched off the Duesy's engine. A man with a big head and vivid features walked by.

"*He* looks like a character type," Berta whispered.

"And he looks like he knows where he's going," Ralph said.

We got out and hurried after the man. Cedric was clasped in my arms; I wouldn't dream of leaving him in the motorcar in this sort of neighborhood.

A line of about two dozen people trickled out the studio doors. They were all distinctive looking: very tall or short, exceedingly corpulent or muscular, or, in the case of the young girls, unusually pretty.

We queued up. The line inched along. Soon, we were inside the studio, in a long hallway. The line ended at a doorway, in front of which a lady took down names and telephone numbers.

"Should we make a break for it?" I whispered to Berta and Ralph. "We can't stand in this line till the cows come home."

"That secretary up there will be sure to put the kibosh on an escape," Ralph said. "Let's see if there's a way we can slip away once we're inside the screen test room."

"Fine," I said. I whispered to Berta, "Exactly who put Mr. Oliver in charge of our sleuthing?"

But Berta was gone. I saw her at a table along the wall, partaking of the gratis lemonade.

Really, why was Ralph here at *all*? He'd convinced me that he wasn't the devil's minion, but he had yet to give me a straight answer about anything.

After ten more minutes—and after Berta had downed three glasses of lemonade—we made it to the secretary. We all gave fake names and telephone numbers. Then we were sent through into a big, bright room marked STUDIO ONE, with concrete floors, brick walls, and light streaming through skylights and burning from floor lamps. A white screen hung on a rack in the middle of the room.

Near the screen, three men stood around a movie camera on a tripod.

"Next!" one of the men yelled.

"Oh, how very exciting!" Berta said. Her eyes danced, and her cheeks were flushed. She went over to the screen, holding her handbag tight.

"Hey," Ralph said in my ear, "I didn't think we'd actually, ah, get ourselves filmed."

"Why, Mr. Oliver—do you have stage fright?"

"No. An aversion to being caught on camera. Doesn't really go with my line of work." He craned his neck. Looking, I guessed, for a way to lam out.

For all I knew, he was a fugitive from Sing Sing.

Berta told her fake name to a man with a handlebar mustache. He scrawled *Letty Lindstrom* on a slate with a piece of chalk. Then he corralled her in a spot before the screen.

"Just try and act natural," he said.

Berta's entire body had gone rigid.

Handlebar held the slate in front of Berta. One of the other men started cranking the camera. "Three, two, one, action," Handlebar said. He whisked the slate away.

Berta stared at the camera like a savannah creature apprehending an oncoming safari wagon.

"Pretend to say something!" Handlebar shouted. "Move around a little! *Blink*, for crying out loud!"

Berta didn't move.

"Cut!" Handlebar pointed to a door marked EXIT.

Berta crept away.

I was next.

Handlebar glanced at me as I walked toward him, Cedric snug in my arms. Handlebar looked away, but then his eyes snapped back. "Hold it!" he yelled.

I froze.

He stared at me with a look of awe. "Those eyes. That hair. Wowie. Just what we're looking for."

"Who, me?" I said. For some reason, I had the urge to pat my bob.

"Naw. The pooch."

"Oh. You mean Cedric?"

"Whatever his name is. Get him over here."

They filmed Cedric. Cedric tipped his head and showed his tiny round tongue and looked altogether adorable. But, since Cedric was so short, they needed to adjust the camera tripod to get a better shot. Then the tripod got jammed, and all three men were bent over it, trying to make it come unstuck.

"*Psst!*" It was Ralph. He and Berta were over by a door on the far side of the room. He beckoned with a finger.

I looked at the film men. They were absorbed in fiddling with the tripod. I glanced out the door we'd come through. The secretary was busy speaking with a dwarf.

I hugged Cedric close and hurried after Ralph and Berta.

We found ourselves in another empty concrete hallway with cracked plaster walls.

"Hey!" I heard Handlebar yell behind us. "Where's the pooch?"

A couple doors led off the hallway, but when we tried them, they were all locked. We went around a corner and found ourselves in an open area, with windows that overlooked some shrubs.

I guessed this was the front of the studio complex.

A secretary sat at a desk equipped with three telephones. She had wire glasses, a frazzled gray bun, and a brown cardigan. She held a receiver to her ear, and she nodded silently as she flipped through stacks of papers on her desk. When she caught sight of us, her eyes narrowed. "Call you back," she said into the mouthpiece. She hooked the receiver on its cradle. "Here for the screen tests?"

"We wish to speak with . . . um . . ." I squinted at the closed doors behind her desk. One brass nameplate said MR. KLINGER. The other said MR. ZUCKER.

He'd know where to find Sadie Street.

"We're here to see Mr. Zucker," I said.

"Mr. Zucker? You? It's Mr. Klinger who handles the bit-part and comic actor screen tests. They're holding them right now in Studio One. Mr. Zucker only handles the stars."

"We have an appointment," Ralph said. He stalked to the edge of her desk.

The secretary gaped up at him. "Well, now, *you*—I can see *you* having an appointment with Zucker." She straightened her glasses. "Now that I see you up close, you have that rugged sort of look. A manly man, kinda."

"We have an appointment," Ralph said. "At four thirty. Which is—" He glanced at the clock on the wall. "—in approximately two minutes, Mrs.—?"

"*Miss* Dudley."

19

George Zucker was reading a sheaf of papers. A script, probably. His desk was piled high with them. His office was large, cool, and bare. Tall windows overlooked a courtyard populated by scrawny plants. He glanced up. "Miss Dudley, I told you, no—"

"Mr. Zucker," I said, stepping forward. "Lola Woodby. We met at the Arbuckles'."

The secretary left.

George blanched. "Oh. That business. Yeah. Sorry, Mrs. Woodby. I'm up to my elbows in—"

"Quite all right," I said. "We only wanted to stop in and say hello—my friend here, um, Letty Lindstrom, was in for a screen test."

George looked at Berta. He didn't seem impressed. Then he studied Cedric. "What about the dog? Looks like he'd show up real nice on film. And—" Now George was staring hard at Ralph. "—where have I seen *you* before?"

"I've got one of those faces, I guess," Ralph said.

"I hate to say it," George said, "but I'm swamped right now. Was there something I could help you with?"

It was now or never. "We're looking for a missing film reel," I blurted. "One that was stolen from Horace Arbuckle the night he was killed."

"Honey, dozens of film reels pass through my hands on a daily basis. Can't help you." George glanced at his gold wristwatch.

Berta said, "We know that Miss Street used to be called Miss Minsky, and that she sang at the speakeasy belonging to Mr. Fitzpatrick."

George slumped back in his chair. "How'd you find out about that?"

"Is it something we should inform the police of?" Berta's look was steely.

"No!" George said. "They don't need to . . . Listen, I'm gonna let you in on a secret. But first, I don't know a thing about Arbuckle's murder, and that's a fact."

Berta, Ralph, and I waited in silence.

"Pantheon bought up Fitzpatrick's theaters, back in December," George said. "There was nothing fishy about it. Except for one thing." He hunched forward.

Berta, Ralph, Cedric, and I leaned in like a barbershop quartet.

George lowered his voice. "I made a deal with Fitzpatrick, all right? I wish I hadn't, looking back. I mean, what kind of schlemiel goes into business with a gangster?"

"What sort of deal?" I asked.

"I'm not so sure I oughta tell you."

"Do not force us to twist your arm," Berta said.

"All right, all right." George Zucker sighed. "Motion pictures are cutthroat, I tell you. Absolutely vicious. It's sink or swim eight days a week. Right now, Pantheon's main competitor is Altus

Productions, though that could change any second, what with all that's happening in Hollywood. Now, Altus has gotten a real good leg up on the competition by buying out theaters. It's not only about productions, see. Distribution is key, too. Gotta control the market."

"You bought Lem Fitzpatrick's chain of theaters," Ralph said.

"That's right. At a real high price, it turns out."

"Something to do with Sadie?" I asked.

"Yeah. The only way Fitzpatrick would agree to the sale of his theaters was if we took his little squeeze Sadie and made her into a star. I said, sure. The bird's just beautiful, and she can act okay, I guess. She's got that husky voice, and what with the talkies coming along, I thought maybe that could come in handy. All my other leading ladies have voices like mice, except for one, and *she* talks like an Italian truck driver."

"What about the feud between Sadie and Bruno?" Ralph asked.

"Don't remind me. Those two have got me between a rock and a hard place, and they know it."

"What do you mean?" I asked.

"Well, I can't very well fire Bruno. He's Pantheon's top-banking star. And that little princess Sadie? I'd be head over heels with glee if we let her go. There are a million girls in America who could fill her shoes. Give me some nice, fresh-faced little miss from Ohio who'll take goddam direction!" He slammed his fist on the desk.

George suddenly seemed . . . violent. My spine prickled.

"But no," he said. "I can't fire her, because if I do, her goddam boyfriend will have me whacked. It's a farce, is what it is."

"Fitzpatrick threatened to whack you?" Ralph asked.

"Don't know if he means it or not, but with that kind of fella, I sure as hell don't wanna find out. Did you hear what happened to that forger who double-crossed Fitzpatrick? Nothing left but a pair of shoes."

Ralph and I exchanged a glance. Berta's hand had made its way to her locket.

"But you've been pretending to be Sadie's beau," I said.

"All for publicity, honey. Gotta play the rags-to-riches game. The public loves it. Look at me: I was just a runty kid from Jersey who everyone picked on, but I made something of myself. People eat my story up. Anyway, Sadie was sneaking off to Fitzpatrick's bedroom every night at the Arbuckles' place. Taking the opportunity for a little zig-zig, if you know what I mean. They aren't able to see each other much, what with her public image to worry about and the reporters hounding her day and night."

"That's why it's so difficult to locate Sadie," I said.

"Sure. Even she needs a little privacy. She's here now, though. Studio Five."

Berta emitted a chirrup.

George glanced again at his wristwatch. "Anything else?"

Just then, I heard the door behind us click open. We turned.

Bruno Luciano posed in the doorway, liquid eyed and suntanned. He gave Cedric a blinding-white grin. "Hi there, little fella."

Cedric growled.

"Bruno," George said. He sounded choked.

"I needed to speak to you, George," Bruno said. "About that . . . thing." He elevated a dramatic eyebrow.

"Okay," George said meekly.

What was going on between these two?

"Say, Zucker," Ralph said, "could we go and say hello to Sadie Street?"

"Suit yourself," George said, not taking his eyes off Bruno. "As long as you don't mention our little conversation here. Miss Dudley will take you."

. . . .

Miss Dudley guided us through a labyrinth of corridors, and along a wider hallway teeming with actors in costume and makeup. The walls were decorated with framed photographs.

"That was easy," I whispered to Ralph and Berta. We slipped around two cigarette-smoking Revolutionary War Redcoats.

"Indeed," Berta said. "Mr. Zucker sang like a canary."

I poked Ralph in the arm. "Maybe *you* ought to take lessons from *us* on how to extract efficient confessions."

"That's kinda the problem," Ralph said. "It was a little too easy."

"Hmph," Berta said.

I said, "You're jealous."

"In my experience," Ralph said, "when someone's that forthcoming, they're hiding something."

"Hiding what?" I asked. "He came clean about a shady deal with a gangster, for Pete's sake!"

"*Shush*," Berta whispered.

A gaunt fellow in face paint, top hat, and tails stared as we passed.

"I'm just saying," Ralph said, "don't believe everything you hear."

Miss Dudley left us in Studio Five. It was even bigger than Studio One, and lit up by skylights, tall windows, and electric lamps. Sets and props cluttered the perimeter.

In the middle of the studio, a motion picture camera sat on a low tripod. A man in baggy trousers, suspenders, and rolled-up shirtsleeves crouched behind it, cranking. A couple other fellows stood nearby.

All eyes were on Sadie Street.

Sadie was dressed, I figured, as Jane Eyre, in a long gown and a brown wig. The backdrop behind her was painted to look like the inside of a grand library. She pretended to read a letter. She crushed it to her bosom and drew an anguished forearm across her brow. Then she stared into the camera with coquettish, pursed lips and wide, vacant eyes.

Berta watched with stony disapproval. I thought Ralph was going to crack up. Cedric was growling again.

"Cut!" one of the film fellows yelled.

The camera man stopped cranking.

"Sadie, sweetheart," the first man said. He must've been the director. "Do ya have to look like you need to swallow an *entire* bottle of Pepto-Bismol? We're running outa daylight here. One more take."

"I'm tired of this!" Sadie shrieked. She threw the letter on the floor and stormed off to the edge of the studio, to a makeup counter. She flung herself into a chair and crossed her arms. Two makeup ladies rushed to her side.

"Let's go speak to her," I said.

"I must find the powder room," Berta said. "That lemonade has traveled right through me."

"Would you take Cedric?" I asked. "He's being a pill, growling at everyone."

Berta compressed her lips, but she took Cedric and trooped off.

"Maybe you'd better talk to Sadie without me," Ralph said. "It'll be less threatening."

"All right. But something tells me it's going to be no picnic."

I went around the edges of the studio, passing an old-fashioned stagecoach, a cluster of fake trees, and a papier-mâché garden fountain on wheels. I came up behind Sadie. She was having her makeup refreshed.

One of the makeup ladies saw me first. She froze, her powder puff suspended in midair.

"Miss Street," I said.

Sadie swung around and looked me up and down. "Who are you? Wait a minute. Where have I seen you before?"

"Cut the monkey business," I said. "We met only a few days ago. Although you did spend much of the weekend hiding in your room."

"I'm simply *unable* to take note of every last person I come across." Sadie plucked a lipstick from the counter. "Have you any idea of the strain I'm under?"

"I know just the person for that. My brother-in-law is a nerve doctor." I smiled sweetly. "At Babbling Brook Hospital."

"I didn't say I'm a *nutcase*, for God's sake." Sadie took up a hand mirror and lipsticked her carnelian Cupid's bow.

You can tell a lot about a lady by the way she wears down her lipsticks. Flat stub, round stub, pointy, or the ones that somehow look like they've never been used. It's an index of personality. My lipsticks always end up flat as pancakes—if I don't lose or accidentally melt them first. Sadie's lipstick was pointy.

"Could I ask you a question?" I said.

"No." Sadie didn't take her eyes off her reflection.

"I'm going to ask anyway."

"Jimmy!" Sadie yelled.

Jimmy?

Something hard and cold pressed between my shoulder blades. A gun barrel, I'd bet.

"Whatcha doing bugging Miz Street?" a man said.

I twisted my neck. Out of the corner of my eye, I saw a fedora tipped down over a mashed-up-looking mug. "Oh. Hello there, Mr.— Was it Mr. Ant?"

"Cut the wise guy routine," he said in his grinding-gears voice. "Never liked it, never will. Step away from Miz Street." He nudged my spine with the gun.

"Um. Okay. Although I'd *hoped* to ask her about a film reel gone missing from Horace Arbuckle's safe." I looked at Sadie and lifted my eyebrows.

The two makeup ladies' mouths were ajar.

"Are you accusing me of stealing?" Sadie said. "Jimmy, get rid of her—if, that is, you can squeeze those hips of hers out the door."

"I'll have you know I'm wearing a top-drawer rubber girdle!" I should've kept my trap shut, but I'd had it up to my bangs with such remarks. Why is it that a girl's chassis is always up for public analysis?

"Your girdle may be top drawer, sweetie," Sadie said, "but your *bottom* drawer is sure sticking out a long way."

That was *it*. I forgot all about Jimmy. I stepped toward Sadie, hands on my much-discussed hips, ready to give her a nice big piece of my mind with extra icing.

"Hold it, dollface," Jimmy said.

I ignored him. "Now, listen here, Miss Minsky—"

"*What* did you call me?" Sadie was on her feet. She leaned in so close, her nose was about three inches from mine. "Where did you dig up that name?"

I closed the distance between our noses to one inch.

"Hold it," Jimmy said to me again.

Again, I ignored him. "Guess I've got a big brain to go with my big hips. Listen, Sadie. Where's the film reel? The butler saw it in your bag."

"I don't know what you're—"

Bang! Short and sharp, right behind me. Something shattered up in the ceiling. I jumped. Sadie screamed. So did the makeup ladies. Glass tinkled on the floor a few paces away.

I spun around.

Yep. Jimmy sure as heck had a pistol. Big and shiny. And aimed straight at me.

I turned tail and sprinted across the studio. Past the old-time coach and the fake trees, past the camera on its tripod, the fellows with their suspenders and slack jaws.

"Hey!" Jimmy yelled after me.

20

....

R alph was waiting for me by the door of Studio Five. He grabbed my hand and yanked me out into the hallway, where the loitering actors did not appear to have been fazed. They probably thought it had been a theatrical gunshot.

We hurried down the crowded hallway.

"What the hell were you egging Jimmy on for?" Ralph said. "He's a gangster, Lola. You know—kills people for a living?"

"What's he *doing* here?"

"Sadie is Fitzpatrick's girl. Jimmy works for Fitzpatrick. Guess Jimmy's been drafted into bodyguard duty."

"Wait!" I skidded to a stop. "What about Berta? And Cedric?" I looked up and down the hallway. I saw Ancient Greeks drinking coffee, a man wearing the rear end of a horse costume, a girl dudded up like a ballerina. Oh yes, and Jimmy, shouldering through the crowd, bandy and glowering. The pistol dangled at his side.

"Holy mackerel," Ralph muttered. He still had my hand, and he dragged me behind a garment rack stuffed with costumes. We had about two feet of elbow room between the costumes and the wall, which was covered with framed photographs.

A moment later, Jimmy strode by. He hadn't seen us.

"We'll just sit tight back here and wait till we see Berta," Ralph said. "Then we'll vamoose."

"Okay." The fright of the gunshot had belatedly sunk in. I felt Jell-O kneed and weepy. I sniffled.

Ralph glanced down. "Hey," he said. He placed a hand on my arm.

I longed to lay my cheek on his shoulder, for him to fold his arms around me. His baggy brown suit looked soft and comforting. He reminded me of a teddy bear. Well, a teddy bear with muscle-rounded arms and a scarred temple. I pulled away.

"What's the matter?" Ralph asked.

"What's the *matter*?" I whispered. "To begin with, I'm a widow of not even two weeks. You're a private detective who's investigating me. I don't know you from Adam. You keep notes about me in a notebook—which is stored next to your *gun*, by the way. And if I don't figure out how to pay my rent, I'm—"

"Hey, hey. Calm down."

"Why is everyone always *saying* that to me?"

My gaze fell on the framed photographs on the wall. At first, the images didn't register. Gradually, it dawned on me that they were ensemble shots of actors in costume. Casts of various motion pictures that had been shot in the studio, I guessed. One of them looked like A Midsummer Night's Dream. Another looked like some kind of Wild West to-do, with a bunch of cowboys and even a cowgirl in a fringed leather skirt, tall boots, and a rifle slung over her shoulder. Too bad the cowgirl had such a sour expression on her face.

"Wait a minute," I said. "Isn't that . . . ?" I poked the glass. "Did you ever see the Arbuckles' nurserymaid? Because I swear that cowgirl looks exactly like her."

Ralph examined the picture. "I saw her in passing, up at the Arbuckles' place. Nanny Potter, right? That does look like her. Same schoolmarm face and everything."

"The likeness is uncanny." My stomach felt all twisty. "She was eavesdropping on Horace and me the night he was murdered, you know. Inspector Digton told me."

Ralph frowned.

"Maybe she's simply a busybody," I said.

"A busybody who, by the looks of this picture, isn't just a nurserymaid, but also an actress?" Ralph's eyes were thoughtful. "Arbuckle was killed by a crack shot, the cops said. With a gun kinda like the one she's got in this photograph here."

"Oh gee whiz," I whispered. "It was *her*. She killed Horace."

"Hold up, kid. This is all circumstantial so far."

"If she *is* an actress, she'd have some kind of reason to want a film reel, right?"

"Sure. But didn't the cops write off all the household staff? Something about the butler providing an alibi for all of them?"

"Yes," I said. "I mean, *no*. She doesn't have an alibi! All of the other help was sleeping in the servants' quarters that night and came down to the kitchen with Hibbers after they heard the gunshot. But Nanny Potter was sleeping in the nursery because the boys had stomachaches. How could I have been so stupid? It was *her*."

"Maybe."

"Probably!"

"Here's Mrs. Lundgren."

I stood on tiptoe and peeked over the garment rack. Sure enough, Berta was headed in our direction. Cedric was slung over one arm, and her handbag was slung over the other.

Unfortunately, Jimmy the Ant was not far down the hallway in the opposite direction, fidgeting. I couldn't tell if he was adjusting his holster, or if he urgently needed better-fitting trousers.

When Berta drew near the garment rack, I burrowed a hole between a clown suit and a tulle gown. *"Berta,"* I whispered.

She stopped and looked around.

"Psst!" I whispered. "In here!"

Cedric yipped.

"Mrs. Woodby," Berta said loudly. "Whatever are you doing hiding in those clothes?"

I squeezed my eyes shut. *"Oh dear Lord."*

Berta tunneled through the garment rack. She thrust Cedric into my arms.

"Hey!" Jimmy yelled. I heard his tiny shoes tapping in our direction. A moment later, he shoved the rack—it was on wheels—and it rolled away to expose me cowering against Ralph.

"Easy there, partner," Ralph said.

Jimmy twirled his pistol around by the trigger guard, on one finger.

Everybody was getting into the Wild West spirit.

I swallowed. "Now, Mr. Ant, there's no need to get so feisty. I was only having a friendly chat with Miss Street back there, and . . ." My voice trailed off. Jimmy wasn't listening. His good eye was looking at Berta. His glass eye lolled in the other direction.

"Why, Mrs. Lundgren," Jimmy said. "You little she-devil, you. Say, that telephone number you gave me last night didn't go through. You wasn't trying to give me the blow-off, was you?"

Berta drew herself up. "Certainly not. You must have told the operator the incorrect numbers. Perhaps you were liquored up when you attempted to call? Perhaps the operator could not distinguish your slurred words?"

"Berta—"

"It is Mrs. Lundgren to you."

"Aw, Mrs. Lundgren. You lovely Swedish tomato, you."

Ralph suppressed a snort of laughter.

"We danced all night last night," Jimmy said. "I thought we was hitting it off real nice."

"Hitting off?" Berta said. "Hitting *off*? Shall I suppose that you joked with your—how do you say?—*pals* about getting to whatever base it is that—that—"

"Naw, doll, nothing like that. It's just, well, you listened to my talk about the farm in Missouri. No dame's ever cared about the farm before."

"There *was* the farm. Boys who grow up in the countryside are so much more *wholesome*, I have always believed. . . ."

Uh-oh. Berta was starting to thaw.

Jimmy sidled up to her. "So I thought we could talk some more, see? That's all. Maybe a nice little drink somewheres, and then we could . . ." At this juncture, Jimmy (quite inadvisably) reached around Berta and gave her backside a squeeze.

Berta's eyes flared. In one fluid motion, she unfastened the buckle of her handbag, drew out a small pistol, and aimed it at Jimmy.

I gasped.

"Whoa," Ralph muttered.

"Back off," Berta said. She pressed the pistol's barrel into Jimmy's lapel and pushed him away. "I am *not* that sort of lady."

"Sure, sure, didn't mean to offend." Jimmy held his hands up. "Hey, is that a .25-cal Colt you got there?"

Berta looked at Ralph and me. "Shall we scram?" she said.

Ralph and I snapped our mouths shut and hurried off down the hallway, Berta close behind.

"So *that's* what you keep in your handbag," I said to Berta over my shoulder.

"Among other things."

"Tomato!" Jimmy wailed after us. "C'mon! Just one drink!"

Berta *tsk*ed her tongue.

....

Back on the road in the Duesy, we talked things over. We'd failed once more to get any closer to Sadie Street's apartment. On the other hand, we may have stumbled upon the identity of Horace Arbuckle's murderer.

"Nanny Potter? An actress?" Berta shook her head. "She seemed such a plain, unassuming girl. Not a glamorous bone in her body."

"I'm sure that was her in the photograph," I said. I swerved into the fast lane over the bridge. Dusk was falling, blue gray and damp. "And she overheard me repeating aloud the combination of Horace's safe, so *she* could've stolen the reel."

"But that does not explain the appearance of the reel in one of the calfskin weekend bags," Berta said.

"Seems to me," Ralph said, stuffed in the backseat with Cedric, "that the first order of business is to confirm that Nanny Potter didn't have an alibi on the night of Horace's murder."

As soon as we got back to the love nest, I telephoned Dune House.

Hibbers answered on the third ring.

"Just the fellow I'd hoped to snag," I said.

"Madam?"

"Billy and Theo's nurserymaid—what is her full name?"

"Miss Vera Potter, madam."

"Vera Potter," I repeated. Berta and Ralph both scribbled the name down in the their respective notebooks. Berta seemed to have replaced Thad Parker with Ralph as her gumshoe exemplar.

How annoying.

"How long has Miss Potter been with the Arbuckles?" I asked Hibbers.

"Since last autumn. October, I believe. As you know, I was still in your employ at that time, so I cannot give an unimpeachable summary of—"

"Okay, okay. Since October. Ever hear any word about Miss Potter being an actress?"

"An *actress*, madam? Heavens no. She is a rather morose and taciturn young lady. Most principled, too, regarding matters of finance. I recall that she refused to accept additional monies offered to her for looking after a friend of young Master Theo's. She said it was tantamount to a bribe. On the rare occasions that I have heard Miss Potter speak in the servants' quarters, she has made reference to her long career as a nurserymaid."

"She could've been fibbing."

"Certainly, madam."

"Any funny business between her and Mr. Arbuckle that you're aware of?"

Hibbers coughed. "Indeed not."

"Listen, about Miss Potter's alibi the night Mr. Arbuckle was shot: The kids were indisposed that night—overindulged in cookies. Miss Potter stayed at the kids' bedsides, swabbing their feverish brows and whatnot. But you told the police that all the household staff were accounted for."

There was a heavy pause on the line.

"Hibbers?"

"Ah. Yes, madam. I was contemplating your suggestion."

"And?"

"And yes, indeed, it appears that I may have made a small . . . error. Miss Potter was absent when I entered the kitchen after the murder."

"I assume you haven't told this to the police?"

"No, madam. It is only now that my attention has been drawn to this oversight. Perhaps I should go to the police station and inform—"

"No!" I cried. If the police arrested Vera Potter before I got to her, then I might never have a chance to speak with her. I might never find out if she knew anything about the film reel's whereabouts.

"Madam, I really must. You see, Miss Potter will travel to Bar Harbor with the children early tomorrow morning."

Phooey. Olive *had* mentioned that.

"Then I'm coming up to the country this evening," I said. "Simply—simply wait, okay? And don't breathe a word of this to anyone." I disconnected. "Pack your suitcase, Berta."

"I never *unpacked* it."

"I'll meet you two at the Foghorn in Hare's Hollow at nine tonight," Ralph said. He was already heading for the foyer. "I have a couple things to take care of here in the city. I've got my own motorcar."

"Wait a minute," I said. "Who said *you* were coming?"

He turned. "You really want to confront a possible murderer on your own?"

"Berta is armed."

"Yeah—I was meaning to ask you, Mrs. Lundgren—"

"I have a permit," Berta said.

"I was actually going to say, do you know how to use that thing?"

"It seemed to do the trick with Mr. Ant," I said. "Mr. Oliver, it's starting to look an awful lot like you're trying to horn in on our turf. Who's to say you aren't going to snatch the reel out from under us?"

"Well now." He scratched his eyebrow. "*There's* a thought."

I narrowed my eyes.

"Mrs. Woodby," Berta whispered, "there is no need to behave in such a prickly fashion to the young man. He is only trying to help."

"You've been utterly taken in!" I whispered back. "Why do you keep forgetting that he's *investigating* me on someone else's dime?" I glanced over at Ralph. *I* kept forgetting that, too. He exuded such a strong air of masculine competence. Seductive, sure, but also exceedingly irritating. Then there were the thoughts that bubbled in my head whenever I looked his way. Thoughts about those big, warm hands.

He grinned at me.

My upper lip felt sweaty. I prayed he wasn't one of those mindreaders I'd heard about.

"I'm not going to steal the reel," he said. "Just helping out, okay? Scout's honor." He pulled open the door. "See you at the Foghorn."

21

It was almost nine o'clock in the evening by the time Berta and I reached Hare's Hollow. I had to park the Duesy a block away from the Foghorn, since all the spaces in front of the inn were taken.

"Looks like the reporters are back in town," I said.

"They probably wish to photograph poor Mr. Arbuckle's funeral in the morning."

"If I know my reporters, they're more interested in angling for photographs of the people up here filming *Jane Eyre*."

We mounted the Foghorn's wooden porch. A rattling motor made us turn our heads. An angular Ford Model T (which was maybe eight years old, but sounded like it was about eighty) double-parked in front of the inn. The engine wheezed off and the headlamps faded to black. Ralph hopped out and slammed the door with surprising violence. He kicked one of the spindly wheels.

"Hi," I called down to him over the inn's porch railing.

He glowered up. "Evening, ladies."

"Nice struggle-buggy," I said.

"Hnh." He stomped up the steps. "Hungry?"

"Famished," Berta said. "From terror."

"Mrs. Woodby's driving that bad?"

Berta shuddered. "Worse."

"You were sleeping the whole way, Berta!" I said.

The three of us had booked the last two rooms. Berta and I would have to bunk together. We took our suitcases upstairs, and then went to get dinner in the Foghorn's restaurant.

"Might I bring my dog?" I said to the lady stationed at the front of the restaurant.

Cedric cocked his head. Who could say no to *that*?

"Long as he stays on the floor," the lady said.

The restaurant was dim and old-fashioned. It catered to holiday-makers on motorcar tours along the coast, but at this late hour, only a sprinkling of shabby-suited men—reporters, I guessed—hunkered over tables. We chose a corner table.

"Any contact with the Arbuckle household yet?" Ralph asked. He draped his jacket over a chair back.

I'd never seen him in shirtsleeves. His shirt was worn but clean, and I noted the bulging muscles of his benders. Tonight, there was no gun in sight. Maybe he'd left it in his motorcar.

"No," I said. "I thought I'd telephone again right after we had a bite to eat."

"You probably shouldn't telephone," he said. "Operators are always listening in."

"This is Hare's Hollow," I said. "Not Chicago."

"Do you suggest that we should go in person to locate Miss Potter at Dune House?" Berta said.

"Maybe you should let me go," Ralph said. "Alone."

"This is my investigation!" I said.

"*Our* investigation," Berta said.

"Right," I said, "*our* investigation. What're you doing, Mr. Oliver, elbowing in like this? We're not going to split the reward with you, if that's what you're aiming for."

Ralph's brow lifted. "Reward?"

Rats. He'd made me blurt things again. I buried my face in a food-stained bill of fare. "Where's the waitress, anyway?"

"I'll go find her." Ralph stalked off around the corner, to the front of the restaurant.

As soon as he'd disappeared, I extracted the notebook from his jacket. "I can't believe he left this unguarded."

"Mrs. Woodby!" Berta whispered. "Put that back this instant!"

"No." I opened the notebook. Its pages brimmed with pencil scribbles.

"Mr. Oliver is our friend."

"Friend? Really, Berta. Do you think Thad Parker would be so gullible?"

"It appeared to me that you had rather hit it off with Mr. Oliver. You must not judge persons by their line of work, anyway."

"Well, I guess *you* certainly don't, considering the way you've hit it off with Jimmy the Ant. You know, the gangster?"

"I rebuffed him."

"Looked like a complicated kind of flirting to me."

Berta pressed her lips together.

What had gotten into me? I wasn't usually so testy. But I didn't have time to make nice with Berta just yet; Ralph would be back any second.

I thumbed through the notebook to the most recent entry. It said *Actress/Nurserymaid: Vera Potter. October.* I backed up a page.

My own initials caught my eye: *L.W. kiss in cinema check.*

"Kiss in cinema, *check?*" I yelped. As though I were an item on a to-do list? He'd planned that kiss!

"Here he comes," Berta whispered. Then, to Ralph, she said, "I do apologize, Mr. Oliver. I told her she should not go snooping through your things."

I slid the notebook into his jacket. Too late. He'd seen.

"You know, Mrs. Woodby," Ralph said in a dangerous tone, "Mrs. Lundgren's right. You *shouldn't* go snooping through people's things. You might see something you don't like." He sat.

"You must be joking," I said, my voice hot. "You make a living snooping through people's things!"

"Ah, but not my friends' things."

"Oh? Then I suppose that means that *we* are not friends, since I now have solid proof that you've been investigating *me*, not Alfie."

"You don't have any proof."

"I have!"

"I was hired to investigate your late husband."

"By whom?"

"Can't say."

"How *dare* you lie to me?"

"Listen," Ralph said, "I'm here with you on this harebrained escapade because this thing's threatening to get way more risky than you realize. There's been a murder, and you've gone and stirred up a snake's nest of gangsters like it's some kinda game. Do you know how gangsters get rid of meddlers?"

"You're trying to scare me." Now I was breathless with fury and, deeper down, humiliation. I'd thought he'd been interested in me as a woman. Not as a mark. *L.W. kiss in cinema check!* I got to my feet. "Come on, Berta. We're going."

"No, thank you," Berta said. "I came here to eat supper, and I mean to do it. If you wish to stomp off like a schoolgirl because your pride has been wounded, you are welcome to do so."

"Fine! Cedric, peanut. Come."

Cedric, under the table, was busy gobbling up fallen scraps.

"Come," I repeated.

Cedric ignored me.

Traitors. Both of them.

I tried to sashay out of the restaurant; it felt more like a limp.

Upstairs in my room, I rummaged through my handbag and dug out the ends of the three chocolate bars Ralph had purchased for me at Wright's. I slumped on the edge of the sagging bed and devoured the lot.

By the last morsel, I'd come to a decision: I couldn't trust Ralph enough to involve him in my confrontation of Vera Potter. And at this point, I couldn't trust Berta not to go blabbing to Ralph about our plans. He'd reeled her in, hook, line, and sinker.

I balled up the chocolate foil and threw it into the rubbish bin.

No, I'd have to confront Vera Potter on my own.

I thought about going to Dune House and finding Vera Potter, but decided against it. I didn't wish to drag in Olive, for starters, and I also figured there were lots of motion picture people cluttering up the place, not to mention whichever members of the Arbuckle clan were there for the funeral in the morning.

I went downstairs and peeked through the doors into the restaurant. Ralph and Berta were still there, eating slices of pie and laughing. Laughing! *Pie.* Cedric sat on the floor, gazing up at their forks. Ralph bent to give Cedric a chunk of pie. Cedric wolfed it down, and his feather duster of a tail swept back and forth.

I felt quite like the Little Match Girl in the story, staring in from the cold.

I went to the call box in the lobby. It was in a little room built under the stairs, with a wooden bench, a bare lightbulb, and a rickety door that folded open and shut. I closed myself in and asked the operator to put me through to Dune House.

Hibbers answered.

"Would you fetch Vera Potter for me?" I asked.

"Certainly, madam. I believe she has just finished putting the young Masters Arbuckle to bed."

I waited for several minutes. I drummed my fingernails on the bench.

Then, I heard a rustle and a timid "Hello?"

I bolted upright. "Miss Potter?"

"Yes. Who's this?"

"Hibbers didn't tell you?"

"No. He only said it was urgent. Is this some sort of prank? Because if—"

"No, no, it's not a prank." I took a deep breath. "Miss Potter, I know about the film reel. *All* about it." I said a quick prayer to the gods of bluffing.

Silence. Then Vera said, her voice muffled as though she'd cupped a hand around the telephone's mouthpiece, "How do you know about that?"

"Um." My feet danced a jig. "Never mind. Do you . . . do you have it?"

More silence.

"It won't do you any good to pretend that you don't," I said.

A slow intake of breath. "Meet me. I'll tell you exactly where you can find it."

"Really? I mean, okay, yes, wonderful."

"The sand dunes to the left of the wooden walkway at the Arbuckles' beach. Tonight. Midnight."

The line went dead.

I stepped out of the call box, and nearly bumped into Miss Ida Shanks.

"The things you see when you haven't got a gun," she said.

"Were you eavesdropping?"

"Now, why would I wish to do a thing like that?" Ida made a show of smoothing the sleeve of her tweed dress. It was an unbecoming shade of green, with orangey-red trim at the cuffs. The colors called to mind a pimento olive.

Have I mentioned I despise pimento olives?

"You know, Duffy," Ida said, "there *are* more interesting people than you. Which you've probably realized, since—" Her eyes, behind her glasses, flicked up and down my black dress. "—you've finally got yourself into some proper widow's weeds. Or have you taken up cat-burgling to make some spare change?"

"Oh, buzz off, Miss Shanks," I said, and pushed past her.

I went upstairs again. It wasn't quite ten thirty. I didn't need to leave for another hour or so. On the other hand, I had no wish to clue in Berta or Ralph on my plans. I decided to change, and then wait out the time elsewhere.

I hulled my torso, at long last, from the rubber girdle. My internal organs lolled in relief. I put on a jersey skirt and a thick woolen pullover—both black. Who would've thought that being a detective and being a widow were so compatible? I pulled on black wool stockings and low-heeled spectator shoes. Normally, I wouldn't be caught dead in flat shoes. But no one would see me except Miss Potter. I strapped on my wristwatch and left the Foghorn through the back.

Main Street was for the most part abandoned. The five-and-dime, the drugstore, the dry-goods emporium, the stationer's, and the tobacconist's were all closed up. Maple trees with tender, new leaves made a shadowy umbrella over the sidewalk. I went through iron gates into the park, and sat on a bench. But in the dim light, the creaking swings were unnerving, so I went back out onto Main Street. At last, it was time to set off for my meeting with Vera Potter.

I'd walk along the beach. Walking in sand is, of course, murder on the calf muscles. But I couldn't exactly motor furtively onto the Arbuckles' gated estate. Even the Duesy's engine didn't purr *that* smoothly, and besides, there was always a guard in the gatehouse. In addition, I'd have a good view all around me on the beach. And considering that I couldn't shake the tingly feeling that someone was watching me from the shadows, visibility was a definite attraction.

22

I accessed the shore from a path behind Hansen's Bait Shop.

The Arbuckles' stretch of beach was about half a mile east. I trudged along, hugging my pullover close. The moon was a bright crescent, lighting up a streak of wet sand before me all the way. Out on the black water, whitecaps glowed, and the gush of the breakers drowned the thud of my heart.

I passed several large houses cushioned in black foliage. Some of them were glorified shingled "cottages," others unabashed mansions. Lights glowed from the windows of a few, but many of them were deserted, their owners off cavorting at other, distant playgrounds.

Presently, the chimneys of Dune House came into view from behind a swell of trees.

I slowed. Cold wind whipped off the water. I squinted at my wristwatch. Three minutes till midnight. I scanned the beach and stared into the shadows of the grass-tufted dunes. I didn't see a soul, but I saw boards laid through the dunes.

The walkway Miss Potter had mentioned.

I headed toward it.

I was twenty yards off. Then fifteen.

Then—*bang!* A gunshot.

I froze.

Behind the feathery dune grass, a black shape sprinted away toward the trees and the Arbuckles' house.

My feet felt like they were trapped in wet cement.

Should I run away down the beach? I *wanted* to. Had that person aimed for me? I wasn't hurt, was I? I did a quick mental scan. No searing pain. Okay. I should run. Turn tail and forget this whole thing and go straight to the luncheonette in Columbus Circle in the morning and sign up—

Wait.

I glimpsed another dark shape, over in the dunes.

Oh dear, dear sweet bejeezus.

It took all of my willpower, but I forced myself into the dunes, floundering through the soft-heaped sand, grass slicing at my calves, and I then saw . . . a large bundle.

No. Not a bundle. A person. A person, on its side, curled up, one arm flung askew.

I dashed over and knelt beside it. I rolled the body gently over.

It was Vera Potter. Eyes wide, a small hole in her forehead, black blood trickling down her neck.

I stared at her in uncomprehending horror for what felt like a month. She wore a cardigan and a blouse, and some kind of long skirt, which was tangled around her ankles. Her canvas tennis shoes jutted at unnatural angles.

My eyes fell on her hand. At the *gun* in her hand. I blinked.

Had Vera shot herself?

No. I was certain I'd seen that *other* figure, running back through the dunes toward the house.

I started shaking and I felt like I might vomit. The black night all around seemed to pulsate with menace, to flicker with spying eyes and furtive movements. I needed to get out of there, before somebody shot *me*—

A golden shine caught my eye. On the sand, about two yards from Vera's body. I crawled over, picked it up, and held it up in the moonlight.

A lipstick tube. Odd. I pocketed it unthinkingly, and got to my feet.

I staggered toward the inky, glistening sea. I would run back down the beach, the way I came. That way, I would see if anybody came at me with a gun.

Fifteen minutes later, I stumbled up the stone steps of the Hare's Hollow police station. I burst through the door.

A policeman lounged with his feet propped on a desk, frozen in the act of biting into a Danish pastry.

"Murder," I wheezed, and then bent over my knees. "There's been another murder at Dune House."

"Humor me, Mrs. Woodby, and explain to me one more time how you found yourself on the Arbuckles' beach at midnight?" Inspector Digton tipped his chair back on two legs and watched me. Cigarette smoke drifted in the light of a hanging lamp.

Digton had shown up about an hour after I arrived at the police station. Roused from a deep slumber, judging by the crushed appearance of his mustache. He was in a surly humor.

"I was out for a stroll on the beach," I told him for the third time. "Fresh air, stretch of the legs, that sort of thing. All the reasons one goes for strolls on the beach."

"At midnight? Sure. Listen, Mrs. Woodby, there aren't too many people who go for healthful strolls at that hour. Something tells me you're not the type. And you just *happened* to hear a gunshot, and just *happened* to see someone running away from the scene of the crime, huh?"

"I won't say anything else until I've got a lawyer present."

"Funny. That's what you said the *last* time I asked you a couple of questions. Seems to me your lawyer's kind of a deadbeat."

"Think whatever you wish."

I was tempted to tell Digton about the film reel. It would explain everything. Sort of. On the other hand, maybe he'd fall off his chair if I told him I'd been trying to steal a film reel from one of the murder victims. For a chorus girl at the Frivolities. For a fee, no less.

"You wanna know what I think, Mrs. Woodby? I think that Vera Potter knew all about how you murdered Arbuckle—"

I made an unladylike grunt.

"—and since you were afraid she was going to spill the beans about that, you bumped *her* off, too."

"The paper-thin logic of your theory, Mr. Digton, makes my head positively ache. Why wouldn't I have killed Miss Potter at an earlier date? Why would I come straight to the police station after finding her body?"

"You tell me."

"I can't, because I'm not the criminal mastermind you take me for." I remembered the lipstick tube I'd picked up in the sand dunes. I pulled it out of my skirt pocket and placed it on the table.

"What's that?" Digton asked.

"I found it beside the—I found it in the dunes, a few paces off from Miss Potter."

He picked it up, uncapped it, and swiveled the lipstick up.

It was a vibrant shade of carnelian. And it had been worn to a point.

"What do you know," I murmured.

"Care to fill me in?"

"That's Sadie Street's lipstick."

"What makes you so sure?"

"See how it's pointy?"

"Yeah."

"Every lady, you see, has her own way of wearing down her lipsticks."

Digton tipped his head back and brayed so heartily, I was able to count the four gold fillings on his upper molars. He capped the lipstick and rolled it back to me. "Here, keep it as a souvenir, why dontcha."

I stared at him. "You're really discrediting this clue?"

"Clue?" He lurched forward, cigarette dangling from his lip. "The only clue I need, Mrs. Woodby, is that you discovered the body. Again. Consider yourself Suspect Number One."

A rap sounded on the door's frosted glass. "Yeah?" Digton yelled.

The policeman thrust his head in and said, "Someone has arrived to fetch Mrs. Woodby."

I followed Inspector Digton to the front of the police station. I supposed, in my groggy state, that it was Berta who'd come to fetch me.

Boy, did I have a bundle of explaining to do.

Yet when I emerged on the porch, the Prig himself was waiting, in a long wool overcoat.

I wanted to shrivel up and die. Or give him a knuckle sandwich. Instead, I adopted an airy tone. "Who telephoned you, Chisholm?"

"I did," Inspector Digton said. He gave Chisholm one of those chummy, gents'-club nods.

"Thank you, Inspector," Chisholm said. "Shall I see you at the Temperance League meeting tomorrow evening?"

Digton said he would, and retreated into the station.

I glared up at Chisholm. "You've got your cronies tattletaling on me?"

He marched in silence down the steps. His long black Daimler idled at the curb. The chauffeur was a mere silhouette behind the wheel.

I hesitated. A mist had rolled in from the sound, and the night was damp and billowy. It smelled of sea brine and vegetation. Frogs peeped out a lively chorus.

Chisholm's pals, keeping him informed of my doings. Chisholm, come to collect me as though I were a truant schoolgirl. Chisholm, who had so very much to lose if word got out that his sister-in-law was a deranged murderess . . . Maybe *Chisholm* had hired Ralph Oliver to snoop on me. Why hadn't I thought of it earlier?

Chisholm turned. "Well? Hurry up, then, Lola."

"What makes you think I'm going with you?"

His smiled. It was the sort of smile you'd give to a mental patient who'd forgotten to button their pajama flap. "You *will* come back to Amberley with me. I have already telephoned your mother. She will arrive first thing in the morning."

I looked up the dark street and considered making a break for it.

"I've got a room at the Foghorn," I said.

"Why, precisely, you have booked yourself into that vulgar establishment is beyond me. No, you must return to Amberley with me. Inspector Digton, you see, wished to arrest you—"

"You're lying!"

"Would you like to go inside and ask him?"

I swallowed.

"He agreed not to make an arrest under the condition that you stay with me. At Amberley."

Cedric. Surely Berta would take good care of Cedric, despite their differences.

"What about my motorcar?" I said.

"Your *motorcar*? For pity's sake, Lola. I didn't come here only to restore you to the very godforsaken rattletrap of sin that has led you down the path of wickedness in the first place." The chauffeur had emerged to open the door for Chisholm. "At any rate," Chisholm said, stepping inside, "your motorcar has been seized as evidence. Now, come along."

I glanced over my shoulder, into the lit-up windows of the police station. Inspector Digton looked out.

I'd been cornered.

I trudged down the steps and into the Daimler.

"Do you not think," Chisholm said, once the motorcar was rolling, "that you have dragged the Woodby name through the mud quite enough for one fortnight? My goodness me, I am going to have to pull quite a lot of strings to keep this hushed up. Quite a lot indeed. I could lose my chairman's seat in the Temperance League! First my brother is called to his maker after leading a life of sheer debauchery—"

"You can hardly blame that on me, Chisholm." I leaned my head against the seat. "In fact, *you're* more to blame."

Chisholm fluttered his eyelids. "I? To blame?"

"Sure. You were his brother. You ought to have led him back to the principled path or whatever it is you call it."

"Ah, but you were his wife." Chisholm held himself still, but his voice quavered. He had a temper, all right. I hoped I wasn't around when he finally blew a gasket. "And a wife, dearest Lola, is the moral arbiter of the family. As is a mother." His eyes flicked to the region of my womb, and back again. "Of course, you were not chosen by the Almighty Creator to bear fruit. Still, you should have done more in the way of tending to Alfred's soul. Planting wholesome seeds, trickling the soil with refreshing rainwater and nourishing sunlight—"

"Stop, or I'm going to be sick," I said. I glowered out the window into the dark.

"You have proved yourself quite unable to take your life into your own hands, Lola. It is rather concerning. You behave like a child."

"Cut the cackle, Chisholm," I snapped.

But, somewhere deep down, I was afraid he was right.

23

My house—*the* house—had been transformed in the days since I left. All the wallpaper had been steamed off, leaving the walls monastery-bare. Every last chandelier had been taken down, every carpet rolled up.

The new butler—who called to mind a prison warden from Transylvania—led me past the good bedrooms on the second story, and up a twisty staircase to the third.

"There must be some mistake," I said. "There are no guest rooms up here. Only servants' quarters."

"Mr. Woodby thought it advisable that you were established in a smaller, plainer chamber," the butler said.

He led me to the puniest of the maid's rooms. It was practically a broom closet, with one tiny window in a gable, and an iron bedstead that looked like it had been nicked from a Charles Dickens orphanage.

"This?" I said.

"Yes, madam. Breakfast will be served at eight o'clock sharp." He bowed and left.

I considered bursting into tears. I also considered storming downstairs and having a row with Chisholm. Both would have been immensely satisfying, but both would've taken more steam power than I had. So I shut the door, closed the curtains, kicked off my shoes, rolled off my woolen stockings, and lay facedown on the mothball-smelling bed.

I collapsed into a thick, headachy sleep.

I was woken by the rumble of a motorcar engine. I pried my eyes open. Bluish morning light slanted through the curtains.

I went to look out the window.

Down below, my parents' butter-colored Rolls-Royce was braking in the front drive. I watched as the chauffeur released first Mother and then Lillian. I detected Mother's Going-to-Battle hustle, and Lillian's Miss Priss flounce.

I pulled the curtains shut.

When I entered the breakfast room fifteen minutes later, Mother, Lillian, and Chisholm were conversing in sickbed tones.

"Lola!" Mother screamed.

"Good morning, Mother," I said. "Lillian." I circled around to the buffet.

"How generous of you to join us," Chisholm said.

It was not yet eight thirty.

"Lola, I am dumbfounded, absolutely *dumbfounded*, by your behavior," Mother yelled. "Have you no sense of responsibility?"

"I see that you are decently clothed for once," Chisholm said.

I'd had no choice but to wear the black jersey skirt, black pullover, woolen stockings, and flat spectator shoes again. The stockings had a few holes from the dune grass, and there was sand in the shoes. My bob was wilted, and I wore no makeup. I felt like one of those sad little ladies who pass out pamphlets about the End of the World.

"You really mustn't wear flat shoes," Mother said. "I thought you knew that. You have your father's mother's ankles."

No, I had *my* mother's ankles.

"Where *is* Father?" I asked.

"At his office, of course."

Probably at his club, trying to forget he had a family.

I surveyed the buffet: slices of dark brown health bread riddled with whole kernels of rye; carrot salad; some kind of pâté-looking thing that was, undoubtedly, vegetable paste; a pot of—I lifted the lid and took a sniff—herbal tea. It smelled like a hay field. What had I done to deserve herbal tea? Without coffee, I'd chug to a stop.

"You've been hiding from me," Mother said. "I telephoned the Ritz, and they told me you are not staying there. You lied to me! To *me*, who labored for thirteen hours to bring you into this world, and nearly died in childbed. And what on *earth* were you doing out there in the Arbuckles' dunes last night?"

"Murdering the nurserymaid, Mother," Lillian said. "Can't you remember anything?"

I swung around. "You truly believe I murdered her?"

Lillian lifted a shoulder. "That's what Chisholm said."

I pointed at Chisholm. "That's slander."

He didn't reply. He merely chewed health bread. Granted, chewing health bread *does* take effort.

"I thought the police said you shot her," Lillian said, "just like you shot Mr. Arbuckle. Who taught you how to use a gun? Was it Alfie?"

"Lillian," Mother said, "of course your sister did not *shoot* anyone.

That is not how she was raised. Besides, didn't you say, Chisholm dear, that the police found a clue this morning?"

"Yes." Chisholm swallowed health bread. "A shred of cloth, snagged on a spike on the Arbuckles' fence.

"Could it have been Lola's?" Lillian asked.

"Don't sound so hopeful," I said. I turned to Chisholm. "What sort of cloth?"

"Green," he said. "Tweed."

"*You've* got a green tweed dress, haven't you, Lola?" Lillian said.

"No!"

Lillian sipped tea, keeping her teacup aloft longer than necessary.

Something sparkled on her finger. A ring, with a diamond hefty enough to be mistaken for a cube of cocktail ice.

"Lillian," I said slowly, "what's that?"

"Oh, this?" She wafted her hand.

"Yes, Lola," Mother said in an accusing tone. "Only yesterday, your sister and Mr. Woodby became engaged. We *would* have told you, of course, had you not been hiding. Why, even Andy, who is up to his eyeballs in exams, found the time to telephone his congratulations."

Guilt sloshed over me. I placed a slice of health bread on a plate and slumped into the nearest chair. "I—I'm sorry. Congratulations, Lillian. And—" I swallowed bile. "—Chisholm."

"I do hope that you'll give me some suggestions on redoing Amberley," Lillian said. "After all, you know the place *so* well, since it used to be yours."

My guilt dissolved, replaced with a silent scream.

"Lillian and Chisholm will travel to Palm Beach in a week's time, to pay an engagement visit to Rose," Mother said.

"My mother will *so* love Lillian," Chisholm said. He threw me a significant look.

Did I forget to mention how much Rose abhors me? The despotic bird-woman had never really met Lillian, since Lillian had been only a small girl at my own wedding. That was the last time Rose had come to New York.

"They shall need a chaperone," Mother said.

Uh-oh.

"I, alas, shall not be able to accompany them," Mother went on, "since the Ladies' Garden Society Gala is drawing near, and of course you know I am *so* consumed by that, and Lillian's maid Dora claims the train makes her deathly ill—so, Lola, *you* must chaperone."

"You want me to go to Florida?" I said. "Next week?"

"It would be advisable for you to get away from the glare of publicity," Chisholm said.

"And you *are* penniless," Lillian said.

"If you wish to return home to live," Mother said to me, "you will have to perform certain familial duties."

This, then, was what returning home would entail. In a flash, I saw it all: hauling around Lillian's luggage. Enduring her prattle. Propping cushions behind her languid head. No highballs on the horizon. Eternally. Even if Inspector Digton didn't have me sent to the electric chair for double murder, a life of playing Lillian's widow-in-waiting would be, itself, death in life.

In the last twenty-four hours, more people than I cared to count had accused me of being childish and spoiled. I had never considered myself so; I'd always figured my life was ruled by a riptide of forces beyond my control.

But maybe Berta, Ralph, Mother, Chisholm—even Miss Ida Shanks—all had a point. Perhaps I *was* allowing Fate to steamroll me. I have to confess, a small part of me longed to surrender to Mother and Chisholm. At least then I'd be assured of a roof over my head, and presumably enough pin money for chocolate.

But. I looked at Lillian's sour-sweet face, at Mother's eyes bright

with expectation, at Chisholm's lip-curl of censure. I looked down
at the slice of health bread on my plate.

And I knew I couldn't do it.

In the past few days, I'd had a taste of freedom. Of poverty, too,
and a dash of peril. But no one had controlled what I did. Maybe
Berta and I really could make a go of this detecting agency. It certainly sounded like a more appealing way to pay the bills than by,
say, filing or typing or accompanying some old, rich fussbudget to
Europe.

The first order of business, then, was escaping Amberley. I'd figure out the rest later.

I stood. "Well," I said, "I simply must go to Horace's funeral—if
you'll allow me to borrow a motorcar, Chisholm? The funeral is at
nine o'clock."

"You should go," Chisholm said, "or people will talk. But you
shan't drive yourself. Bartell will take you."

I tracked down Bartell, the chauffeur, in the garage. He was crouched
on a wooden crate behind Chisholm's Daimler, gulping coffee and
smoking a cigarette.

"I'm glad to see Mr. Woodby has kept you on," I said.

"Just barely." Bartell stamped out his cigarette in a tin can. "Don't
tell him you saw the coffee and the smoke, Mrs. Woodby, all right?"

"My lips are sealed."

Instead of instructing Bartell to take me to the chapel in St.
Percival's Cemetery, I asked to be delivered to the Foghorn in town.
My first order of business was to find Berta. Maybe she'd have an idea
of how to get the Duesy out of the clink.

But Berta had already checked out of the Foghorn. Ralph had,
too. Although for all I cared, *he* could take a trolley straight to Hell.

Berta had taken my luggage.

"And the dog?" I asked the front desk clerk.

"Yup," he said. "She took the pup, too. Cute fella. Oughta be in pictures."

I went back to the waiting Daimler and asked Bartell to drive on to the cemetery. By the time we arrived *there*, Horace's burial was over.

I thought about begging Bartell to motor me all the way back to the city. After all, I didn't have my handbag, so I couldn't purchase a train ticket. But I knew Bartell would lose his job if Chisholm found out.

So I asked him to take me to Dune House. I'd pay my respects to Olive and see if I might hitch a ride back to the city from someone there.

24

Hibbers opened the door. Jazz caterwauled from behind him, and I heard girls' laughter. "Oh. Mrs. Woodby," Hibbers said. "I did not, at first, recognize you."

You know you've hit rock bottom when you show up at a Society Matron's fête in flat shoes and a woolen pullover.

"Hello, Hibbers. Under a bit of nervous strain?"

"I cannot fathom what you mean, madam."

"You've got raccoon circles under your eyes. Is it about, you know—" I leaned close. "—Miss Potter getting herself murdered?"

He sighed. "Two murders in one week is nothing when compared with the motion picture people, madam."

He led me through to the crowded drawing room.

You'd never have guessed that a funeral had just taken place, and that another member of the household had gotten fogged the night before. Cigarette smoke hung in swathes. The furniture was haphazard. The gramophone throbbed out a King Oliver record, and a couple of jazz babies in fringed dresses and shiny lipstick fox-trotted together across the carpet. Where were Horace's family and friends?

And where could I get one of those cocktails?

Olive and Eloise Wright emerged from the haze. Olive's black dress twinkled with beadwork, and she held a cigarette in a long ivory holder. Her face was radiant. Eloise held a martini, and she'd done something different with her steel wool hair.

"Lola, darling!" Olive kissed the air next to my ear. "Just *look* at you, poor thing. Oh my. All in wool, and those flat shoes! I suppose tripping over Nanny Potter last night was simply devastating."

"Mrs. Woodby, how nice to see you again." Eloise said, "You are not wearing the new rubber—"

"How is Gerald?" I asked loudly.

Eloise and Olive exchanged a glance.

"Eloise," Olive whispered, "is, well, dropping the pilot—"

"I am not ashamed." Eloise looked at me. "I am divorcing Gerald."

"Oh. Goodness," I said. "So sorry."

"Don't be," Eloise said. "I've been liberated from a newt in glasses."

Hibbers appeared with a highball on a tray.

I grabbed it and took a gulp. "Do you have any idea who, um, shot Miss Potter?" I asked Olive.

"Oh, *I* don't know. Probably some jilted boyfriend."

Miss Potter? Jilted boyfriend? Hard to picture.

"You don't think it's in any way linked to Horace's . . . demise?"

"Why would it be?" Olive puffed cigarette smoke. "It's all a wretched bore, darling. I simply can't wait till the police are done poking about. They're completely in the way."

Apparently, Olive hadn't heard that I was Suspect Number One. Yet.

"How are Billy and Theo?" I asked.

"Wonderful. They loathed Nanny Potter. My maid is looking

after them now—they're starting off for Maine this afternoon. She's probably stuffing them with sweets, but I simply can't be bothered about it. *Let* them be fat little dumplings. I give up."

"Are you returning to the city today?" I asked Eloise. A forty-mile drive with her wouldn't be a cakewalk, but it would do the trick.

"No," Eloise said. "I plan to stay here and keep dear Olive company."

Rats.

"Well, I must go mingle," Olive said. She swayed off.

"I'm famished," I said, staring down into my fizzing glass. "Is there to be a luncheon?"

"Oh, these motion picture people don't really *eat*, dear," Eloise said. "That must be difficult for a healthy girl like you to fathom."

Peachy. The conversation was once more careening in the direction of my undercarriage. "There is nothing wrong with a bit of pot roast or chocolate cake," I said.

"You *do* like your chocolate, don't you?" Eloise sauntered away.

Eloise was taking her divorce rather well. And, come to think of it, Olive seemed pretty cheery for a woman who'd not only buried her husband that morning, but whose nurserymaid had been murdered as well. Maybe it was shock.

Or maybe it was something—or some*one*—else. I watched Bruno Luciano, dashing in white shirtsleeves and dark trousers, chatting with a fellow I recognized from the film studios. Bruno must've felt me gawking, because he glanced up. He came toward me.

"Hello, Mr. Luciano," I said.

"Call me Bruno."

Thank heaven the movies were silent.

"Dreadful business last night," he said. "I understand you found the body?"

"As a matter of fact, yes. But I'd rather not talk about it."

"Nobody would. Nasty little crime. I heard it was a jilted boy-friend."

Who had started that rumor?

"Now everyone's got their backs up," he said. "Sadie refuses to film with me, but of course, that's nothing new. Holed up in her room upstairs."

"Sadie Street is here?"

"Yes. We're supposed to film our scenes together, come hell or high water. George said he's ready to break both of our contracts."

Bruno gave no sign that he knew about George's deal with Lem Fitzpatrick. But then, Bruno was an actor.

"George is around, too?" I asked.

"Upstairs. Rubbing Sadie's feet or something. Naturally, he's only bluffing about *my* contract, but he means business with Sadie."

Interesting. Both Sadie and Eloise were currently in residence at Dune House. I ought to have a little poke-about in their rooms to see if either of them had the film reel in their luggage.

I sipped my drink. "Oh, look," I said. "Auntie Arbuckle."

Auntie stood by the drinks cabinet. She wore a long, old-fashioned black gown, complete with bustle. Her antique-granny image, how-ever, was ruined by her brimming whiskey glass.

"That old biddy is a real fright," Bruno said. "Olive says she's angry about her picture on the pork and beans cans. They say she hasn't been right in the head after some kind of yachting acci-dent."

Yachting accident? What about being dropped on her head as an infant? And having first cousins for parents?

"By the way," I said, "are you motoring back to the city today?"

"No. We're filming here for several more days."

Rats again.

....

The next time Hibbers passed by with a drinks tray, I took him aside. "Which bedroom is Sadie Street in?" I asked.

"The bedroom overlooking the swimming pool, madam. The one you stayed in last weekend."

"And Eloise Wright?"

"Two doors down from Miss Street's room." Hibbers paused. "Madam, might I be so bold as to caution you against making further inquiries regarding the . . . item you are searching for? There have been two murders, and although I cannot claim to have been greatly attached to either Mr. Arbuckle or Miss Potter, it would be a blow indeed if something were to happen to you."

"I can look after myself, Hibbers, but that's awfully sweet of you to say." Truth be told, I was worried something *would* happen to me. But I wasn't about to admit to being a fraidy cat. I plucked a gin rickey from his tray and headed upstairs.

Sadie's room was first. I knocked on the door.

"*Go away!*" she screamed inside.

All right, then. I wouldn't be searching *her* room.

I went two doors down to Eloise Wright's room. It was unlocked.

Inside, everything was as neat as a pin. No gun, no film reel, no incriminating anything. Nothing of interest whatsoever except, hidden under a folded blouse in an open Louis Vuitton suitcase, a big pile of GooGoo Clusters in white-and-red wrappers.

Well, well.

Don't get me wrong—GooGoo Clusters are lumps of chocolate and marshmallow divinity. But let me put it this way: They went with a Louis Vuitton suitcase the way a tractor goes with a ballroom.

With great effort, I backed away from the GooGoo Clusters, and tiptoed downstairs.

. . . .

The party migrated outside to the swimming pool. The morning had warmed up and the mist had burned away.

I parked myself on one of the teak lounges in the shade of the house. I sipped a drink, and willed that somebody I knew would show up so I could get back to the city.

Some of the movie people had changed into bathing costumes. They splashed and squealed in the pool. Hibbers wheeled the gramophone onto the pool deck, and a maid came around with a tray of fresh cocktails.

This wasn't so bad, was it?

My gaze drifted to a hedge beyond the swimming pool. I started upright, sending my drink slopping.

A row of reporters peeked over the hedge. They wore trilby hats and brandished cameras. In the thick of the reporters was Miss Ida Shanks. I'd know that wilty-flowered hat anywhere.

She grinned at me.

I heaved myself off the lounge and went in search of Hibbers again. I found him in the butler's pantry.

"Did you know there's a whole army of reporters on the property?" I asked.

"Indeed, madam. Mrs. Arbuckle instructed the gatekeeper to allow them in. They have even been so audacious as to use the lavatory in the carriage house, I am told."

"Why on earth would Olive allow them to intrude?"

"I could not say, madam."

But I knew the answer: Olive wanted her name and photograph splashed in the movie magazines.

I returned to the poolside lounge chair. I still held out hope that an acquaintance would turn up. An acquaintance with an especially cushy motorcar.

I lay my head back and stared up gloomily at the house above me, the stone facade, the gargoyles aloft, the blue sky. How silly, really, for a house in Long Island to have gargoyles. My eyelids sagged.

Then they flew open.

One of the gargoyles was . . . moving.

I jumped up. My glass went flying. I stumbled on my own flat-shoed feet and went face-first into the swimming pool.

I was swallowed up in cold blue, and everything sounded gurgly and muted. When I burst back to the surface, my ears were filled with shrieks.

I wiped water from my eyes and looked over at the lounge chair. Splintered teak jutted up around a three-foot-tall gargoyle, stone wings spread, snout leering.

Drunken yelping, dashing about, and general pandemonium ensued. Even though *I* was the one who'd nearly been smashed to death by a gargoyle, two flappers in bathing costumes were in hysterics. Nobody had turned off the gramophone, which was now dinging out Jelly Roll Morton.

I dragged myself out of the pool.

I stood shivering for a few moments. Water puddled around my spectator shoes. My sopping pullover felt like lead. Then Hibbers appeared with a highball.

"Madam," he said.

"Did I ever tell you you're the cat's pajamas, Hibbers?" I took a sip. Water dripped off the tip of my nose.

"On more than one occasion, madam." Hibbers left.

I found a towel and blotted my hair.

"Here, let me help you." A puffy towel enfolded me. I found myself gazing up into Bruno Luciano's ravishing mug.

"Thanks," I said. I tipped my chin.

Maybe it was the pose. Maybe it was only the booze. But for a second, I was Jane Eyre gazing up at Mr. Rochester.

"That gargoyle nearly fell on top of you," Bruno said. His hamster voice shattered the silver screen moment. "Could I get you any-thing? Hot tea?"

"I think I'll go . . ." I'd almost said, go home. But I didn't have a home anymore.

The fright of the falling gargoyle finally clobbered me. Tears sprang to my eyes. My whole, soggy body went trembly.

"There, there," Bruno murmured. He wrapped an arm around me.

"I'll go find my motorcar out front," I said. Bartell was waiting somewhere. I'd take a hot bath at Amberley and cook up a new es-cape strategy.

"I'll escort you to your motorcar, then."

Bruno guided me along. He had his arm around my shoulders to keep the towel on, and he carried my highball. What a gent.

We rounded the corner of the house.

Smack into Miss Ida Shanks.

Now, usually, Ida scribbled in her notebook while some potbel-lied sidekick snapped the photographs. But this time, she was doing the camera-snapping. At me.

"Taken up photography, Miss Shanks?" I said. "Expanding your horizons?" I pushed past her.

"It rather looks like you are expanding your horizons, Duffy—or is it merely that you're wearing flat shoes?" Ida lowered her camera lens and snapped a picture of my ankles.

I barged across the side lawn. Bruno scurried at my side, still man-aging to hold the towel around me and hold my highball.

We reached the front drive. A battered brown Model T idled in the driveway. Berta roosted in the passenger seat with Cedric on her lap. I caught a glimpse of Ralph through the windshield.

"There she is!" I heard Berta say. She rolled down the window. "Mrs. Woodby!" she yelled. "Come quickly! The gatekeeper told us not to enter, but I instructed Mr. Oliver to gun it when—"

The rest of her words were lost under the roar of Ralph revving the Model T's engine.

I turned to Bruno. "Thanks ever so much, Bruno. You're an absolute peach. Give Olive my regards, won't you?" I shrugged off the towel and placed it in his arms.

His face looked almost . . . boyish. "But when will I see you again, Lola—may I call you Lola?"

"Sure." I felt Berta's and Ralph's eyes boring into the back of my head.

"You're a . . ." Bruno's face softened. "You're a real girl, Lola. I don't meet real girls like you too often anymore. I'd love to see you again. Would you give me your telephone number?"

"Well, I—"

He delivered another heart-stopping Mr. Rochester look.

"It'll be listed under Alfred Woodby," I said. "In Washington Square. But don't tell anybody where I'm staying, all right?"

"Why would I do a thing like that?" Bruno ambled away.

Had the world-famous Latin Lothario really asked me—*me?*—for my telephone number? While I was wearing flat shoes, no less?

The horn beeped.

"Are you coming, Mrs. Woodby?" Berta yelled.

I roused myself from my dazzle and clambered—still soaking wet—into the backseat of the Model T.

25

I *did* so hope we would find you here," Berta said as we tooled down the drive. "We waited for you at the funeral, but you never arrived. Why in heaven are you all wet? And what was Mr. Luciano saying to you?"

"Yeah," Ralph said. "I've gotta hear this."

"To begin with, I had a brush with death," I said.

Berta gave a cry. Cedric propped his front paws on the seat back, and I lifted him over. I burrowed my face in his warm fluff. He licked my face. "Why does Cedric feel so heavy?" I asked. I heaved him up and down like a dumbbell. "What have you two been feeding him?"

"What about this brush with death?" Ralph glanced over his shoulder. His eyes were filled with concern. Not picturesque chivalry, as Bruno Luciano had displayed; Ralph's eyes were keener, and sort of bruised. "Are you kidding?"

"No, I'm not kidding. And don't look at me like that, because you're on my X-List. Permanently." Humiliation about *L.W. kiss in cinema check* still stewed on the back burner of my mind. More per-tinently, I was abuzz with the suspicion that Chisholm had hired Ralph to spy on me. But I couldn't let those things boil over. Too much was happening. Besides, it looked like Ralph was my ride back to Manhattan.

"X-List?" He chuckled. "Okay, I think I can live with that." He steered through the gates and took a right onto the coastal road.

"What happened?" Berta asked.

I described how the gargoyle had come crashing down onto my teak lounge, and how I'd tripped into the swimming pool.

"Hang on a minute," Ralph said. "You're saying the gargoyle just *fell?*"

"What are you suggesting? That someone pushed the gargoyle?"

"Seems more likely than it simply falling, wouldn't you say?"

I felt icy cold. "Someone tried to . . . kill me?"

"Does that come as a surprise," Berta said, "considering the events of last night?"

"You heard, then. About Miss Potter," I said.

"You forget we were staying at the Foghorn with all of those news-paper and magazine reporters," Berta said. "For them, a murder is a feast."

"Who was at that party back there?" Ralph asked. "Who could've pushed the gargoyle?"

I racked my brains. It wasn't easy. What I hadn't drunk in coffee that morning, I'd made up for in giggle juice. "Well, honestly, I didn't know most of them. They were motion picture people, mainly. Olive was there, of course. And Eloise Wright—she's divorcing her husband, by the way. Sadie Street and George Zucker were in the house somewhere, but I didn't see them."

"Horace's family?" Ralph asked.

"Not that I know of . . . wait. Yes. Auntie Arbuckle."

"What about Luciano?" Ralph said. "Could he have pushed it?"

"After he's been so chivalrous! I'll bet you're jealous." The truth was, Bruno *could* have pushed it. He'd been out of my sight, anyway, at the right time. But why would he want to bop me off?

"Jealous? Naw." Ralph's shoulders were rigid.

"No woman can resist Mr. Luciano," Berta said. "I read about it in *Movie Love*."

"*What?*" I said. "Well, maybe as long as he keeps clammed up."

Ralph snorted.

Berta swiveled around. "Mr. Oliver is suspicious only because Mr. Luciano is a motion picture star, and you are, well . . . oh dear me. You are not going to cry, are you?"

"I want to change into some dry clothes and have a cup of coffee," I mumbled into Cedric's fur.

We motored into Hare's Hollow. The Model T shuddered to a stop in front of the Foghorn.

I took my suitcase and handbag, which Berta had jammed in the backseat, and went to change in the washroom off the lobby. I moved Sadie Street's lipstick from my skirt pocket to my handbag. My dip in the pool didn't seem to have damaged it.

It was a relief to be back in dry clothes. And in mascara, lipstick, and high-heeled shoes. There wasn't much I could do about my beaver-lodge hair.

I met Berta, Ralph, and Cedric in the Foghorn's crowded restaurant.

Between bites of gristly pork chops, oversalted scalloped potatoes, damp string beans, and sludge-strong coffee, I described how I'd arranged the meeting with Vera Potter, and how I'd heard the gunshot and found Miss Potter's body in the dunes.

"Vera Potter had a gun?" Ralph said. "It could've been for her own protection, but maybe she meant to shoot you."

"I *know*," I said. Would it cause a scene if I catapulted string beans at him with my spoon?

"Perhaps she carried the gun because she indeed knew something about the film reel," Berta said. "Perhaps, Mrs. Woodby, she intended to kill you because of whatever secret the reel holds."

Fear made me fork up my potatoes with gusto.

"We must unmask the murderer before you are killed," Berta said.

"What about you? You're as deep into this as I am."

"Indeed, but I am told I have an innocent face. No one would suspect *me* of having anything to do with murders and stolen film reels."

"That reminds me," Ralph said. "I got ahold of my junk-dealer buddy, Prince, last night. He told me the fleur-de-lis mark on the film canister was the imprint of a now-defunct film company out of New Rochelle. Pinnacle Productions. They made news reels, advertisements, that sort of thing."

"News reels?" I said.

"How peculiar," Berta said. "I was certain the film contained filth."

"Inspector Digton wants to arrest me, by the way," I said. I explained the chummy deal Chisholm had struck with Inspector Digton. "But *you*, Mr. Oliver, probably already know all about that, don't you?" I speared a potato without taking my eyes off Ralph.

But Ralph seemed genuinely surprised. "Chisholm?" he said. "You mean your brother-in-law? What's it to him?"

"You mean he didn't hire you?" I said.

"Nope. And it doesn't sound like he'd need a private eye, anyway, if he's got the police force doing his dirty work for him."

True. My balloon popped. If Chisholm hadn't hired Ralph, who the heck had?

"I probably shouldn't even be here," I said. "Who knows who else Chisholm has enlisted to snitch on me."

"Then you are on the lam," Berta said. Her eyes sparkled.

"Yes. Oh. And I found this." I dug out the gold lipstick tube from my handbag, and set it on the table.

"A lipstick?" Berta said. "Nanny Potter did not wear paint. At least, not when I saw her last weekend at the Arbuckles' house."

"She wasn't really the type," I said.

"She was an actress, though," Ralph said.

I hunched forward, tapped the lipstick, and whispered, "This belongs to Sadie Street." I removed the cap and showed them the pointy wear pattern. "Digton laughed it off, but I think this is our pivotal clue."

"You think Sadie shot the nurserymaid and dropped a lipstick in the process?" Ralph asked.

"It's a theory. Don't forget that Hibbers saw the missing film reel in Sadie's weekend bag."

"Or Eloise Wright's bag," Berta said.

"Eloise is the more suspicious of the two," Ralph said. "All of a sudden she's managed to scrape together enough dough to leave her husband."

"Maybe she's so anxious to be rid of Gerald, she'd rather be broke," I said.

"That doesn't happen too often," Ralph said. "Does it, Mrs. Woodby? Seems to me, usually ladies stick to rich hubbies like glue, no matter how rotten the fellow happens to be."

My lips said nothing. But my eyes said, *X-List*.

"If it is indeed Sadie Street's lipstick that you found," Berta said, "then—"

"Shh, not so loud." I looked around. Nobody appeared to be listening.

The waitress arrived. She plopped a thick wedge of banana cream pie in front of me.

There was still a God, then.

"If it *is* Sadie Street's lipstick," Berta said in a whisper, "you must prove it. Then you will be off the hook, and she will be arrested."

"How can I prove it?" I asked.

"There's only one thing to do, the way I see it." Ralph sipped coffee. "Break into Sadie's apartment."

"We never learned her address," Berta said.

I dug into my pie. "Back to square one."

A lady at the next table spiraled around.

My forkful of pie hung in midair. "Miss Shanks," I said. "I didn't notice you without that flea-ridden fox fur."

"Oh, it's not *fox* fur, Duffy." Ida leered at Cedric. At his lovely, fox-colored fur.

"You need to be straitjacketed!" I cried. "And, by golly, why are you always *following* me?"

She dragged her chair over to our table and sat. "Because, Duffy, you are where all the excitement is. Isn't that right, Mr. *Oliver?*"

Ralph eyed her lazily, but his fingers clenched his coffee cup. "How'd you figure out my name?"

"Sources, my dear. Sources. Now—" Ida turned to me. "—what's this I hear about Sadie Street's lipstick?"

Berta grabbed the lipstick, dropped it into the handbag on her lap, and snapped the clasp. "What lipstick?" she said.

"I'm not stupid," Ida said. "Or blind."

"Could've fooled me, with that dress you've got on," I said. It was the same one she'd had on last night: green tweed with orangey-red trim at the cuffs. I frowned. "Wait a minute." I bent to peer under the oilcloth. "I knew it!" A few inches up from Ida's hem was a rip. She'd repaired it with a safety pin. I straightened. "Sneak over any sharp fences lately? Say, anytime last night around midnight?"

"I don't know what you mean." Ida adjusted her glasses.

I lowered my voice. "Stop bluffing. The police found a bit of your dress on the Arbuckles' fence last night. Why didn't you *change?*"

"I left the city in a hurry. Didn't pack a spare." She glanced over her shoulder.

I hadn't seen Ida Shanks flustered since around the time we were learning our multiplication tables.

"I was only trying to take photographs of the motion picture people in the house," Ida said. "How was I to know there would be another murder? But, since you have a rather savage gleam in your eye, Duffy, I'll make you a deal."

I glanced over at Berta; Berta made a slight nod. I looked back to Ida. "Go on."

"I'll turn over Sadie Street's address if you keep your lips locked about seeing my torn dress."

"You really must be desperate, striking a deal like that with me," I said.

She shrugged. It came off a little jerky.

Could Ida really be a murderer? What motive could she have?

"Deal," I said.

Ida took a dog-eared notebook from her satchel. She flipped through—it was chock-full of smeary scribbles—licking her fingertips as she went. She found the address, jotted it on a separate scrap of paper, and passed it to me.

I glanced at it. *Suite 12D, the Plaza.* I stuffed it in my handbag. "This had better be accurate, or I'm going to the police about your torn dress."

Ida stood, leaned over, and picked up my fork. She took a huge bite of my banana cream pie. *"Delicious,"* she said, and left.

"Wowie, Mrs. Woodby." Ralph sipped more coffee. "You drive a hard bargain, don't you?"

I squinched my eyes at him and shoved my maimed pie away.

26

....

When we arrived in the city, the air was gritty and stagnant. What a relief. Fresh sea breezes would only remind me of Vera Potter's corpse.

We planned to break into Sadie Street's rooms at the Plaza that afternoon, but we needed to leave Cedric at the love nest. Cedric turned heads. I'd reluctantly agreed that Ralph could come. After all, Ralph was the only one who knew how to pick locks.

Once we arrived at the love nest, I went into the bathroom to change. I yanked on a sturdy girdle—steel-boned, not rubber, thanks very much—a black silk dress, and my favorite black cloche. The hat hid my beaver-lodge hair nicely. I pulled on stockings, buckled on my highest André Perugia T-straps, brushed my teeth, and touched up my lipstick.

The gussying-up had nothing to do with Ralph Oliver. Nothing whatsoever. Although, if he happened to glance my way and notice what he was missing—well, that was none of my affair.

In the kitchen, Berta told me that she had decided not to partici-
pate in our excursion to the Plaza.

"I'll stay here and tidy up the kitchen," she said. She clattered
dishes in the cupboard.

"But it's already tidy—more than tidy." I pulled on black wristlet
gloves. "You could eat off the floor in here."

"Good heavens, I think not," Berta said. "And Cedric needs to
be walked, come to think of it. He has been cooped up all day."

"Say, why are you acting so . . . jittery? And it's not like you to be
so concerned with Cedric's welfare."

"What?" Berta yelled over her shoulder. Now the faucet was
running full blast. She ambushed the sink with a sponge and a can
of Bon Ami cleaning powder. "I cannot hear you."

"Fine. I'll be back later. Don't give Cedric anything starchy. He's
getting fat."

I collected Ralph from the sitting room. "Nice dress," he said. His
glowing eyes hinted that he meant it.

"What, this old thing?"

"I knew I'd get you to smile at me again. No more Z-List?"

"It's not a Z-List. It's an X-List. And you're still at the tippy top."

We went down to the street. "Berta is acting funny," I told him
once we were walking along.

"Sure. She doesn't want to break into a suite at the Plaza. Makes
sense. She's still squeaky clean. You're suspected by the police for two
homicides."

"Don't remind me."

We rode the Fourth Avenue Line. Ralph said ducking into a subway
station was always the smoothest kind of getaway. I hoped it wouldn't
come to that.

The subway car was jam-packed, so we stood and clung to hand straps. It was the first time Ralph and I had been alone together all day. I sensed the stiffness in Ralph's bearing, his unwillingness to meet my eyes, although my face was about an inch from his lapel.

Dandy. Because I didn't want to meet *his* eyes, either. What was he doing, acting wounded, anyway? *I* was the one he'd kissed in order to check it off some list. *I* was the one who was being spied on.

The subway rattled along. People shuffled off and on. It wasn't till after we'd passed the Grand Central Station stop that I noticed the man.

He was halfway up the carriage, on the opposite side, on one of the benches. He wore a drab suit and hat. His distinguishing characteristics were (1) a too-short torso, which brought the waistband of his pants, exposed beneath his open jacket, to the latitude of his underarms; and (2) dried-currant eyes, which were fixed on my face.

When I first noted him staring at me, I glanced away. New York is a big city. People stare.

I glanced back.

Mr. Highpants was still staring.

I elbowed Ralph. "See that man?" I whispered. "The one with his pants pulled up past the equator?"

Ralph's eyes slid around. "Nope."

I scanned the crowded carriage. Mr. Highpants was gone.

When Ralph and I emerged from the station at Fifty-ninth and Lexington, the sun had dipped behind the high buildings to the west. Lexington was a canyon of shadows.

We headed on foot along Fifty-ninth. Fellows in suits and hats streamed down the sidewalk, a few young girls in secretarial garb mixed in. Every pair of eyes was hidden by hat brims. From the street came chugging engines and horn beeps.

The Plaza came into view, rising up from the corner of Fifty-ninth and Fifth Avenue. The Plaza was a monumental, modern French château of creamy stone, with steep green roofs and hundreds of black-edged windows. A big paved square, planted with frail young trees, sprawled in front.

"Suppose you've been here a bunch of times," Ralph said when we'd stopped at the curb, waiting to cross the street. His jaw was tight.

Did my high society past make him edgy?

"Yes, I've been here," I said. "Cotillions, banquets, wedding receptions, galas, luncheons, you name it. But I've never visited in the capacity of a burglar."

"First time for everything."

We were still waiting at the curb, and a flock of pedestrians had bottlenecked around us.

My spine prickled. I cut a glance to my left.

Mr. Highpants stood off to the side, half hidden behind two businessmen, his dried-currant eyes fixed on me. The crowd started migrating, and he was swallowed up.

My greasy lunch churned in my stomach. "I saw him again!" I whispered to Ralph as we were swept along. "The man from the subway. He's following us."

"Where?"

"I don't know. He has a way of vanishing."

"Maybe it's a coincidence."

"You don't often see the same stranger twice. Not in this city. And he was *staring*."

"What can I say, kid? You're a knockout."

We reached the entry of the Plaza, with its broad steps, white columns, and ornate glass and gilt canopy. I kept a lookout for Mr. Highpants, but I didn't see him again. Only swanky motorcars and darting bellhops.

"Shall we go in?" I started up the steps.

Ralph grabbed my hand and dragged me back down to sidewalk level. "Just a little pointer—this is if you and your Swedish sidekick are crazy enough to try and set up an agency—"

"Berta told you about that?"

"Sure. Last night. We had to kill time after you ditched us. And the pointer is, use the service entrance." He pulled me along. True, he was on my X-List. But his hand felt too reassuring to let it go.

We went around the corner and down a short stair to the ground floor. A door was propped open to let out puffs of starchy, soapy steam. The hotel laundries.

Inside, we crept around whitewashed basement hallways until we found a bare, concrete service staircase. No one noticed us.

Ralph started up the steps. I winched myself up the banister behind him. Flight after flight we went. It was the Mount Everest of staircases, but I was no Sherpa. And the steel boning of my girdle was digging into my cupcakes. Maybe I should've worn Eloise Wright's rubber girdle, after all.

Ralph glanced back at me. "Holy Moses, Lola. Are you okay?"

A bead of sweat rolled down my forehead. "Of . . . course."

By the time we reached the twelfth floor, I was pretty certain I'd developed asthma.

Mental note: Reduce cinnamon roll consumption. Perhaps eat health bread instead? Nix that. May as well eat cardboard.

"Here we go," Ralph said. He knocked on a paneled door.

"What're you doing?" I asked, panting. "Sadie's filming at Dune House."

"Here's another tip: Don't go crashing down doors when you can get someone to open it for you. Saves energy."

"We're going to crash the door down?"

"Not if we don't have to." He gave the doorknob a jiggle. "Locked." He fished in his trousers pocket and pulled out a funny little instrument, much like a pocketknife. Except in lieu of blades, it had steel pokey bits of various shapes and sizes.

"Where did that come from?" I whispered.

"My motorcar. I always keep a spare."

"*I* need one of those."

"Shh."

"But I do. If I'd had one of those to begin with, I could've picked my way into Horace's safe."

The lock gave way with a *click*. Ralph folded the gadget, stuffed it back in his pocket, and pushed the door open. "You can't pick that kind of safe. If it has a dial, you either have to use the combination, or blow it open with nitroglycerin. I could teach you about that. Later."

Something about that word—*teach*—brought on a belly-swooping memory of our kiss in the movie palace. Then there was *later*. Were Ralph and I going to have a *later*?

Oh—and then there was the bit about blowing things up.

"Come on," he said.

We crept in, and he shut the door.

We were in a marble foyer. White statuettes of sylphs stood in niches. The chandelier was modern, gold, and sharp looking. Ladies' shoes were strewn across the floor.

We went through to the sitting room. Sculptural furniture of blond wood and steel, huge mirrors, glinting gold, geometric motifs on the wallpaper. Tall windows offered a staggering view of the angular black skyline and the salmon-colored sunset beyond. But the place was a pigsty.

"Doesn't she have a maid?" I said. "She must have a maid."

Gilt-rimmed plates with half-eaten crackers, empty drinks glasses, cascading ashtrays, and open magazines littered every surface that wasn't scattered with slinky garments and jewelry.

Ralph poked through a pile of sheet music on the grand piano. "You'd be surprised how people live when they think no one's looking. It's something you figure out in my line of work. When you're a detective, you're not usually showing up with an engraved invitation."

Empty booze bottles cluttered the sideboard. I sniffed through them. Gin, gin, and more gin, with a few bottles of vodka and rum to spice things up.

I wandered into the bedroom. White satin and gold velvet snarled the bed. The carpet was ankle-deep with evening gowns, furs, and high-heeled shoes. I poked around Sadie's vanity table. She had an ample supply of depilatory cream. Well, guess you wouldn't want any stray hairs cropping up when the movie camera came in for a close-up.

I found a lipstick. I pulled off the cap and screwed it up.

Pointy as a pin. I *knew* it.

And then I saw it. In the corner. I think my heart stopped for a few beats.

It was a weekend bag. *The* weekend bag. Hermès Frères, fawn-colored calfskin.

I hurried over, knelt, and pulled the bag open. Clothes and shoes were stuffed inside. I recognized the sleeve of the yellow golfing suit Sadie had worn last weekend. Nestled inside the dirty clothes was a round, flat, metal canister.

The moment called for brass band music.

"I found it!" I yelled.

Ralph appeared in the doorway. "You're kidding me, right?"

"No. I mean, this *must* be it." I held up the canister. Something inside clanked.

"Careful." Ralph said. "Look at that—the fleur-de-lis imprint. It was just sitting in that bag there?"

"Yes." I jimmied the lid with my fingernails. "It looked like Sadie just tossed the bag aside when she returned from the Arbuckles'. She'd never even unpacked the bag—the clothes she wore last weekend are still in there." The canister lid popped free, and I lifted it.

A big, flat metal spool lay inside, with a shiny black ribbon of film looped around.

Ralph let out a low whistle. "You've got it, kid. Let's get out of here."

I replaced the lid and tucked the canister under my arm. Ralph pulled me to my feet. As he did so, he grunted with effort.

Note to self: Although health bread tastes like stuffing exhumed from an antique teddy bear, *eat it.*

We made a break for it.

Halfway down the service stairs, I stopped in my tracks. Ralph stopped, too.

"Did you hear that?" I whispered. "I heard footsteps above us. But they've stopped."

I couldn't get Mr. Highpants out of my head. I held tight to the banister and stuck my head out into the middle of the stairwell. Up above, flights of stairs coiled around and around. Dizziness rocked through me. I didn't dare look down.

"I don't hear anyone," Ralph said.

"Maybe he's following us. Maybe he's waiting for us to start walking again."

Ralph shook his head. "Don't let some creep from the subway get under your skin."

27

B ack outside the Plaza, evening was huddling down. The air
  smelled of burnt peanuts, horse manure, and motorcar exhaust.
Traffic gushed past. Across the way, Central Park was green, shadowy, and serene.

"What next?" I said, pretending not to pant. I mean, is one supposed to get breathless going *down* stairs?

"Do you want to see what's on that reel?"

"I'm not certain." Part of me wanted to get it out of my hair and
into Ruby's hands as quickly as possible. On the other hand, the film
likely contained clues to the murderer's identity. And I needed to
collar the murderer before I took the fall—or before the murderer
murdered *me*. "I can practically feel Inspector Digton breathing down
my neck, and I've never felt so twitchy in my life," I said, "so, yes. I
want to view the film."

"Okay. Remember my buddy I told you about, who owns the junk
shop? Prince?"

"The one who identified the fleur-de-lis symbol. Sure." Prince was, as far as I was concerned, a name for a borzoi.

We stopped at the corner. Ralph whistled for a cab.

My eardrum was quite possibly shattered.

"Prince might be able to rig together some kind of film projector," Ralph said. "That is, if he doesn't already have one. Prince loves that kind of thing. He's real good with his hands, and he knows doohickeys like most people know their own belly buttons."

"A mechanical genius?" I asked.

"Kinda. Yeah, he is."

"Can we trust him?"

"With your life. When I met him, he was in the Army Signal Corps. Over in France. It was his job to lay telephone lines between the trenches. Every time the Jerries hit the lines with fire, Prince had to run out and lay new ones. He kept the telephones in the trenches working, too. Kept a lot of us alive that way."

Then Ralph, just like that, went quiet. His hands were stuffed in his trouser pockets. He gazed out into the river of traffic with eyes that were watching memories.

I'd met shell-shocked men. The bombs and tanks and machine guns over in Europe would keep nerve specialists like the Prig in business for years to come. But Ralph didn't seem shell-shocked, exactly. He was simply a man who'd seen too much.

I knew that Ralph's Too Much was probably terrible, but I wished he'd tell me about it, anyway. I wasn't sure why. He was on my X-List, after all.

Ralph did his taxi whistle again.

This time, a taxicab veered to stop in front of us.

"Whereyawant?" the driver said.

"Orchard Street," Ralph said. "Lower East Side."

....

Inside the taxi, I hugged the film canister tight. "Sadie might've shot Horace," I said softly—I didn't want the cabbie to overhear. "Maybe whatever is on the film could ruin her career, the way Ruby says it'll ruin *hers*. Sadie shot Horace, and then grabbed the reel and brought it back to her suite at the Plaza for safekeeping."

"The reel wasn't exactly safe in that weekend bag," Ralph said. "Looked like she hadn't even noticed it in there."

"What do you mean?"

"Look, if I murdered a guy over something, like this reel, I'd sure as heck lock it up tight after all was said and done. In a safe deposit box, maybe. Come to think of it, I'd want to destroy it. I wouldn't leave it lying around in a bag."

"You're suggesting Sadie wasn't the one who put the reel in her bag?"

"It's possible. Maybe someone *else* stole the reel—maybe Vera Potter, because don't forget she's the one who overheard you saying the safe combination out loud. When the cops started crawling all over the Arbuckles' place, maybe she panicked and dropped it into Sadie's bag. Heck, she might've thought she was dumping it into Eloise Wright's weekend bag, since hers looked just like Sadie's."

"This is giving me a headache." I slumped against the seat. "What about the lipstick? The lipstick on her vanity table matched the one I found by Vera Potter's body."

"Oh yeah? You didn't tell me that."

"They matched *perfectly*."

"Okay. Maybe too perfectly. Think about it. We went to the Plaza looking for two things—the reel, and lipstick matching the one you found by Vera Potter's body. And, as luck would have it, we found exactly those two things."

"Well, you said it yourself—it's lucky."

"Something's fishy. Things get planted. Anyone who had access to Sadie's makeup could've stolen her lipstick and left it by the body. And since Sadie's an actress, that's a lot of people."

"Hold on," I said when we were halfway to Orchard Street. "What about Berta? She's been looking high and low for this film, too. She and I are partners in this. If we view it without her, she'll be awfully upset." *Upset* wasn't quite the word. She'd be white-lipped with fury. She might even cut off my cinnamon roll supply.

"All right," Ralph said. "Let's stop and get her, then. I'll tell the driver."

A few minutes later, the taxi stopped in Longfellow Street. I dashed upstairs.

Except, Berta wasn't there.

Only Cedric was home. He was too lazy to get up from his pouf in the corner of the kitchen.

"Are you all right, peanut?" I said to him.

He closed his eyes for a snooze.

I went back down to the taxi. I told Ralph that Berta was missing.

"She might have gone down to the corner store," Ralph said.

"That must be it," I said. But I still felt uneasy.

Presently, we lurched to a stop in front of a row of brick apartment blocks. Fire escapes crisscrossed the walls like bad sutures. Laundry flapped between open windows. Laughter, cooking onion odors, and warbling gramophone music wafted through the night. At street level, tattered awnings stretched over shops. Folding grilles protected a hardware store, a tobacconist's, and a bakery. One restaurant was open. Light and a piano waltz spilled out.

Ralph paid the driver, and we climbed out.

"That joint is delicious," Ralph said as we passed the restaurant.

"The cook is French. I fought in his village, it turns out. He always gives me a dessert on the house."

"Dessert?" I craned my neck.

"This here's Prince's place."

Prince's shop was next door to the French restaurant. The grimy display window read PRINCE KNIGHTLEY, ESQ. CURIOS ETC. in crackled gold lettering. The window was lit by a single, dangling lightbulb, which illuminated, well, junk—a row of porcelain doll's heads, three dusty gramophone horns, mismatched china chargers, grubby brass lamps, bicycle gears, dingy little watercolors.

"Prince Knightley, Esquire?" I said. "How very grand." My mental picture of the borzoi was replaced with an image of a tweedy English lord with a pince-nez.

"Prince *is* grand, in his own way. You'll see." Ralph pushed the doorbell.

The scent of steak and *pommes frites* floated over from next door. My belly rumbled.

Ralph pretended not to notice. I supposed he was gentlemanly, in his swaggery, shabby kind of way.

Not, mind you, that I'd forgiven him for being a sneaky cad.

Bolts and chains rattled, and the door cracked.

"Ralph!"

"Prince, brother. Wondering if you could be of some help."

"Come in, come in. Always glad to help you with one of your cases." The door swung wide.

So did my eyelids. Prince Knightley, Esq. was a corpulent man. He wore a stained undershirt that didn't fully conceal the curving flesh of his ponderous belly, and patched dungarees. He was perhaps thirty-five years old, although he was so baggy-eyed, he might've been decades older. I couldn't picture him dashing about from trench to trench amid explosions, laying telephone wire.

"Who's this?" Prince asked, smiling at me. He was missing a tooth in the upper right-hand corner.

Ralph tugged me forward. "Mrs. Woodby."

"Nice meeting you, Mrs. Woodby." Prince led us inside. "I was just settling down to a tinker with an old music box I found in the alley. Someone took it for rubbish. Can you imagine?"

"No sirree," Ralph said. "But folks don't know their et ceteras like you do, Prince."

The shop was dim. I made out lampshades, springs, the silhouette of a dressmaker's dummy. We passed through a fusty curtain into a rear room.

A downy white cat hovered over a plate on a table and glared at us with defiant yellow eyes.

"Persephone!" Prince said to the cat. "Scram, you little villainess."

Persephone thunked to the floor on tiny paws and swished off into the shadows.

"Drink?" Prince said. He went to a shelf crammed with old books. He slid a huge atlas aside, revealing a half-filled bottle of clear liquor.

"Sure," Ralph said.

We sat. I laid the film canister on the table. Prince poured gin into chipped teacups with—ugh—brown rings inside. We drank to Persephone's health. Then Prince went over to a gramophone and selected a record. I waited for jazz.

Instead, the cushiony sounds of an orchestra blossomed, and then, gliding above the cellos and harpsichord, a soprano.

I hadn't pegged Prince as an opera-goer. Although he *did* have that Carnegie Hall voice and the proportions of a tenor.

Prince closed his eyelids and appeared to liquefy in ecstasy.

I wondered which opera it was. Something baroque, maybe. I opened my mouth to ask.

Ralph's finger flew to his lips, and he gave me a warning look.

I clamped my teeth.

Prince kept swooning.

I sipped more gin. I noticed a row of mismatched cameras on a mantelpiece. Surely Berta would approve of me purchasing a camera, as a business expense. If we were really going to give that retrieval agency notion a go, we'd need a camera, right?

After a bit, the aria ended.

"Still stuck on 'Dido's Lament,' brother?" Ralph said. "I was sure you'd be over it and turning to some of those Schumann art songs."

"How do you know so much about opera?" I asked Ralph.

"Took me for a philistine, did you?"

"No," I lied.

"Schumann art songs aren't opera," Prince said to me.

"Oh."

Prince turned to Ralph. "I shall never get over 'Dido's Lament.' Never."

"Suit yourself," Ralph said.

"Mr. Knightley," I said, "would you sell me a camera?" I gestured to those on the mantelpiece.

"They aren't new," Prince said. "I rebuilt them with bits and bobs that I salvaged."

"Do they work?"

"Of course."

"How much for the small brown one?"

"That's an Eastman Kodak Brownie. Simple to use. About ten years old, but I fixed it up myself. Good as new. On the house."

"Really?"

"Any friend of Ralph's is a friend of mine."

"Thanks!"

"Say, Prince," Ralph said, "you don't think you could do us a favor, do you?"

Finally.

"Depends," Prince said.

"We've got this reel of film, here—" He gestured to the canister on the table. "—and we want to view it."

"May I?" Prince said.

I slid the reel over. Prince pried the canister open and inspected the reel. "Yes," he said. "I have a projector—I cobbled it together myself—that will run this."

Inside of ten minutes, Prince had rearranged the back room into a cramped movie palace. He'd gone upstairs—there was a stair through a doorway at the back—and brought down a wrinkled bed-sheet. He hung it over the bookcase, making a screen. Then he set up a film projector on the opposite side of the room. He spooled the film onto the projector and flicked on a light. A yellow beam shot across the room, over the table, onto the bedsheet.

"Ready?" Prince said.

"Yes," I said. My palms sweated.

"Ready," Ralph said, and finished off his gin in one gulp.

We'd never talked it over, but there was a pretty decent chance that the film contained things that were, well, a bit, shall we say, *French* in nature. You know. Racy. Or worse.

28

....

Prince flipped a switch.

First, crackly black, and then the film flickered into motion. Glowing white words on a black background: EVERYONE LOVES AUNTIE ARBUCKLE'S PORK AND BEANS!

"What?" I said.

Next, two women smiling and waving at the camera. They wore white factory workers' uniforms—smocks and caps. They stood in front of a big pale building without windows, beneath a spacious sky. The cogs of the Manhattan skyline rose in the background.

Ralph leaned forward on his chair.

"That's Ruby Simpkin, on the left," I said. "And . . . and oh my word, that's Vera Potter!"

More words: COME ALONG AND JOIN US! IF THIS TOUR DOESN'T WHET YOUR APPETITE FOR DELICIOUS AUNTIE ARBUCKLE'S PORK AND BEANS, NOTHING WILL!

Ruby and Vera traipsed up a ramp and through the factory doors.

Shots of whirring, whizzing factory machinery. Conveyor belts and cans and crates. The two actresses pointed and gestured at it all with enthusiasm.

More words: BUT WHAT'S THE DELICIOUS SECRET OF THIS HOME-MADE FAVORITE, JUST LIKE AUNTIE MAKES?

A shot of a gleaming white industrial kitchen, with a large cook-stove beside a counter. Ruby and Vera stood behind the counter. They took turns measuring ingredients and dumping them into a big pot. Vera stirred the pot and smiled coyly. Ruby stuck a spoon in and gave Vera a taste. Ruby winked hugely at the camera.

Words: SCRUMPTIOUS! SHHH! DON'T GIVE AWAY THE SECRET RECIPE!

Then, a shot of them going out the factory doors, smiling and waving at the camera.

Words: THE END.

The film whapped off the reel. The entire film had lasted less than two minutes.

Ralph spoke first. "Not exactly what I expected."

"I can't believe that Vera and Ruby knew each other," I said.

"Well, they are—or, I ought to say, *were*—both actresses," Ralph said. "It's interesting—by the position of the city skyline in the background, I can tell the factory is over in Brooklyn."

"But it's just a *factory*," I said. "Yet now Arbuckle's dead, and one of the actresses on the film is dead, too. It's all tangled up together, but I don't see how. The film seems so innocent. Although, Auntie Arbuckle did mention a recipe to me."

"Oh yeah?"

I nodded. "Last weekend. She hinted that Dune House's butler had been fired over it."

"Maybe we missed something," Ralph said. "Let's watch it again."

But a second viewing revealed nothing more, except for the briefest flash, during the kitchen sequence, of a third person's hand, passing a spoon to Ruby from outside the shot. Prince stopped the film, and we studied the hand.

It was a man's hand, wearing a round signet ring of some kind. Whoever the man was, he'd been wearing a white smock, too.

And when Vera and Ruby dumped the ingredients into the pot, it was impossible to tell what the ingredients *were*, let alone the precise measurements.

We all sighed.

Prince removed the film from the projector and replaced it in the canister. He handed it over.

"Do you want to take the reel to the police?" Ralph asked me.

"After all my hard work? No. I'm getting paid. Besides, Inspector Digton would laugh this film off, exactly like he's laughed off everything else I've told him." I stood. My legs felt like overcooked noodles. Bathtub gin. Whoops. "I wish to go to the Frivolities." I would give Ruby Simpkin the film reel and collect my kale. I'd be able to think more clearly once I knew I could pay the rent.

Twenty minutes later, Ralph and I were backstage at the Unicorn Theater. However, there was no sign of Ruby Simpkin in dressing room three.

"Excuse me," Ralph said to a red-sequined firecracker who was bustling by.

"Yeah?" She looked annoyed, but once she'd flipped her fake eyelashes down and up Ralph a couple times, she put on a cute smile. "Who you looking for?"

She seemed to be blind to my very existence.

"Ruby Simpkin," Ralph said. "Is she onstage?"

"Naw, it's funny you're asking, because Ruby didn't show tonight."

My breath caught.

"Ill?" Ralph said.

Firecracker toyed with a peroxide curl. "Maybe."

"Do you know where she lives?" Ralph asked.

"Say, you ain't one of them crazy obsessionals, are you? The kind that stand under the streetlamp and gongoozle up at a girl's window all night?"

"Not the last time I checked."

"Yeah. You're too handsome for that sorta thing, ain't you? Guess you got obsessionals after *you*?"

I tapped my toe.

"Places!" someone shouted down the hallway. "Places for 'Yankee Doodle Dandy'!"

"I gotta go," Firecracker said to Ralph. "Come back again, okay?"

"What about Ruby Simpkin?" Ralph said.

Firecracker dashed away with an excess of swerve in her bumper. "Ruby cleared out all of a sudden," she called over her shoulder. "Said she needed a holiday real, real bad."

Ralph and I looked at each other. I was pretty certain he was thinking the same thing I was: *What if Ruby Simpkin had been killed, too?*

Ralph and I rode the subway back to Washington Square.

I was hungry, exhausted, annoyed, and a little paranoid when we turned down Longfellow Street. The film canister was heavy in my hands. "I went through so much trouble to find this reel," I said, "and Ruby ups and skips town?"

"Let's just hope she's all right," Ralph said.

"My rent is due the day after tomorrow! I'm going to have to go home to my parents. Do you have any idea how awful that's going to be?"

"Yeah. Real tough. A double apartment on Park Avenue. A bunch of servants, a Rolls-Royce, and piles of cash."

I spun to face Ralph. "Take that back!"

We stood in the conical puddle of a streetlamp, but Ralph's eyes were hidden by the shadow of his hat. "No."

"Good-bye, then," I said. My tone was haughty. But my feet wouldn't go.

"You've been lucky, Lola," Ralph said softly. "You *are* lucky. You live in a city packed with people just scraping by. Now you're one of us."

My eyes flooded with tears. One of them spilled down my cheek. *Rats.*

"And you know what?" Ralph said. "It's mostly not that bad. You're going to be okay. You're smart." He smeared the tear away with a fingertip. "You're beautiful."

More tears trickled. What the heck was the matter with me? Wait—he thought I was smart? And beautiful?

"Besides," he said, "you've got your Swedish sidekick."

"Berta's only in this because I owe her several months' worth of salary."

"Nope. She cares about you. She'll never admit it, but she does." Ralph held my face in his hands and smeared more tears with his thumbs. Then he kissed me, right there in the pool of the streetlamp, with the big, dark, noisy city circling us all around.

I gave myself a mental shake, and pulled away from him. "Wait a minute. You're doing it again."

"Doing what?" His voice was hot. His arms fell to his sides.

"Tricking me into smooching you. So you can check it off the list in your horrible little notebook."

His lips twitched.

"It's not funny," I said.

"I think you might've misread something."

"Your note said, clear as day, 'L.W. kiss in cinema check.'"

"Okay." He sighed. "I shouldn't have written that, but—"

"I knew it!" I *had* known it. But now he'd admitted it. My ribs ached, and not because of my girdle, either. I stomped down the sidewalk.

He caught up with me at the steps of number 9. He took my shoulder and turned me around. "I'm not going to let you go like that." His voice was rough, but his hands were steady as he dragged me close and kissed me again.

I dissolved. I had amnesia. My only cogent thought involved wanting to unbutton Ralph's shirt.

He pulled away too soon. "Give me a thumbs-up out the window to let me know Mrs. Lundgren is back," he said. "Don't forget to lock your door tonight, and I'll come by in the morning. We'll figure out what to do with that film reel."

I looked at the canister.

"I could take it," Ralph said. "I've got a safe at my place, if that would make you feel better. If you trust me with it."

Good point. Why should I trust him with it? On the other hand, two people had been killed because of it, and I sure didn't want to be next.

"Okay," I said. "I trust you. With the reel, anyway." I pressed it into his hands and teetered up the steps. Would I ever see him, or that film reel, again? Who knew? I wasn't thinking straight. I wasn't even *walking* straight.

The scent of almond and butter unfurled from the apartment when I opened the door. A radio program clamored in the kitchen.

Berta had returned.

I closed the door, shucked off my shoes, dropped my handbag with the Brownie camera inside it on the floor, and yelled "I'm back!" I went to the window and gave Ralph a thumbs-up. He tipped his fedora, pushed his hands in his pockets, and strolled away.

My gaze trailed after him until he melded with the shadows. A snippet of my heart abandoned me then. The snippet was going to follow Ralph all the way home. Wherever he lived.

Whoever he was.

Suspicion smacked me. Ralph knew an uncomfortable lot of details about my parents. When had I ever mentioned their double apartment? He hadn't really come clean about that notebook entry, either. All he'd given me was a fever. And a missing snippet of heart.

Mr. Ralph Oliver certainly knew his business.

Damn him.

29

I padded to the kitchen. "Hi, Berta," I said.

"Not so loudly. Ed Wynn is on the wireless."

Golden cookies lay cooling on the table. Berta sat in her quilted robe by the open window, head propped in hand. A comic routine crackled through the radio. But Berta wasn't laughing. She looked . . . dreamy.

Uh-oh.

Cedric lay on his side on the pouf. His tummy bulged.

I chose a cookie. "I found the film reel."

Berta snapped the radio off. "In Miss Street's Plaza suite?"

"Yes. In her weekend bag."

"Quite in the nick of time. The landlord is due back in one more day. Did you tell Miss Simpkin you have found it?"

"No." I told Berta what we'd seen on the film, including the hint that the factory was over in Brooklyn, and how Ruby Simpkin had scarpered.

Berta's eyes blazed. "The little cheat! Unless, mind you, she has kicked the bucket. If *that* proves to be the case, then I shall only say that I believe it *is* possible for harlots to get past the pearly gates if they exhibit the proper amount of remorse." She tipped her head. "The secret pork and beans recipe was demonstrated on the film, you say?"

"Yes, but we couldn't really make out what was going into the pot."

"Perhaps we ought to locate the Japanese butler Auntie Arbuckle mentioned. He must know something, do you not think? Remember, you told me that Auntie Arbuckle said he was fired over something to do with the pork and beans recipe, and that is precisely what the film is about. The recipe."

"What's the point? Ruby's gone. We're still tapped out."

"Have you forgotten that you are on the lam? That Inspector Digton might have a warrant for your arrest? That there is a murderer at large who has attempted to crush you with a gargoyle?"

Oh. That. I bit into my cookie.

"We could telephone the domestic agencies in the morning," Berta said. "Perhaps the butler has found a new position."

"I'm really worried something happened to Ruby. I mean, the other actress on the film has been *murdered*. I've got the willies. And what *will* we do about our finances?"

"We'll solve the murders, of course."

"What has that got to do with finances?"

"If we solve the murders, the story will be in the newspapers."

"Believe me, Berta, having your name in the papers isn't all it's cracked up to be."

"You do not understand. We shall become famous. These two murders, because they concern film stars, are being covered in newspapers all around the country, from here to San Francisco. Go see for yourself at the newsstand. If we succeed where the police fail, we will become famous lady detectives. Our names will be made. Our discreet retrieval agency will be launched."

It was far-fetched. Yet, there are times when you have to allow yourself to be swept up in somebody else's conviction and let it carry you through.

"Okay, Berta," I said. "We'll solve the murders. But I'm not sure what we'll do when the landlord comes knocking."

"We shall stay with my dear friend Myrtle, uptown. She has only a bedsit, but her bed is quite roomy."

"Sounds wonderful." I bit into a second cookie. In one short week, I'd gone from a four-poster in a mansion to the prospect of bunking with two aged ladies in a bedsit. Maybe we'd have three matching nightcaps.

I went over to the icebox. I did a double take. Berta was wearing petal-pink lipstick. I hadn't noticed it before. Lipstick! And now I realized that her hair wasn't in its customary bun. It had been curled into a shoulder-length row of waves.

"Did you go out?" I said.

"What?"

"You've got lipstick on." I sniffed the air. Somewhere below the haze of almond and butter was another scent. Sharper, floral. "Are you wearing *perfume?*"

"Cannot a lady do herself up a bit without having the screws put on her as though she were a Bolshevik prisoner? If you must know, I did not wish for the miniature bottle of Le Jade to go to waste."

"That was a business expense. You said so yourself." I opened the icebox and dug out a bottle of milk. "Why so secretive? I wouldn't begrudge you a beau or two. Or three." I poured milk into a glass.

Berta threw her hands up. "That is *precisely* why I did not tell you. Because—"

"So there *is* a beau." I gulped milk.

"—because you would insinuate that my having an innocent meal with a gentleman was somehow on par with your wild flapper ways!"

"Who's the sheik?"

"Never you mind."

"So there *is* a he." I crunched down on a third cookie. "You know, Berta, you've never told me about your marriage. You were married once, right?"

"Why, yes. I was. To a lovely gentleman. But he—" Her fingers crept to her locket. "—he perished. In Sweden. It was so long ago, really, and I was quite young."

"Oh. I *am* sorry." I kicked myself for asking. But then, Berta could write a laundry list of all my foibles, yet I knew next to nothing about her. She was a walled fortress.

"Shall we return to business?" Berta said. "While you and Mr. Oliver were locating the film reel, I gathered some interesting facts about Bruno Luciano."

"Still going on about him?"

"Your head has been turned. *Movie Love* was correct. No woman can resist Mr. Luciano."

"No, I simply see no good reason to waste time investigating him. Why would he murder Horace Arbuckle? Or Vera Potter?"

"Blackmail. Blackmail gone wrong."

"That's a laugh—Bruno's probably as rich as Midas. He's a film star."

"Oh, but he has not been for long. You told me that, last weekend, Sadie Street made a cryptic remark about Philippe's restaurant."

"Yes."

"Well, Miss Street mentioned Philippe's because Bruno Luciano used to work there. As a taxi dancer."

"What? One of those fellows who's paid to dance with the rich old biddies and whisper sweet nothings in their ears?"

"One small step away from a gigolo."

"I didn't know you *knew* those sorts of words, Berta."

"Simply because a lady does not say things aloud does not mean she is unaware."

True. "Go on—Bruno was a taxi dancer. When was this?"

"He ended his dancing career about a year ago."

"Then he must've worked at Philippe's right up until he started making motion pictures."

"Precisely. What is more, the story of Mr. Luciano's background that one reads about in the movie magazines is, like Sadie Street's, utterly fabricated."

"You mean his Italian *contessa* mother, and his horse polo hero father, and the orphanage, and—"

"Goodness me. Did you believe that claptrap for a second?"

I supposed I had.

"I obtained a description of Mr. Luciano's mother's tobacco shop on Mulberry Street," Berta said. "The shop has two painted wooden Indians standing in front. Mr. Luciano was reared above this shop. My source believes that Mrs. Luciano still runs it."

"Bruno is from Little Italy? Here in New York? *Where* did you say you got all this information?"

"From a source."

"Not from Mr. Ant?"

Berta laid a palm over her bosom. "I know many people, Mrs. Woodby. Long ago, before I worked for you, I was employed in a household in Annandale-on-Hudson, upstate. I became dear friends with the housekeeper there, and her cousin Paul's wife's brother's uncle is employed at Philippe's. As a doorman."

I couldn't crack that puzzle. Not tonight. "Okay. I hope that's not a fib. Because we're business partners, right? So we've got to be square with each other."

"Of course." Berta snapped the radio back on.

I trudged off to bed.

The next morning, my gritty eyes were greeted by a plate of bacon, a pan of cinnamon buns, and a bubbling percolator of coffee. Oh yes, and blaring across the front page of the newspaper on the kitchen table,

SECOND HIGH SOCIETY MURDER: *Society Matron Lola Woodby questioned in murders of Tinned Foods Tycoon and Family Nurserymaid*

Below was a grainy photograph of me. Bundled in a towel, wet hair mortared to my skull, holding a highball. My mouth in a crooked O, two front teeth showing like a rabid woodchuck's, squinty eyes.

"Not the most flattering likeness," Berta said, placing a cup of coffee before me.

"That nasty Ida Shanks! This is her way of getting the last word after our little bargain yesterday."

"She will always get the last word, will she not? Miss Shanks's words are printed in thousands of newspapers."

Didn't I know it.

"There are some interesting facts pertaining to Miss Potter in the second column," Berta said. "I would avoid the column about yourself."

I had to chomp through three slices of bacon to work up enough nerve to look at the newspaper again.

Naturally, I started with the column about myself.

I was a "possible suspect" who had disappeared without a trace.

"Without a trace?" I said. "Bruno saw me leaving Dune House with you and Ralph. So did Miss Shanks."

"Then she is a lady of honor," Berta said.

"Honor? Are we talking about the same Miss Shanks?"

I returned to the newspaper. I was wanted for further questioning, according to Inspector Digton of Hare's Hollow. There was also a choice quote from Dr. Chisholm Woodby: "The possible suspect is erratic, but not dangerous," he'd told the reporter. "She has suffered great nervous strain as the result of her husband's recent demise, and as a natural result of her barren condition. I have diagnosed her as a clinical hysteric, and any information regarding her whereabouts would be most appreciated."

"Hysteric?" I yelled. "Clinical *hysteric?*" I crumpled the entire newspaper into a large ball.

Berta smoothed out the newspaper. "I told you not to read the article about yourself." She tapped a fingertip on the paper. "Read this one. About Miss Potter."

What I really wanted to do was climb into a boxing ring with Chisholm and sock him in the jaw. I was sure I could take him down. I ate bacon. He ate turtle food.

The gist of the second article was, Vera Potter had indeed been an actress. First in vaudeville—her parents were actors, too—and then as a bit-part player in the motion pictures. She wasn't cut out for the job, though, and around October of last year, she had put together a bundle of phony references and managed to get a job as nurserymaid in the Arbuckle household.

"I smell a rat," I said.

Berta nodded. "Thad Parker always says, one coincidence is one coincidence too many. It does not sit well, for me, at least, that Vera Potter starred in a film set in Horace Arbuckle's factory, and then just so happened to find employment in Arbuckle's house."

The doorbell buzzed.

I headed to the foyer.

"Ask the landlord to give us another week," Berta called after me.

When I opened the front door, I sighed in relief. It wasn't the landlord; it was a boy in a courier's uniform. He held a parcel wrapped in brown paper. "Mrs. Woodby?"

"Yes?"

"Delivery for you. From a secret admirer." He thrust the parcel in my hands, tipped his cap, and skittered away down the stairs.

I carried the parcel to the kitchen and placed it on the table. It was tied up with twine, but it had no labels or markings. I shook it. It rattled dully, as though there were rocks inside. I found scissors and cut the twine.

Berta fluttered beside me.

I tore off the brown paper, revealing a jumbo floral box with golden lettering and curlicues all over. It read, MCALLISTER'S ASSORTED CHOCOLATE CREAMS.

"Mr. Oliver certainly knows the way to your heart," Berta said.

I stared down at the box. "Really? You think he . . . admires me?"

"He appears to hold you in high regard. He was beside himself with worry when you went missing from the Foghorn."

"He was?" I couldn't picture Ralph being beside himself about *anything*. I opened the box.

The doorbell buzzed again.

"I'll get it," Berta said, and went to the door.

I heard voices, and rapid footsteps.

I rustled through the pink waxed paper and selected a nice, plump milk chocolate cream.

Berta burst into the kitchen, Ralph behind her, just as I bit into the chocolate.

"Stop!" Berta cried.

"Spit it out," Ralph said.

I stared, but spit out the bite of chocolate into my palm.

"Rinse your mouth with water," Ralph said.

"Mind telling me why?"

"I didn't send those."

"Oh." I went over to the sink and rinsed my mouth under the tap. Then I threw the chocolate into the dustbin.

"These have been tampered with." Ralph was examining the bottom of one of the chocolates. "Look."

"I see a hole in the bottom. What of it?"

Ralph inspected the entire top layer. Each and every chocolate had a puncture in it, and a couple of the holes had traces of white powder. "I'd put my money on arsenic," he said.

Berta squawked.

"*What?*" I said. I sank into a chair.

"Lola," Ralph said, "come on—are you really surprised? Someone has already tried to kill you with a falling gargoyle."

"*Maybe* tried to kill me," I said. But I knew how naïve I sounded.

"And now," Ralph said, "they're giving it another try. What's surprising to me is that you'd eat chocolates sent by a person unknown."

"The delivery boy said they were from a secret admirer." I felt myself blush.

Ralph grinned. "And you thought it was me?"

"Maybe."

"Aw." He leaned over and chucked me lightly on the chin. "That's kinda sweet."

"We must report this to the police," Berta said.

"I'm not so sure about that," Ralph said. "Lola is wanted by the police for murder, and this won't convince them of anything. Heck, they might even say she poisoned the chocolates herself to create a distraction. But it's up to Lola."

Berta and Ralph looked at me.

"We'll keep the chocolates as evidence—put them up high in a closet where Cedric can't reach them," I said. "And we'll keep mum."

30

Berta, Ralph, and I discussed our next moves over a fresh pot of coffee.

I'd decided to stay quiet on the question of why Ralph was still hanging around. After all, he had just saved my life.

"You say Luciano's past is a bundle of lies?" Ralph said. He was putting away his third cinnamon roll. "It might be worthwhile to check up on his background a little more, then. I could go down to Mulberry Street and see if I can learn anything else about him. See if I can dig up some kind of motive for murder."

He was muscling in on my investigation. Again. "*We'll* go to Mulberry Street," I said.

"No way, kid. I saw the papers this morning. One false step, and it's into the slammer for you."

"I'm going to Mulberry Street," I said. "Why would *you* go? I'm the one whose life could be on the line."

But I knew why Ralph wanted to go to Mulberry Street, and it wasn't out of the kindness of his heart. He was a private investiga-

tor. In an infamous case like this one, plastered across all the newspapers, fame and fortune were at stake. Berta had been right.

"Do you know how to get to Mulberry Street, Mrs. Woodby?"
Berta asked.

"Of course," I lied.

"She doesn't know," Berta said to Ralph.

Ralph grinned.

I glared.

"You'll need a disguise," Ralph said. "A good one."

Fifteen minutes later, I was disguised, in brief, as Berta: I wore her
dumpy Edwardian hat, no makeup, my low-heeled spectator shoes,
woolen stockings, and one of Berta's floral-print dresses under her
rubberized raincoat.

"Well, now," Berta said, "you *do* cut quite the figure of a lady,
Mrs. Woodby."

Secretly, I was depressed. I was filling out Berta's clothes far
better than I'd anticipated. And, although Berta somehow pulled
off the calico-and-dimity look with aplomb, on me it was just plain
dowdy.

Ralph looked me up and down. "Nice," he said, and winked.

I treated him to the Double-O.

Berta stayed behind, in order to telephone household staffing
agencies and attempt to track down the Japanese butler the Arbuckles had fired. Ralph and I walked the several blocks to Mulberry.

Mulberry Street was the thumping heart of Little Italy. Brick
buildings jutted with balconies, fluttering awnings, and fire escapes.
Shabby men pushed carts piled high with rainbow-hued fruits and
vegetables. Women chattered in Italian, wicker baskets on their arms.
Children darted about at their games. Horse carts outnumbered motorcars, and I smelled garlic, incense, toasting nuts, and sweat.

"Never been down here?" Ralph asked as we walked along, searching for the tobacconist's shop. "You look a little dazed."

"It's Berta's raincoat," I said. "It's hot. Besides, why would I come here? People say it's dangerous." It didn't actually feel dangerous. Only a little motley. But then, many gangsters were Italian.

"Immigrant neighborhoods can be dangerous," Ralph said. "Lots of desperate people. I grew up in one myself."

He'd never mentioned his childhood before. "Where?" I asked.

"South Boston. Irish. My dad worked in the shipyards."

He clammed up again.

Halfway down the second block, we found a tobacconist's with a door flanked by cigar-store Indians. The shop's display windows were stacked high with Italian newspapers and colorful boxes of cigarettes, cigars, and sweets.

"This must be it," I said.

We went inside. A scowling, leather-faced man puffed a cigarette on a stool behind the counter.

"Mr. Luciano?" I said. "I am Lola Woodby."

Ralph gave me an *Are you off your rocker?* glance.

Right. I supposed private investigators didn't give out their names willy-nilly.

"Eh?" the old man said.

"Are you Mr. Luciano?" I asked.

"Luciano? No. Signora Luciano gone." The old man made shooing motions. "I buy shop. This my shop. You wanta cigarette? Cigar?" He made a sweeping gesture along the display counter.

The counter held packets of different kinds of gaspers, and some bright candies in little glassine bags. I pointed at those.

"Business expense," I whispered to Ralph. "We've got to sweeten him up."

Ralph dug out three pennies from his baggy pocket. "More like

sweeten *you* up." He plopped the pennies on the counter. "I'm keeping track, you know."

"Sure," I said. I winked.

Ralph scratched his temple.

Oh. I'd nearly forgotten. I was disguised as a rubberized chintz
ottoman.

The old man pulled out one of the glassine bags and slid it to me
over the counter.

"When did you buy this shop?" Ralph asked the man.

"*Che?*"

"Which month?"

"Ah, month. *Sì. Agosto.*"

I almost choked on a cherry lozenge. "August?"

Ralph gave me a slap on the back.

"August is when Arbuckle started writing those big checks," I
whispered.

Ralph gave me a *shut your trap* look, and turned back to the man.
"You purchased the shop from Signora Luciano?"

"*Sì.*" The old man gusted smoke from hairy nostrils. "She sold to
me for very good price. She old lady. She said her son take care of
her now, she needa not work no more."

"Where does Signora Luciano live?" Ralph asked.

"In fancy house now, my wife say. *Mia moglie*—my wife—say
Signora Luciano wear fur coat to Mass! Say she too—" He waved
his cigarette. "—how you say, too big for britches now. Rich lady now."

"Because you purchased her shop," Ralph said.

"No, no, I not pay her *that* much. No, the money from her son.
Big film star now." He poked his cigarette between his lips and used
both hands to make a kind of theatrical master of ceremonies gesture. Rolling the *r*, he cried, "Bruno Luciano!" He waited for our re-
actions.

"You don't say," Ralph said. He tipped his fedora. "Thanks, signor."

We went back out onto the noisy sidewalk.

"You've got to learn to keep your cool, Mrs. Woodby," Ralph said. "Don't give the game away. You've just got to keep people talking."

I sucked my cherry lozenge. "You're a know-it-all, aren't you?"

"If by that you mean that I know everything, then, yeah, I am."

I beaned his temple with a spice gumdrop. It bounced onto the sidewalk and was promptly gobbled up by a dog lounging in a shop doorway.

Cedric didn't know how good he had it.

I glanced up from the dog. A face was watching me from inside the shop window. Two dried-currant eyes in a blank face, peeping out between towers of red-and-white cans.

Fear slashed through me.

Mr. Highpants.

He shifted away, out of sight behind the tower. I was left staring at the red-and-white cans. DA PONTE TOMATO PASTE, the labels repeated again and again and again.

"Lola," Ralph was saying. "What's the matter?"

"I saw him." My throat was dry. "Mr. Highpants."

"Where?"

"In this shop."

Ralph sprang through the doorway. I forced myself to follow.

But inside the shop, no Mr. Highpants. Only a handful of crabby-looking old ladies in black dresses. Silence fell; the old ladies glowered.

Ralph and I legged it out of there before one of them put a hex on us.

Back at the love nest, Berta was bursting with news.

"I telephoned around to every household staffing agency in the city," she said. "I strong-armed the secretary at the Mrs. Hartwicke Household Staffing Agency into admitting that a gentleman of Japanese extraction had passed through their doors a few weeks ago."

Berta, strong-arming? Okay, it made sense.

"But," she said, "I could not get anything else out of the secretary. Even a bribe was not going to work."

"I could visit the agency in person," I said. "I could throw my name about and force Mrs. Hartwicke to tell me where the butler has found his new position."

"Throw your name about?" Ralph said.

I'd nearly forgotten; my name was mud.

"I'll go anyway," I said. "Maybe Mrs. Hartwicke hasn't seen today's newspapers yet. And even if she has, well, I'm still Lola Woodby, aren't I?"

"Sure," Ralph said.

Berta wrapped her fingers around her locket.

Before we went to the staffing agency, I needed to see if I could get ahold of Bruno Luciano at Dune House. I wished to pry into his sudden influx of cash last August. Sure, probably all that dough had come from his film contracts. But maybe, just maybe, it had come from secret checks written by Horace Arbuckle.

"Just don't make any of your direct accusations," Ralph said.

"Quite," Berta said. "Or, if Mr. Luciano is a blackmailer and a murderer, he might shoot you, too."

What a soothing pair Ralph and Berta made.

Olive answered the telephone. "Oh, hello, darling. I thought you'd run off to Panama with that Swedish cook of yours. The police are simply *fuming* that you've disappeared. I said that *I* don't know where you are, and surely you didn't pop off Horace and Nanny Potter. I mean, why ever would you? Your dreadful brother-in-law, Chisholm,

Maia Chance

has been stopping by, too. Good heavens, what a scrummy face to be wasted on *such* a stuffy mind, and so I told him—"

"Could I speak with Bruno?" I asked.

She paused. "Bruno is filming."

"Filming there, at your house?" I knew this, but I wished to confirm it.

"Yes, of course. The motion picture people are to be here for *days*. It's a good thing, too, because with Billy and Theo gone to Bar Harbor, I'd be absolutely *stranded* in the house with nobody for company but nasty old Auntie, and *she's* gone on a bender. She's going to run out of bootleg whiskey, and then where will she be?"

"I thought Eloise Wright was staying to keep you company."

"Oh, she is. But she talks of nothing but her dreary divorce, and of her Girdle Queen company. Ladies oughtn't do business, I think. It makes them so *tedious*, so—"

"Would you tell Bruno that I telephoned?"

"Of course, darling."

"Thanks."

The Mrs. Hartwicke Household Staffing Agency was on the sixth floor of a fashionable Midtown building. I left Ralph and Berta on a sofa in the lobby and took the elevator up.

Inside the agency, I marched up to the reception desk, where a young secretary sat filing her nails.

"Have you an appointment, madam?" she asked.

"I do not need an appointment. I am Mrs. Woodby. Mrs. Alfred Woodby. And I require a new butler. Please inform Mrs. Hartwicke that I must see her at once."

"Yes, madam."

It was gratifying to so easily command respect. Granted, I'd changed from Berta's clothes into full Society Matron regalia: mink-collared coat (only slightly crumpled by my suitcase), diamond stud earrings, and a hat that could've doubled as a hassock. At the same time, commanding respect from skittering young girls is a sign that oneself is aging. One of life's tragic trade-offs.

The secretary returned. "Mrs. Hartwicke will see you."

Mrs. Hartwicke was a plump lady in periwinkle, with a white bun and rectangular reading glasses. The gold chains drooping down from the sides of her glasses matched exactly the droop of her cheeks.

"Mrs. Woodby, what a pleasure!" Her voice was shrill.

She'd read the newspapers, then.

"Hello," I said. I sat, and perched my handbag on my knees. "I require a Japanese butler."

"Japanese?"

"Yes. Is it terribly eccentric of me?"

"Japanese. Well, I don't know." Mrs. Hartwicke fluttered through dossiers on her desk. She also sneaked a few glances at the telephone.

Did she worry that I, in the capacity of Clinical Hysteric, was going to hurdle over her desk and throttle her? Probably.

"We *had* one gentleman of Japanese extraction pass through the agency recently," Mrs. Hartwicke said. "But he has already found a situation."

"Oh dear," I said. "But I *must* have him."

"Ah. Here we are." Mrs. Hartwicke spread open a dossier. "Yes. Mr. Takanori Hisakawa. Such a lovely gentleman. He was quite snapped up by one of my clients. He had glowing recommendations, you see, and the most impeccable—"

"Yes, yes." I twiddled my fingers. "I must have him for my own household."

"I'm afraid that's—"

I leaned forward. "Who hired him?"

"We never disclose our clients' names, so—"

"Mrs. Hartwicke, you are perhaps aware that my mother, Mrs. Virgil DuFey, is in the process of restaffing her Park Avenue household?" A complete fabrication.

"Oh, indeed?"

"Mother will do her utmost to spread the word about your excellent agency."

"Well—"

"However, if you were not the most *helpful* agency, well, perhaps Mother would be forced to seek out an alternative."

Mrs. Hartwicke pursed her fuchsia lips. I could practically hear her thoughts: On the one hand, I was (reportedly) a murderous cuckoo on the loose. On the other hand, recommendations from the Woodbys and the DuFeys would be priceless.

Mrs. Hartwicke slid the dossier across the desk toward me.

I spun it around. I glanced at it long enough to see, printed at the top, MRS. ST. AUBIN.

I knew Mrs. St. Aubin. Doddering battle-axe in oyster fruits and a whalebone corset. Her niece Posy had been in the class below me at Miss Cotton's Academy for Young Ladies. "Thank you, Mrs. Hartwicke." I hurried toward the door.

"You cannot simply march into Mrs. St. Aubin's home and steal away her butler," Mrs. Hartwicke called.

I turned. "Such thefts have been known to happen."

Mrs. Hartwicke's hand was already reaching for her telephone.

31

Out in the corridor, I hastened toward the elevators. When I was a dozen paces off, an elevator pinged and someone stepped off.

I stumbled to a halt.

Mr. Highpants.

I took off in the other direction.

I didn't know if he was chasing me or not. I didn't *want* to know. Without a doubt, he was tailing me, although *why* I wasn't sure.

I ran down the corridor, around a corner, and to the end of the line, where there was a door marked EXIT.

I pushed through and found myself in a stairwell. I bolted down five flights of stairs and burst out into the lobby.

Berta and Ralph were still side by side on the sofa, looking bored.

"Come on!" I whispered, *tick-tick*ing past them. "Hurry!"

They followed me. Outside, we zigzagged through shoppers and businessmen on the sidewalk.

I swung one last look over my shoulder before we ducked down the subway stairs at the end of the block. A dark blue paddy wagon roared around the corner, heading toward the building we'd just fled.

Mrs. Hartwicke had ratted me out.

Thirty minutes later, I was safe at the love nest and cradling a highball.

"You ought to stay inside for the time being," Ralph said. He looked through the kitchen window, down into the narrow brick alleyway.

Berta agreed.

"But it'll be so dull," I said. I stretched out my hand to nab a butter almond cookie from a plate on the table.

"No!" Berta cried. "The rest of the cookies are for—I am saving them. For someone else."

"He'll adore them," I said.

"What makes you think it is a *he?*"

The telephone jingled.

"Ah, that will be the police," Berta said. She went to answer it.

I removed the diamond stud earrings and stuffed them in my handbag for safekeeping. "Wouldn't the police simply break down the door?"

"Beats me," Ralph said. "I've never been in your position. I never get caught."

"It's for you, Mrs. Woodby," Berta called.

Turned out, it wasn't the police. It was Bruno Luciano.

"I hear you've been checking up on me," he said.

My guts twisted. How had he learned about our trip to Mulberry Street? Was he in league with Mr. Highpants? "Um," I said.

"Olive told me you called."

Oh. *That's* what he'd meant.

"I'm not some dingledangler," Bruno said. "You *did* tell me how to telephone you."

True. "I wished to speak with you, yes," I said. "But come to think of it, I'm not so sure we ought to do it over the telephone. Are you still at Dune House?"

"I am, but you know, I wouldn't mind a jaunt into the city. We've all got cabin fever up here. Olive's quite the hostess, if you know what I mean. No room to breathe. And that batty old auntie is giving everyone the jitters. Staggers around drunk, won't stop going on about the goddam pork and beans, talks about burning this place to the ground. Say, how about meeting me for a drink tonight?"

"Oh. I am, at the moment, somewhat, um, wanted by the police, so—"

"Okay, how about at my apartment?"

"Your apartment?"

I glanced up. Ralph was making a *cut* gesture across his throat.

I blurted the first place that came to mind. "Blue Heaven. Have you heard of it?"

Ralph clapped a palm on his forehead.

Maybe it was crazy to go back there. On the flip side, if the police showed up at Blue Heaven, I wouldn't be the only one getting handcuffed.

"Okay, Blue Heaven," Bruno said. "Ten o'clock tonight?"

"Perfect."

I'll come clean. I've got my pride. And I'd spent the day dressed first in Berta's housewifely togs and then in my own worst Society Matron armor. So can you blame me if I spent forty-five minutes sprucing myself up for Blue Heaven?

When Berta, Ralph, and I arrived in Harlem at ten o'clock, I wore my short sable coat, my peach Coco Chanel, gold peep-toes, and triple helpings of mascara, kohl, and poppy-red lipstick. My bob was back in order, shiny and bedecked with one jeweled hairpin.

Ralph got us past Blue Heaven's door without even saying the password. Maybe it should have bothered me that he was known by a speakeasy guard, but I had other things on my plate. Inside, Blue Heaven was just as rip-roaring and gin drenched as it had been a few nights back, and the jazz band was at it full steam ahead.

We settled into a table with our backs to the wall. I slid off my sable and looked around for Bruno Luciano. No sign of him.

"How do you think Bruno will get past the guard?" I asked Ralph.

"Easy. He's famous," Ralph said. "Drink?" A waiter had appeared.

"No, thanks," I said. "I've got to keep my head clear."

Berta ordered a gin blossom. Ralph asked for neat whiskey.

Fifteen minutes later, Bruno still hadn't shown, and Berta was submerged in her second gin blossom.

"Hey there, you juicy Swedish tomato, you." Jimmy the Ant sidled up to our table. He only had eyes—or, I should say, *an* eye, since one of them was glass—for Berta.

"Jimmy," Berta said. "Goodness. I did not expect to see you here."

Judging by Berta's freshly ironed rosebud-print dress, her lipstick, and her waved hairdo, I fancied she *had* expected to see him.

"Wanna dance?" Jimmy said. Before Berta could protest, he'd swept her to her feet.

"Mrs. Woodby," Berta whispered. "Would you manage my handbag?" She plonked it in front of me, black, hefty, and square.

I propped my chin in my hand and sighed.

"Buck up, kid," Ralph said.

"I'm thirsty."

"Well, okay." Ralph signaled the waiter.

Three minutes later, I had an extra-extra-strong highball in hand. In another three minutes, half the highball was coursing through my bloodstream, and I was having trouble ripping my eyes off Ralph's mouth. At the next table, a flapper was getting *really* comfortable with her fellow. Hands and lips weren't exactly being kept to themselves.

Ralph glanced over at the couple. He looked at me, lips quirked, eyes smoky. "How about it?"

My body yelled *Yes!* I said, "Certainly not," straightened my spine, and looked haughtily away.

I gave a start. Mr. Highpants! Again. Leaning against the bar on an elbow, nursing a drink. He wore the same drab suit and hat, those same pleated trousers pulled up to his sternum. For once, he wasn't staring at me. His empty little eyes were on the jazz band.

I almost keeled off my chair.

Ralph put a hand out to steady me. "Hey, I was only joking about a smooch. I know you only kiss me when you're real, real mad."

"Look," I whispered. "It's Mr. Highpants. At the bar."

"I see why you call him Highpants. Jeez. Those suspenders of his couldn't be more than four inches long."

Mr. Highpants leaned and sipped. After a few minutes, the throng around him parted. Everyone kept chatting, but their eyes were shifty. Something was happening.

Lem Fitzpatrick, in pinstripes, with a caveman shadow on his jaw, strutted into the space the crowd had made. Sadie Street clung to his arm.

"Huh," Ralph said.

Lem wrapped a hand around Highpants's shoulder. Highpants stared down at his own feet, bobbing his head.

"Mr. Highpants is acting like a *peon*," I said, "like a—"

"Like a hired hand," Ralph said.

My eyes met Ralph's.

"*Lem*," I said. It sounded like a swear. I got up and slung Berta's handbag in my elbow. The handbag was heavy, I realized, because her gun was in there. Her .25-caliber Colt.

Dandy.

"Hey, where are you going?" Ralph said.

"I'm going to give Lem a piece of my mind," I said over my shoulder. "He's scared me half to death, siccing his spooky little bloodhound on me!"

"Don't go over there." Ralph was on his feet. "Are you crazy?"

Evidently, I was.

I barreled through the tables, turning heads as I went. Lem was still giving Mr. Highpants a talking-to when I made it over. Neither man had seen me coming.

Sadie Street noticed me, though. Her nostrils flared. "I simply *can't* remember your name," she said to me, "but I do adore that handbag. My, it's big enough to carry around at *least* six extra girdles for your—"

"I've got to carry a big bag," I snapped, "on account of all the dropped lipsticks I find next to dead bodies."

Sadie's eyes were as blank as a cartoon bunny's. That sealed the deal. Her lipstick must have been planted next to Nanny Potter's corpse.

I tapped Lem on the shoulder. He stiffened, and turned. "Yeah? Oh. Mrs. Woodby. Hi there."

"Hi there?" I said. "*Hi there?* Why, I ought to slap you, you low-down, rotten skink! What do you mean by sending your spy to follow me all around the city?"

Sadie tittered. Ralph was just behind me; I felt his hand on my shoulder. I shook it off. "It's an affront to my freedom," I said to Lem. "I ought to telephone the police."

"Yeah, real funny," Lem said. "You, call the police on *me*? I seen the papers, dollface." He touched the side of his jacket, west of his pin-striped lapel. Something bulged there. A gun.

The people around us had gone silent. In the background, the jazz band kept wailing, and the crowd kept up its hubbub.

"You really shouldn't bring up the fuzz in a joint like this," Lem said. "They ain't welcome. And snitches ain't welcome, either." His hand lingered over the gun bulge. "Unless, of course, they wanna be Swiss cheese."

My hairline misted. Lem wouldn't shoot me, would he? Not in front of all these onlookers.

"Come on, kid," Ralph whispered in my ear.

"It's about Eloise Wright, isn't it?" I said to Lem. "You're in business with her. I know she telephoned you after I visited her office at Wright's. She said I was a meddler, and that something had to be done. So then you set *this* piece of work—" I prodded a finger toward Mr. Highpants. "—on my tail. Right?"

Lem unbuttoned his suit jacket.

Dear sweet bejeezus.

Berta's handbag was still in the crook of my elbow. I inched my right hand to the handbag's clasp. I snapped it open.

I heard Ralph pull in a breath.

"Okay, Mrs. Woodby," Lem said. "You got me. I'm doing business with Eloise Wright. If you can call it business. We had a kinda deal, see, about staging Sadie here's little discovery. Sadie wanted a real cute, high-publicity place to take photographs for that dumb discovery story she cooked up with the film studio. Mrs. Wright agreed to let the movie reporters photograph Sadie in the store. For a fee."

"If that's all there was to it, then why send Mr. Highpants here after me?"

Mr. Highpants jerked his chin, offended.

"Show a little respect," Lem growled. "His name—" He shoved his face right up to mine. "—is Morrie." Lem's hand was inside his jacket now.

I shoved my hand deep inside Berta's handbag, feeling for the cool hard Colt. Where was it? I peered down into the handbag's shadowy abyss.

The crowd gasped. I heard a *snick*.

I looked up. Lem was aiming a big silver pistol at my chest.

I rummaged blindly in the handbag. My hands wrapped around something, and I whipped it out.

Lem burst out laughing.

I stared at the object in my hand. It was a waxed paper parcel of butter almond cookies.

"No!" Berta shrieked from somewhere. "Those are for Jimmy!"

Lem shoved his gun back inside his jacket. His shoulders shook with laughter. "I wasn't gonna shoot you," he said. The sparks in his eyes told a different story. "I just gotta show you dames who's in charge. Right, Sadie?" He gave Sadie's cheek a hard pinch.

Ralph drew me away. "Let's blouse," he said in my ear. "I don't care to wait up for the fireworks. Let's get Berta, get your coat, and go."

I was too shaky to argue.

Berta intercepted us at our table. "What did you mean by that?" she said to me. She swiped the waxed paper parcel of cookies from my hand, and grabbed her handbag, too. "Not every last cookie in the world was baked for you, Mrs. Woodby."

"We're heading out, Mrs. Lundgren," Ralph said.

"Oh dear. But I must say good night to Jimmy."

Ralph tossed me my coat. He shoved his fedora down low over his eyes and grabbed my hand. "Maybe you ought to skip the Romeo and Juliet routine tonight, Mrs. Lundgren. Lola's gone and made Fitzpatrick upset."

Berta sighed. She gathered up her raincoat and followed us.

We'd made it halfway to the exit when Bruno Luciano came through the door. He wore a dark suit. His hair was brilliantined, his face placid.

"I've got to talk to him," I whispered.

Ralph flexed his jaw. "Why do I feel like a baby-minder?"

"Take that back."

"Last time you said that, I got a kiss."

32

I edged up to Bruno at the bar. People were watching Bruno, of course. Especially the girls. Bruno was a star. But Blue Heaven's customers were too slick to make a fuss.

"Hi there, Lola," Bruno said. "Wow. Being on the lam sure looks good on you." Bruno's piping voice made everything sound like a puppet show.

"I've taken it upon myself to poke around a little," I said. I situated my rump on a barstool. It wasn't the easiest thing to do in my thigh-length girdle, with my sable coat balled in my arms. "Into your, um, past."

"You wouldn't be the first girl to do that."

"No! Not—I'm not some kind of crazed fanatic."

"Course not."

It suddenly hit me: Bruno Luciano was what nerve doctors like the Prig called a narcissist. The world, to their kind, was one big mirror.

"I know you're not really from Italy," I said, lowering my voice.

"You're from *Little* Italy, and your mother used to run a tobacconist's shop down on Mulberry Street, and you worked as a taxi dancer at Philippe's."

Bruno's eyelids flittered. He ordered a gin gimlet from the bartender and turned back to me. "Okay, okay." He held up his hands in mock surrender. "Boy, you sure are one great sleuth. Mind if I ask *why* you're poking your nose into other people's business?"

"Because Inspector Digton thinks I murdered Horace Arbuckle and Vera Potter, and I don't especially relish the possibility of going to the electric chair, that's why."

"What's the big idea? Trying to pin the murders on me?"

"Where did you get enough dough to buy your mother a new house and fur coats, and to allow her to sell off her shop?"

Bruno looked past me. Was he thinking? Or showing off his magnificent profile?

The bartender slid over a gin gimlet. Bruno took a swallow. "It's like this," he said. "That money that I used on my mama was an advance, sort of."

"From Pantheon Pictures?"

"No. Pantheon didn't start paying me big till after *The King of Sheba* came out. The money was from Fitzpatrick."

"*What?*" I glanced down the bar. Lem Fitzpatrick was lording over a herd of cool characters. Sadie perched beside Lem, smoking.

"Yeah," Bruno said. "Fitzpatrick hatched a scheme, see. Sadie and I would pretend to have this feud, and then the studio would be forced to beef up our contracts."

"I *knew* it was all a big sham," I said. "All that posing for the photographers at the golf links."

"Fitzpatrick knew we'd have Pantheon over a barrel, because Zucker had made a deal with him, buying out all his movie palaces under the condition that Zucker groomed Sadie into a star."

George Zucker had said the same thing, to a T. Except—something seemed off. I couldn't put my finger on it.

"If the studio fires Sadie," Bruno said, "they'll be dropping their end of their deal with a, you know—" Bruno tipped his head in Lem's direction.

Gangster.

My palms went moist. "Wouldn't want to do that."

"Anyway," Bruno said, "it's a good deal. Everybody gets what they want."

"Everybody, except for George Zucker." I thought of George's defeated shoulders, of the desperation in his voice.

Bruno swallowed more gimlet. "Oh, yeah. Except for Zucker."

Things seemed neatly wrapped with a frilly bow on top. Lem Fitzpatrick and Eloise Wright were in cahoots, but not over anything to do with the film reel or the murders. Bruno Luciano hadn't been blackmailing Arbuckle; he'd got his sudden crop of cabbage from his *own* deal with Fitzpatrick.

Although people lie. They lie through their teeth.

It was around midnight when Berta, Ralph, and I arrived at the love nest. Ralph wanted to see us safely inside, since I'd gone and fizzed off a notorious gangster.

I dug the key from my handbag and reached out for the lock. Except that the door was already ajar.

"Rats," I said. "The landlord must have come."

We crowded into the foyer.

Ralph whistled. "Unless you've got the rottenest landlord in New York City, I'd say he had nothing to do with this."

The apartment was in shambles.

The hall tree was on its side, and coats and hats flowed across the floor. In the sitting room, desk drawers were ripped out, lamps were toppled, and leopard-skin cushions had been slashed open to disgorge cotton wool and feathers.

"Where's Cedric?" I cried. "Cedric?" I rushed down the hallway and checked the bathroom and the bedroom. Both rooms had been ransacked. No Cedric.

I stumbled into the kitchen. The light was on. Shattered glass sparkled on the floor tiles. The window gaped open, and cold wind puffed in. I crunched over the glass shards and put my head out the window.

A small form cowered on the fire escape. Two eyes gleamed up at me. Puffy fur waved in the breeze. "Peanut!" I gathered Cedric in my arms. "Are you frightened, puppy boy? Poor sweet precious. Mommy's here."

Ralph and Berta were watching from the kitchen doorway.

"She never talks to *me* like that," Ralph said to Berta.

"Who *did* this?" I said. "Do you think it was Lem Fitzpatrick? Maybe one of his goons?"

Ralph shook his head. "Maybe someone's looking for the film reel. Or maybe someone's just real peeved. One thing's for certain: You ladies aren't safe here anymore. You'll have to stay at my place till things blow over."

It turned out that Ralph lived only six blocks away, in a leafy street on the other side of Washington Square Park. His building was another brownstone—a little frayed, but respectable. He lived on the second floor.

"Good heavens, Mr. Oliver," Berta said, parking her suitcase in Ralph's entry foyer. "I suspected you would be in someplace one notch up from the YMCA. This is actually habitable."

Ralph's sitting room was cramped, and furnished with a hodge-podge of tattered antiques and smooth-jointed wooden pieces. A real—and to my eye, at least, quite good—expressionist painting hung above the fireplace, and the objects on the mantel were natural history museum in character: a wooden mask with googly eyes; a seal carved from bone; a round box of delicately grained wood; three arrowheads of some shiny, black stone. One wall was crammed with books, and a gramophone squatted on a mahogany buffet. The wallpaper was curling off, and the Oriental rugs were threadbare.

"I'll sleep on the sofa here," Ralph said. "You two will have to kip together in the bedroom."

"I shall go to bed directly, then," Berta said. "If I do not fall asleep first, I could be kept awake by the snoring."

"You snore?" Ralph asked me.

"She means Cedric," I said quickly.

Ralph went to ready his bedroom—he'd muttered something about clean sheets and dirty socks—and several minutes later he reemerged. Berta bade Ralph and me good night and toddled off, suitcase in hand.

"How about a bite to eat?" Ralph said to me. "Are you hungry?"

"Starving."

"Yeah. Run-ins with gangsters will do that to you."

Ralph's kitchen was tiny, but it appeared to be well used—especially for a bachelor's kitchen. Boxes and tins lined the open shelves. A bowl of apples sat on the table. Everything was spick-and-span.

"Pull up a chair, kid," Ralph said. He shrugged off his jacket and draped it over a chair, and rolled up his sleeves. His shirt was wrinkled, and he wore dark blue suspenders. "I'll fix you up."

I sank into a chair. Cedric hopped down to beg for scraps at Ralph's feet.

Ralph washed his hands in the cracked sink and whipped a clean kitchen towel over his shoulder. He poured gin into a tiny juice glass painted with daisies. "Sorry I don't have any ginger ale and whiskey," he said.

"This'll do."

"Normally, I make something special when ladies come over." He winked. "But it's kind of late. Sandwich okay?"

"Wonderful."

Ladies came over? Well, of course they did. In droves, probably.

Ralph brought out a loaf of bread, mustard, pastrami, a tomato, and a brick of cheese, and got to work.

"Okay," I said, "you grew up in South Boston. With—" I glanced around the kitchen. "—without a mother. So you learned to cook."

He smeared mustard on bread. "Practicing your sleuthing on me?"

"Am I correct?"

"Yep. I learned to cook from the neighbor downstairs. She was Portuguese. So even though I'm Irish, I couldn't cook corned beef and cabbage to save my life. Ma lammed off when I was small. Left me and my two brothers alone with Dad. Kind of a rough-and-tumble childhood."

By the clench of his jaw, I guessed *rough-and-tumble* was putting it mildly.

"Then what?" I said.

"Well, I'd grown up working with my hands, what with Dad in the shipyards." Ralph sliced the tomato. "But I wanted to learn a real trade, so when I was sixteen, I took myself up to Maine, to Bath, and learned how to build ships."

Shipbuilding. So that's how he'd gotten those muscles.

"Never finished school," he said. "It's tough for me to sit still. But I made that table you're sitting at, and the chairs, too."

I ran my fingertips over the pine boards of the table, almost seamlessly joined. He was a good carpenter.

Why did that make me want to slide my hands under his suspenders?

Ralph finished making the sandwiches. He plated them, and pushed one over to me. He sat down with his own sandwich. But he didn't take a bite.

He leaned forward on his elbows. "Lola. I've got to get something off my chest."

I lowered the sandwich from my open mouth. "Yes?"

He twisted his hands. The sight wrung my heart.

I knew what he wanted to say. I felt it, too.

I stood, and circled the kitchen table. I lowered myself onto his lap and wrapped an arm around his neck. "You needn't say anything," I whispered, my lips brushing his. I slid my fingers down his chest, under his suspender.

"Lola," was all he said. He wrapped his arms roughly around me. I sank into him.

If our two previous kisses, in the Zenith Movie Palace and under the streetlamp on Longfellow Street, had been surprise parties, then *this* kiss was an all-out gala ball. Before I knew it, Ralph had a hot palm wedged under my garter, and my own hands had fumbled open his shirt buttons. His sandwich crashed to the floor. I was dimly aware of doggy-gobbling noises under the table, but I was too enfolded in the kiss to care about Cedric's figure.

Ralph drew his mouth away from mine. "Wait," he murmured. "I've really got to tell you."

I frowned. I'd assumed what he meant to tell me was that he wanted to kiss me. That, maybe, he was starting to fall in love with me. "Go on, then."

"It's about, ah, work."

My fire poofed out. I pushed his hand from my garter. "Oh?"

"About my investigation."

"I already know quite well that you've been investigating me."

"Okay. And who would you say hired me?"

"I haven't the faintest notion. I'd thought Chisholm, but then, when he couldn't find me . . . it's *not* Chisholm, is it?"

Ralph sighed. "I need to tell you, Lola. I can't—well, this just isn't right. You being here, and us—well, you know."

"Who is it?"

He swallowed. "Your mother."

"What?" I jumped to my feet. "My mother hired you to *spy* on me? And you didn't bally *tell* me? You're an absolute—an absolute *monster!*"

"I feel bad about it."

"You should've told me before!"

"I've got bills to pay, kid."

"*Don't* call me kid."

"Trust me, I feel guilty about all this. You and Mrs. Lundgren have been real nice."

"Nice?" I narrowed my eyes. "*Nice?* Is that what you call—call this?" I swept my hand between us. "Oh, sure, yes. How could I have been so stupid? You're exactly like Alfie—you're a ladies' man. I, of all people, ought to be able to spot a—a Don Juan when I see one!" I made a humorless cackle. "I've seen the way the girls circle around you like—like buzzards."

"Buzzards?" He scratched his eyebrow. "So I'm some kind of road-kill?"

"You said it. Only tell me this: Why did my mother hire you to snoop on me?"

"She wired me from Italy, shortly after she'd received word of Alfred's death. Said she got my name from a client of mine, an American fellow who was staying at the same hotel in Rome, and she wanted to enlist my services. Asked me to just keep an eye on you."

"But why?"

"I'm not exactly sure."

"Did she think that I killed Alfie?"

"No, I don't think so. Although I checked on that."

"*What?*"

"The doctor's report was clean as a whistle. Unless, of course, you figured out how to make his death look like a heart attack with digitalis or something, but I—"

"You're suggesting that I murdered Alfie."

"No. I'm not. I mean, I'm a professional. I look at every angle. But I ruled murder out early on. You just don't have it in you."

"Funny you should say that, because I feel like I could murder *you.*"

I dragged Cedric from his half-eaten pastrami sandwich. I marched out of the kitchen, through the apartment, and flung open the bedroom door. Berta was sitting in bed, reading in the glow of a lamp.

She gave me the up-and-down.

"We're leaving," I said.

"Leaving?"

"You can't go back to that apartment," Ralph said behind me. "It's not safe. Come on. Stay here. We'll talk it over again in the morning. You'll feel better then."

I pushed past him to the foyer and dug for my coat. "The hell I will, you two-faced, conniving—"

"Mrs. Woodby," Berta fluted from the bedroom, "calm yourself."

"I'm *calm!*" I whisked Cedric under my arm, grabbed my suitcase, and stormed out. "I'll wait for you outside, Berta," I said.

Berta joined me on the front steps a few minutes later. She carried her suitcase. The hem of her quilted robe poked out from beneath her raincoat.

"Did Mr. Oliver take liberties?" she asked.

"Worse. He's been working for Mother."

Berta *tsked* her tongue.

33

First thing the next morning, after eating breakfast and tidying the ransacked love nest, Berta and I prepared to go to Mrs. St. Aubin's house. I had looked up her address in the 1920 copy of the *New York Social Register* I found in Alfie's bookcase. Tracking down Dune House's fired butler, Hisakawa, was our only good lead. There *was* Sadie Street's incriminating lipstick. But without a motive or any other clues to tie Sadie to the murders, we were up against a brick wall on that one.

I buttoned on one of Berta's dresses—brown flowers with a high lace collar. Even though I was wearing one of Eloise Wright's rubber girdles, I filled out Berta's dress a treat. Wonderful. I covered my hair with a floppy hat. I added scratchy wool stockings, the flat-heeled spectators, reading glasses, and one of Alfie's cardigans. Queen of the Frumpy Fishwife Pageant.

Mrs. St. Aubin had never laid eyes on Berta before, so Berta didn't need a disguise.

I walked Cedric, and left him on his pouf in the kitchen next to a bowl of fresh water and a Spratt's Puppy Biscuit. As though he'd eat it. I was uneasy leaving Cedric alone after the apartment had been pillaged last night, but Cedric would blow my cover. *Everyone* in my social set knew Cedric.

The St. Aubin mansion was a splendid row house—white stone, bow windows, groomed shrubs, licorice-black railings—one block off Central Park. Berta and I stopped on the sidewalk.

"Are you certain Mrs. St. Aubin will not recognize you?" Berta asked.

"Fairly certain. I haven't seen her since Lillian's cotillion last winter, and that was only the briefest hello. Besides, *look* at me."

"I think you look rather nice."

We mounted the mansion's steps and rang the doorbell.

After a minute or so, the door swept inward.

A short, plump man in butler's livery and white gloves stood before us. He had smooth silver hair, black almond-shaped eyes, and a serene expression. "Good morning," he said with a lilt of Japanese accent.

Hisakawa.

"Hello," I said in an adenoidal voice. "We are from the Maiden Ladies' Orphanage Fund, here to see Mrs. St. Aubin."

"Does Madam expect you?"

"Not as such," I said. "But we have been referred to Mrs. St. Aubin by Mrs. Virgil DuFey."

"If Madam does not expect you, then you must write first," Hisakawa said. "Good morning." He began to close the door.

Just before the door hit home, Berta wedged her boot in the crack.

Hisakawa shoved harder.

Berta grunted, but held her ground.

"Madam," Hisakawa said, "if you do not remove your appendage from the premises, I must telephone the police."

"Go right ahead, Mr. Hisakawa," I said, scrapping the adenoidal voice.

He stiffened. "How do you know my name?"

Berta and I exchanged a glance. Berta's face was burgundy—Hisakawa was still bearing down on her foot with the door.

"Oh, we know lots of things," I said. "About Auntie Arbuckle."

"Miss Clara?" Hisakawa said.

"Yes. And the secret pork and beans recipe."

Hisakawa let up on the door.

Berta extracted her foot with a wince.

Hisakawa glanced over his shoulder into the marble foyer. He looked up and down the street. "You must come inside," he whispered. "Through the kitchen entrance, in the back. Go around to the alley, and through the gate with climbing rosebushes. Five minutes."

"Did you see the look on his face when I mentioned the secret recipe?" I whispered to Berta. We went around the corner in search of the alley.

"I did indeed. Thad Parker would be proud of your conning abilities."

Walled gardens lined the alley, which was overlooked by the rear windows of row houses. We found an iron gate festooned with climbing rosebushes, and crept through into a courtyard with a mossy fountain, potted topiaries, and vine-draped walls. The kitchen door was down a short stair, concealed behind a tortured-looking espalier bush.

The kitchen door swung inward just as Berta lifted her hand to knock.

"Be quick," Hisakawa whispered. "Cook has gone to take stock of the pantries, and the kitchen maid is out to market."

Berta and I piled through the door, and Hisakawa shut it.

"What do you want?" he asked. "Who sent you? Fitzpatrick?"

"Do we really look like the sort Fitzpatrick would hire?" I said.

And what could Fitzpatrick, of all people, have to do with a pork and beans recipe?

"Then you know him." Hisakawa took a step back. "Please. I do not—"

"Listen," I said. "I need your help. I suppose you've read in the papers about the murder of your former employer, Horace Arbuckle?"

"Yes, of course," Hisakawa said. "And Nanny Potter, too."

"We're trying to get to the bottom of all that. Now. Auntie Arbuckle mentioned something to me about a secret pork and beans recipe, and she also told me that you were fired over something to do with the recipe."

Hisakawa stared at me. "You do not understand what 'recipe' means?"

"What it means?"

"When Miss Clara says pork and beans recipe, she means—" Hisakawa glanced over his shoulder, and then leaned in closer. "— she means *bootleg*."

My tongue went dry. "Bootleg? You were fired over bootleg? Doing a spot of illegal trafficking, perhaps?"

"Of course not," Hisakawa said. "I was fired unfairly, but not because I was a bootlegger. It is true, I did procure cases of Canadian whiskey for Miss Clara from time to time. She was good to me, and not so crazy as they say."

"Where did you get the bootleg?" Berta asked.

"I have connections. But I did not take a profit. Procuring whiskey was a courtesy to Miss Clara, something any good and loyal servant would do."

"Okay. And what about Arbuckle? What did he have to do with this?"

"Why should I tell you? I merely wish to carry out my duties in this household, and leave that unfortunate business in the past."

"If you don't speak up, Mr. Hisakawa," I said, "innocent people might end up in the poke. Or worse."

"Mr. Hisakawa," Berta said, "I quite understand your dilemma. I have been a domestic servant myself for many, many years, and I know how servants are often unwittingly pulled into their masters'— and mistresses'—" She gave me a sidelong glance. "—absurd predicaments. Yet, this case is of the most pressing importance. We shall not tell a soul what you know about Arbuckle and the bootleg. Not a soul."

Hisakawa was ashen. "Fitzpatrick has ways of making people tell. I have heard tales."

"Please," I said. "I'm begging you."

He studied me. Pity glimmered. "Very well. I shall tell you, and then you will go."

Berta and I bobbed our heads in agreement.

"One day about two weeks ago," Hisakawa whispered, "I procured a new crate of Canadian whiskey for Miss Clara. Because she is a feeble, elderly lady, it was my custom to crowbar new cases open for her, in her private sitting room. No other servants could be trusted with such a task. Well, at that time, two weeks ago, I crowbarred the crate open, but instead of bottles of whiskey in the crate, there were cans. Cans of Auntie Arbuckle's Pork and Beans, with Miss Clara's own face staring back from the labels. I cautioned Miss Clara, but she was upset. She went to Mr. Arbuckle to demand an explanation. I was given notice later that day."

I frowned. "But I don't quite see what—"

"Oh, *there* you are, Hisakawa," a lady's voice warbled from the far end of the kitchen. "I forgot to tell Cook that I wish new potatoes for dinner tonight. Not whipped, since Mr. Van Goor cannot abide the cream that—Oh dear. Who's this?" Daphne St. Aubin's voice trailed off. She was a rangy dowager, draperied to the nines in maroon silk. "Who are these women, Hisakawa?"

"Madam," Hisakawa said loudly, "I do not know who allowed these women into the house. They are selling subscriptions of some kind. I shall see them out."

Mrs. St. Aubin peered at me hard. A little *too* hard.

Hisakawa herded Berta and me out of the kitchen. He slammed the door. The bolt thunked home.

"I think Mrs. St. Aubin recognized me," I said to Berta as we swung through the garden gate into the alley.

"We have bigger fish to fry than that, Mrs. Woodby. For heaven's sake. Why must your mind incessantly wander to the outskirts of the matter? I understand that you have had a lovers' quarrel with Mr. Oliver, but you must focus!"

"All right," I said, "then explain to me why Hisakawa had his trousers in a twist over seeing a crate of Auntie Arbuckle's Pork and Beans."

We hurried down the alley.

"I would have thought, Mrs. Woodby, that you would be a bit quicker on the uptake. Do you not see? If Hisakawa opened a crate that he expected to be Canadian whiskey, and found instead cans of Auntie Arbuckle's Pork and Beans, then the crates were mixed up somewhere along the way."

It sank in slowly. Then comprehension—and fear—flumed through me. "Arbuckle was smuggling *bootleg*." I stopped in my tracks. "Hiding bottles of booze in crates labeled pork and beans."

"Precisely." Berta had stopped, too. She was breathing hard. "What is more, Hisakawa mentioned Mr. Fitzpatrick."

"Do you suppose Arbuckle and Fitzpatrick were in business to-gether?"

"That does seem to be the logical conclusion."

"The crates must've been mixed up at a place where there were shipments of bootleg *and* shipments of pork and beans," I said. "But where? If only Mr. Hisakawa had told us where he procured those crates of whiskey."

"One possibility of the location springs to mind."

"Oh. Right." Neither of us needed to say it aloud: *the factory in the film.* I said, "I'd bet you anything that Ruby and Vera Potter, when they were filming that reel at the factory, saw something that made them realize it was a bootleg operation. I'd bet it was either Ruby or Vera who was blackmailing Arbuckle."

"We must go to that factory," Berta said. "With the camera. We shall photograph evidence of the illicit operation and turn over the pictures to the newspapers."

"No! Are you off your rocker? We've got to notify the police. This is a federal crime we're talking about. And two murders, and gang-sters, and—"

"Would you rather hand all of the hard-won fruits of our sleuth-ing to the police and let them solve the crimes?" Berta said. "After which you, with nothing to show for yourself, can go to live with your mother and father and go about after Miss Lillian, picking up her soiled handkerchiefs and Chisholm's health bread crumbs? Or would you prefer to join me in cracking this case ourselves, taking it to the newspapers, and receiving enough fame and adulation to open a proper detective agency and live as financially independent ladies?"

I stared at Berta. "Okay," I finally said. "Okay. The only wrinkle is, how the heck will we find the factory?"

"It appeared to be in Brooklyn, you said, near the river. So, we shall hire a taxi, and motor past every riverside factory in Brooklyn until we find it."

34

We Pony Expressed it back to Washington Square, and stopped by a newsstand to purchase a city map. My old map was in the Duesy, and the Duesy was in the clink.

Back at the love nest, I had gathered up the Brownie and checked its spool of film before I thought of Cedric. I looked around the sitting room. No Cedric. I whistled down the hallway.

No scamper of tiny paws. I went to the kitchen.

Cedric's pouf was empty.

I dashed to Alfie's bedroom. Berta was fixing her bun. "Is Cedric in here?" I asked.

"Why, no. I thought he was in the kitchen."

"He's not." My insides wrenched. I checked the bathroom and the foyer, and then went and looked in the kitchen again.

Only then did I see the note.

It looked straight out of a Thad Parker novel: mismatched letters snipped from newspapers and glued crookedly to a sheet of typing paper, at once carnivalesque and sinister:

tHis IS yOUr laSt ChaNce: StoP MEDdlinG oR You'Re
A GoNEr 2

I tasted bile. My hands shook. I read and reread the note, but it wasn't soaking in.

Then Berta was at my side, reading over my shoulder. She clutched her locket. "Poor little mite."

Eleven years ago, when the RMS *Titanic* slid to her icy grave, only three shipboard dogs survived. Two were Pomeranians. Perhaps this fact only suggests that first-class dogs, like first-class passengers, have better survival odds when lifeboats are in short supply. But I liked to think that those two Pomeranians on the *Titanic* survived because of the breed's particular verve.

And I needed to believe that Cedric could weather a kidnapping in style.

The telephone rang.

Berta went to answer it. I didn't pay attention as she spoke in low tones with someone. All I could think of was Cedric. How I'd neglected him during the past few days. How I'd foisted those horrid Spratt's Puppy Biscuits upon him.

Berta appeared in the kitchen doorway. "That was Eloise Wright, telephoning from Dune House. She said that she procured this telephone number from Mr. Luciano, and she wished to know if you would care to join Mrs. Arbuckle and her this weekend at Dune House. I told her you were indisposed."

Who cared about Society Matron soirees at a time like this?

I managed to speak. "You don't think Cedric's really a goner, do you?"

"No. *No.* Who would do such a thing? No, surely he is safe and sound somewhere. . . ."

I wadded up the note and I blotted the picture of Cedric from my mind. I latched on to a single idea. "We'll find the bootleg warehouse," I said. "We'll get those photographs and pinpoint the murderer. We'll find Cedric. We *will*."

Except . . . there was a tiny glitch in that plan.

I dug into my handbag, rummaging past the Brownie, and found my coin purse. I snapped it open. Empty. I'd spent all my money, down to my last cent. "Have you enough money for a cab ride to Brooklyn?" I asked Berta.

Her lips made a small O. "No. No, indeed I do not."

"What about bus fare?"

"I am very sorry, Mrs. Woodby. I am utterly, as you so succinctly put it once, on the nut."

"But we have to get there. It's the only way to find Cedric!"

"Mrs. Woodby," Berta said slowly, "it occurs to me that Mr. Oliver has a motorcar."

We rushed the six blocks to Ralph's. I thumped my fist on his door.

Ralph cracked it. We'd woken him. His ginger hair was tufted like a guinea pig's, his eyes were bleary, and he was shirtless. "Here for your film reel?" he said. "It's still in my safe. I'll—"

"No, Mr. Oliver," I said, breathless. "Would you, um, show me the key to your motorcar?"

"*Show* it to you? Are you kidding me?"

"It's a—it's about a clue. About Ruby Simpkin's Model T. It's *ever* so important."

He lifted an eyebrow.

"Hurry," I said.

"Fine, fine." He scratched the back of his head and padded away. In a moment, he was back, a small brass key dangling from his fingers on a narrow leather strap. "See?"

"Come closer," I said.

He came closer. The key was stamped with the cursive word *Ford*.

I snatched the key and stampeded down the stairs. Berta huffed and puffed at my heels.

The Model T's engine would be cold, but there was no time to crank it. We slammed ourselves in, I started it up, and we peeled away from the curb.

Ralph leaned out a window. "Hey!" he shouted. "Where are you going?"

Berta poked her head out the passenger window, holding her hat with one hand. "To the factory in Brooklyn!"

I gunned the Model T around the corner. "Why did you tell him?" I said. "I don't want to see Mr. Oliver again. Ever."

Berta settled into the seat. "You might change your mind."

I nosed the motorcar through the traffic and over the Brooklyn Bridge while Berta inspected the city map.

"Oh my," Berta murmured, her nose buried in the map. "Oh my, my, my."

"What?" I sped around a delivery van. *"What?"*

"Do you recall that Mrs. Wright had an address jotted on a sheet of paper on her desk, when we visited her Girdle Queen office on Tuesday?"

"Yes. Seventeen Wharfside. But what's that got to do with—? Oh! Don't tell me that—"

"Indeed, Mrs. Woodby. Wharfside is a road abutting the river. In Brooklyn. Go left after the bridge. And, if you do not mind me saying so, let her rip."

We zigged and zagged and found Wharfside, a desolate dirt street lined with swaybacked wooden buildings. The midday sun bounced off broken machinery. Across the river, Manhattan was a sparkling mirage.

I slowed the Model T to a chug. "These buildings don't look like the factory on the film. It was all white and gleaming, and had a big sign that said 'Auntie Arbuckle's Pork and Beans.'" The only sign that wasn't too faded to read said HENRY & SONS. "Maybe the address on Eloise's desk has nothing to do with the factory we're looking for."

"The pork and beans sign may have been erected only for the film," Berta said, "and then removed. After all, the place we are searching for is being used for criminal purposes. It might not be a real factory."

We drove along. We didn't see a soul, except for a bunch of seagulls squawking on abandoned sheds.

"Wait." I slammed on the brakes. "There it is. Third building on the left."

Berta had guessed correctly: The pork and beans sign was not there. But I recognized the pale concrete walls, the eerie lack of windows, and the ramp leading to the truck-sized wooden door.

"You are certain?" Berta asked.

"Yes. That's the ramp in the film." My breath caught. "Someone's over there."

"Oh dear," Berta murmured. "It is Jimmy."

"Jimmy the Ant?"

"He does *so* dislike that name. Mr. Fitzpatrick insists upon it, as he feels it gives Jimmy the proper air of menace. But Jimmy prefers to be—"

"Could we talk about this some other time?" I reversed the Model T and drove around a bend. I parked in a weedy lot. "What are we going to do?"

"I have always, Mrs. Woodby, considered myself a lady. However, these are desperate circumstances. I must step into the character of the trollop."

"Trollop? *You?*"

Berta tore off her hat, unpinned her bun, and shook her silver waves free. "Have you any lipstick? Jimmy did so like the pink shade I wore last night."

Berta dolled herself up with the lipstick, cake mascara, and jeweled hairpin we found in my handbag. I checked the Brownie's film-winder and shutter to make certain they were in working order. I nestled the camera in my handbag, shoved the Model T's key down my brassiere for extra security, and we left the motorcar.

We crept on foot along the shadows of two abandoned buildings, to the side of the warehouse where we'd seen Jimmy standing guard.

We peeked around the corner.

Jimmy sat at the top of the warehouse ramp, legs dangling over the side in minuscule shoes. He wore a three-piece suit and a fedora, and an outsized tommy gun lay across his knees. He stared into space.

"I shall distract him," Berta whispered, "and you sneak inside and get the photographs. Do not dilly-dally. I am not willing to advance to the next base with Jimmy. Not today, at any rate."

Oh boy.

Jimmy almost fell off the ramp when he saw her. "Berta?" he said in his gravelly voice. "Tomato! Whatcha doing here? Say, don't *you* look swell."

Berta said something in low tones and fondled his lapel.

Jimmy's face suggested a man riding the conveyor belt to Paradise. He set his tommy gun aside and wrapped his pipe cleaner arms around Berta.

It was now or never.

I tiptoed around the corner and up the ramp, hugging my handbag to my chest. I was halfway up when Jimmy, who was nuzzling Berta's neck, lifted his head.

If Jimmy turned his head even a single inch, he'd see me.

Berta's eyes bugged. She wrapped her fingers around the back of Jimmy's head and thrust his face into her bosom.

I ran the rest of the way up the ramp and tried the door. It opened.

I found myself in a lofty, dim space with a concrete floor. Light from a high window showed me that the room was empty.

But—I squinted—there was *another* room, through a doorway on the other side.

The next room was filled with stacks and stacks of wooden crates, piled in a half dozen haphazard, six-foot-high rows. Some kind of factory machinery ran along one wall. Double cargo doors filled another wall, and I saw the sunlit, flowing river through the crack. The building must've been some kind of storage hold, or transfer point, for the crates.

I moved closer to the crates. Black lettering said AUNTIE ARBUCK-LE'S PORK AND BEANS.

I flicked open the Brownie's lens and twisted the film-winder. I aimed the lens at a crate, squinted through the viewfinder, and snapped three pictures.

I set the Brownie on the floor and tried to heft a crate down. It was heavy. It rattled and clinked. It didn't sound like metal cans of pork and beans. It sounded like . . . glass.

I yanked at the crate.

The crate tipped, and wobbled, and the entire stack of crates crashed to the floor. One of the crates split open, and glass bottles splintered. Liquid sprayed up into my face.

I licked a drop at the corner of my mouth. Good Canadian whiskey.

A rather unforgivable hankering for a highball washed over me.

I grabbed the Brownie—luckily, it seemed to be unscathed—and aimed the lens at one of the broken bottles.

That's when I heard the muffled shouts.

"Hey!" a man yelled in a castrato's soprano. "What the hell was that?"

"Dunno," another man said in a slow bass.

Doors squealed as they were pushed open. I saw a spreading fan of light.

I seemed to have lost the use of my legs. They simply wouldn't move. Was this punishment for all the unkind thoughts I'd had about my ankles?

I peeked around the crates.

Two men had entered through the cargo doors. They were mere silhouettes: one medium-sized, the other shaped like Frankenstein's monster. And they each had a large pistol braced low against a hip. They advanced toward the fallen crates, toward me.

My legs still wouldn't budge.

The distance between us shrank.

My legs finally switched back on. I scuttled, crablike, to the side, away from the fallen crates. With one hand, I clutched the Brownie. I put my other hand to the floor to brace myself, and I squelched a cry; splinters of glass bit into my skin. I scampered around the corner of the row.

Not a second too soon.

"Wouldya look at that?" the bass voice said. "Them crates just fell down."

There was a smacking sound.

"Ow!" Bass cried. "What you do that for?"

"Don't be a sap," the castrato voice said. "Someone's in here."

I heard a *click*. Then a deafening burst, a *zing*, and a *thunk* as a bullet lodged in a wall somewhere.

I stifled a whimper.

"Come on out," the castrato voice crooned. "Or we're gonna come and get you."

Then footsteps pattered farther off, and I heard Jimmy the Ant. "Hey! Tomato! Come back! You ain't supposed to go back there!"

"Mrs. Woodby?" Berta cried.

If I got out of this alive, Berta and I were going to need to have a little chat about blowing one's cover.

"Hey, Jimmy," the castrato voice said. "Who's the dame?"

"My lady, that's who," Jimmy said. "Put them guns outa her face. What's going on here? Look at this mess. Boss ain't gonna be pleased."

"Mrs. Woodby?" Berta called again.

"Mrs. Woodby?" the castrato voice said. "Say. I know her. I know her *real* well."

He did?

I peeked around the corner.

Mr. Highpants. I'd never heard him speak before; that castrato voice belonged to *him*. He stood with Frankenstein's Monster, Jimmy, and Berta. They stared down at the shattered bottles of bootleg.

I dodged into the next aisle. This aisle was stacked, not with wooden crates, but with large brown cardboard boxes.

I knew that goal numero uno was, now, to get out of this warehouse alive. But I had a sudden vision of Cedric's toy-bear face, and I realized that if I didn't get photographic proof of Arbuckle's bootleg scheme, I might never see Cedric again.

The three gangsters and Berta were engaged in a back-and-forth about Berta's identity. I might have a couple moments to snap more photographs. I lifted a cardboard box down from the stack and removed the lid.

I'd expected more whiskey bottles. What I saw were rubbery white mounds of . . . girdles.

I glanced up and down the row of cardboard boxes. Each one was printed with the image of a crown and the words GIRDLE QUEEN.

I dug into the box.

It turned out that the box *was* filled with whiskey bottles. Whiskey bottles wrapped in perforated white rubber girdles.

Eloise Wright had found a profitable use for her girdle seconds, after all. Profitable enough, it seemed, for her to divorce her husband and establish herself as financially independent.

I aimed the Brownie's lens and snapped away, trying to catch angles with enough stray light.

But the gangsters—and Berta—must've heard my camera shutter whapping and the film-winder clicking. Four sets of footsteps came closer.

I stuffed the Brownie down my bodice and ran to the end of the aisle of boxes, away from the footsteps. Just as I reached the end, Highpants yelled, "Hey!" A bullet whizzed by my ear. I sprinted past the factory equipment along the wall. I had the wild idea that I could outrun bullets, I guess.

But then, something snagged against my side, and I was flung to a stop. A piece of the factory machinery, some sharp protuberance, had sliced through my dress and snagged into my rubber girdle.

I yanked and thrashed, but the gummy material only stretched.

"There she is," Frankenstein's Monster said behind me.

Another bullet whizzed by.

"Leave Mrs. Woodby alone!" Berta cried. Then she said *"Oof,"* and there were thundering sounds.

I corkscrewed around to see a pile of cardboard boxes shower down onto Highpants and Frankenstein's Monster.

Oddly, there were no sounds of shattering glass.

"Run!" Berta screamed to me.

I struggled and twisted. With a twang of the metal machinery and a long *ziiiip* of ripping dress, I finally wrested my girdle free. I ran through the room with the crates, across the other big empty room, out the front door, and down the ramp.

I fled down the street and across the weedy lot. The Brownie joggled inside my bodice. I leapt behind the wheel of the Model T, dug the key from my brassiere, and fired up the engine. I skidded the motorcar along to the warehouse. Berta was bouncing down the ramp. I slowed down just enough for her to leap into the passenger seat. I slammed my foot on the gas before she'd even shut the door.

Yells and gunshots rang out behind us. Bullets dinged off the Model T's bumper. Another hit the rear window, and it shattered. Then I two-wheeled it around a corner, and we were safe.

35

E loise Wright," Berta said a few moments later. She was still wheezing for breath.

"You saw the boxes?" I asked.

"Indeed I did."

"Eloise telephoned us from Dune House earlier," I said. "I'll bet she called to make sure we'd found her note, and to see if we'd realized that Cedric was missing." I clenched the steering wheel. "I'm driving straight to Dune House. And then I'm going to throttle her."

"Did you obtain photographs of the bootleg operation?" Berta asked.

"Yes. I hope they turn out. It was kind of dark in there."

"The girdles must prevent the bottles from clattering. The bottles did not break when I pushed the boxes on top of those dreadful men," Berta said. "The rubber acts as cushioning."

"And there's no telltale noise when the boxes are transported. That's how Eloise Wright has been disposing of all her troublesome seconds. Letting Lem Fitzpatrick have them, and allowing him to use her labeled Girdle Queen boxes. They *are* in business together. Do you think Eloise could've really killed Arbuckle, though? And Vera Potter?"

"Mrs. Wright was a desperate lady. She longed for financial independence from her husband in order to divorce him. Desperate ladies are capable of far more than people might suppose."

True. Berta and I were desperate ladies, and look at the soup *we'd* dipped ourselves into.

Around the thirty-mile mark down the highway toward Hare's Hollow, the Model T's engine started clanking.

"Rats," I said. "We're out of gasoline."

I pulled over at the next gas station. While the attendant was filling the tank, I saw a Cadillac Phaeton across the highway.

The Cadillac crouched on the grassy verge, long, black, and wicked. I saw the silhouette of Frankenstein shoulders behind the wheel. Mr. Highpants was riding shotgun.

Quite *literally* shotgun, in fact: the barrel of a tommy gun poked out the passenger window.

I rummaged in my purse for money to pay for the gasoline, and then remembered that I hadn't a cent. A sparkle at the bottom of the handbag caught my eye. One of the diamond stud earrings I'd worn to Mrs. Hartwicke's staffing agency. I dug it out.

"Keep the change," I said, and dropped the earring into the slack-jawed attendant's hand. We roared out of the gas station.

Berta clung to the dashboard. "What on God's green earth has come over you, Mrs. Woodby?"

I glanced in the rearview mirror. The Cadillac eased onto the highway.

"They're back."

"What?" Berta turned. "Insolent men."

"What do they *want*? And do you think they'd really—" I swallowed. "—really use a machine gun? On us?"

"Of course."

"But why?"

"Do not whine. It is most unbecoming. They want the camera. You photographed the bootleg operation they have been entrusted to guard. Mr. Fitzpatrick will have their hides." Berta shook her head. "Jimmy told me never to trust a gangster."

I swerved around a delivery hack. "I hate to break the news, Berta, but Jimmy's a gangster, too."

"Only temporarily."

"Oh, okay. He became a gangster to pay for—what? His mother's operation?"

"He wishes to buy back the family farm. In Missouri. They were swindled out of it."

"He told you that because he knew it would impress you, and then he'd have a better chance of getting to second base."

"Good heavens, what a terrible thing to say. Apologize at once."

"Sorry," I mumbled. I glanced in the rearview mirror again. The Cadillac was stuck behind the delivery hack. I pressed still harder on the gas. In another minute, we would lose them.

But suddenly, the delivery hack turned off the highway. The Cadillac roared up on our tail. Bullets clanged against our fender.

Berta sighed. "I had *so* hoped I would not have to do this." She unfastened her black handbag. She pulled out her Colt, rolled the window down, and leaned out. "Do try to stay within the lines, Mrs. Woodby," she said. She spiraled her torso halfway out the window and squirted metal.

I guess I hadn't believed Berta would actually shoot. Not really. I white-knuckled the wheel and concentrated on staying on the road. The speedometer quivered as it crept past sixty, then on to seventy. . . .

Berta fired again. I heard squealing tires. "Gotcha," she muttered.

"You shot a gangster?" I yelled.

"Indeed not. I shot his tire."

We burst around a bend in the highway, out into a sweep of road with a meadow along one side. A low stone guardrail lined the other side of the road. Below the guardrail crashed a rocky surf, about two stories down. *Straight* down.

We soared around the curves, mile after mile. I was getting the hang of it, and I realized we were within half a mile of Dune House.

Without warning, Berta unloaded the Colt's last three bullets in quick succession. My nerves frizzled. I lost control of the motorcar. The curve of the road was too sharp, and I didn't turn the wheel in time.

With yawning horror, I saw the guardrail hurtling toward us and the blue glitter of water beyond.

"Jump!" I screamed. I somehow unlatched the door and hurled myself out. I landed with a painful thud on the edge of the road and rolled into a ditch. As I rolled, I hit my hip, hard, and then my head, and my elbow and my ribs, and crumpled to a stop in a puddle at the bottom.

A stretched-out, metallic groan was followed by a moment of eerie silence. Then a series of bangs, screeches, and clatters as the motorcar smashed into the rocky surf below the wall.

I had the shakes. I turned my head. Berta, a few yards away in the ditch, lay in a tangle of raincoat.

Relief surged through me and I felt tears in my eyes. "Are you okay?"

"I believe so."

How Berta had managed to keep a grip on her handbag through all that, I'll never know. On the other hand, *I* still had a camera stuck down my bodice, so I suppose I was not one to judge.

I crawled to the top of the ditch. The Cadillac was stopped by the guardrail with a flat tire. Mr. Highpants and Frankenstein's Monster stood with their backs to us, staring over the guardrail where the Model T had plunged to its final parking lot.

"*Hurry,*" Berta whispered. She was scrambling up a narrow ravine that led from the ditch into the meadow above.

I followed.

Up in the meadow, the wild grass and flowers were tall enough to conceal us, as long as we kept low. We crawled all the way across the field. By the time we stopped at a fence, my stockings were shredded and my hands smarted with grass cuts. My shoulder throbbed where I'd landed on it when I jumped out of the car. Something sticky-warm was trickling down my face, too, and my scalp was oddly numb.

When we climbed over the fence, we saw the gates of Dune House across the road.

"Almost there," I said.

"Good, because I fancy I broke my wrist."

When the gatekeeper saw us, his mouth fell open. Probably thought we were a couple of swamp monsters. I racked my brain, trying to remember his name. Slink? Strump? Oh yes—

"Mr. Strom!" I said airily, shoving the Brownie more snugly down my front. I smeared my face with my palm. "How good to see you!"

He blinked.

"I'm here to see Olive—she's expecting me, you know."

He blinked again.

In the distance, I heard the purr of an engine.

"It's me," I said. "Lola Woodby."

"Mrs. Woodby? That you? Why, what in tarnation's happened to you? You're bleeding."

I looked down at the palm I'd touched to my face. Bright blood glistened.

I simply stood there, staring at my hand. My teeth began to chatter.

The engine purr grew louder. Louder.

"Mr. Strom," Berta said, "we have been in a motorcar crash. Please allow us through the gates this instant so we may telephone a doctor."

"Yes, yes, of course." Strom unlocked the gates and let us through.

The engine pulsated to a roar behind us.

"Close the gates, Mr. Strom!" I shouted.

Berta and I ran up the drive toward the house. The iron gates clanged shut. Yelling. Gunfire.

I prayed that the gangsters hadn't shot Mr. Strom.

When Dune House came into view, I noticed in a blur lots of motorcars and trucks scattered around the drive, and people milling around.

I dug the Brownie from my bodice and handed it off to Berta. I burst through the front door. I stood, wheezing and trembling, in the foyer, and screamed at the top of my lungs, *"Eloise! Eloise Wright, come here this instant!"*

My voice bounced off marble.

Hibbers materialized. "Mrs. Woodby. Good heavens. What has happened to you?"

"Where is she?"

"I presume you mean Mrs. Wright? I am not quite certain. I last saw her at luncheon. Perhaps she has gone for a lie-down. Shall I telephone an ambulance for you?"

"Maybe I can help," someone said in a treble clef voice.

I spun around. Bruno Luciano lounged in the doorway, wearing an old-fashioned frock coat, knee breeches, tall boots, a cravat, and side whiskers.

"Oh," I said. "Mr. Rochester. You're filming today."

"Yes." Bruno came closer and wrapped an arm around me.

I went limp. I stared up into Mr. Rochester's face, and he, with his smoldering dark eyes, his haunted slash of eyebrow, his gritted jaw, his tortured soul, stared back into my—

"I saw Eloise," he squeaked.

Daydream shattered.

"Upstairs," he said. "Allow me to escort you to her."

"All right," I said.

But Bruno did not, at the top of the grand staircase, turn toward the guest wing. Instead, he turned toward a wing of the house that I'd never entered before.

We passed a room crowded with costume racks and babbling people. The next room was cluttered up with girls applying actors' makeup. I saw Sadie Street, in her Jane Eyre wig and a nightgown, having rouge brushed onto her cheeks.

"We're filming in the bedchamber," Bruno said. "The scene where Jane is awakened by a fire set by the madwoman in the attic."

"Oh," I said. It was tough to focus my eyes. Warm blood dripped into my ear.

Bruno led me past another open door. I made out, in a muddle, a four-poster bed, a movie camera on a tripod, a clutch of murmuring men, and George Zucker. George glanced up as we passed, and Bruno gave him the slightest head-tilt of acknowledgment.

"Where's Eloise?" I asked.

"I think she was watching the filming," Bruno said. "But we're taking a break, and I saw that she came up here." He opened a door. A narrow flight of stairs led, ladderlike, upward "Come on."

"To the attic?"

"Not exactly." Bruno gave me a nudge.

I started climbing. Bruno was right behind me. "What on earth is Eloise doing all the way up here?" I asked.

"She wanted a little peace and quiet. To smoke a cigarette."

"But she doesn't smoke." I'd reached the top. We were inside a gable, facing another door. I twisted the doorknob.

"Oh, she's started up smoking again," Bruno said. "Because of her divorce."

I pushed the door open and fresh air gusted in.

"Go on, then," Bruno said.

I stepped outside onto a narrow walkway that ran along the roof-line, with iron railings at hip height.

I heard the door shut. I turned. Bruno leaned on the door and smiled. It was a rakish, Mr. Rochester smile. But his gaze was a cold abyss.

"I don't see Eloise," I said.

"No? Silly me. I could've sworn this is where she'd gone." He took a step toward me.

Instinctively, I backed up a step. Steep roofs slanted down on either side of the walkway. On the far end, the walkway simply ended. Down below, the Arbuckles' green lawn, gravel drive, hedge maze, tennis court, and swimming pool sprawled like a map in a hotel brochure.

Bruno took another step toward me. He grabbed the rail to steady himself.

And then I saw it. A glint of gold on his hand. A signet ring with a flat round face.

I'd seen a ring like that before. On a hand like his.

36

For a long moment, I was speechless. "It was you," I finally said to Bruno. "On the film."

From somewhere in the distance came muffled screams and yelling. I smelled the faintest whiff of smoke.

"You got me, Lola. Yes. It was me. I ended up on the cutting room floor in that one. Not good enough to be in a pork and beans advertisement, they said. My smile was too cheesy, the director said." Bruno laughed. "I'll bet that director's kicking himself. Passed over Bruno Luciano! What a fool." His lip curled. "But that's all in the past. Before I became a star."

"Then *you* saw the bootleg, too. In the warehouse. You were there with Ruby and Vera." I edged back. "You *did* blackmail Arbuckle. That money wasn't from Fitzpatrick, like you told me last night. It couldn't have been."

That's what had seemed off: Bruno and Sadie's feud was only a few weeks old, but Bruno had said he received money—because of the feud—from Fitzpatrick way back in August.

"Arbuckle had bucks to spare," Bruno said.

"But he didn't need to die. Why did you kill him?"

"I didn't."

"Where's Cedric?"

"I don't know a Cedric."

"What about Ruby Simpkin?"

"Haven't seen her in ages."

"Stop lying! What about Vera Potter?"

"She knew too much. Way too much. Might as well tell you, since now we're going to have to get rid of you."

We? I backed up some more.

"I *tried* to keep that shrew Vera quiet," Bruno said. "I knew that if the gangsters found out what we actors knew about that warehouse, they'd kill us, see. But Vera refused to take any of the blackmail money, out of some prudish idea she'd got in her head. Ruby was different. Ruby knew how to keep her trap shut. Sure, she was kind of crooked—I mean, what kind of girl goes and nicks a film reel from a studio in the first place? She was always looking ahead for the next opportunity. With Vera, I kept her happy by getting her that job as a nurserymaid. She wanted out of acting, see, and it was easy enough for me to make Arbuckle hire her. All it took was one more anonymous letter. I shouldn't have told Vera that reel had wound up in the Arbuckle house, but I lost my head when Ruby told me Arbuckle had bought it."

"And Vera was the one who stole the reel from the safe that night."

"I don't know anything about that."

But I did. Vera Potter had overheard me reciting the safe's combination out loud. Once Horace had been killed, she jumped at the chance to get rid of the reel—which was evidence that she'd gotten the job in the Arbuckle household through shady means. Then, when the cops had come, she must've panicked and dropped the reel in Sadie Street's bag to get rid of it. I remembered seeing her herding Billy and Theo through the drive the morning after Horace's murder.

The screaming was growing louder. Acrid smoke hit the back of my throat.

The door behind Bruno opened. Smoke billowed out. I coughed, and tears pooled in my eyes. Yet I was able to make out, through the smoke and the tears, George Zucker. He emerged from the churning smoke like a sorcerer.

"Thank God!" I coughed. "Mr. Zucker, Bruno has cornered me. He's—he's dangerous!"

"Auntie Arbuckle has set fire to the house," George said. He placed a hand on Bruno's shoulder. "Darling. Please. Allow me. You've got your career ahead of you, your glorious, glorious career. Go. Don't forget, whatever comes of this, that I've done everything for you. That I love you, and I always will."

In a flash I recalled the head-tilt Bruno had sent to George when we passed the doorway downstairs. It had been a signal. Bruno had brought me up here so George could . . . what?

Bruno disappeared.

I doubled over, coughing.

Two shoes appeared in my line of vision. I covered my mouth and nose with my cardigan and looked up.

George smiled, a little sadly, down at me. "Sorry it's gotta be this way, Mrs. Woodby."

"*You?* Why?"

"For Bruno. The love of my life."

Oh. George and Bruno were gentlemen who preferred not blondes, but other gentlemen.

"Does Bruno know what you've done?" I asked.

"Of course. Killing Arbuckle and Vera Potter was my gift to him. My sacrifice."

"But was it worth it?" I asked, bargaining for time.

"I dunno," George said. "He never did say thanks. People as beautiful as Bruno don't learn to really love. Don't need to. But that's something that you and I, Mrs. Woodby, are never gonna have the luxury of understanding."

"Where's Cedric? What have you done with him?"

"Oh, don't you worry about the pooch. He's at the film studio. In Queens. He's gonna be a star."

"You're a loon!"

"No, really. The Spratt's Puppy Biscuits people saw his screen test and want him for their advertisements. He's just gotta lose a little weight."

"You pushed that gargoyle, didn't you," I said. "And sent those poisoned chocolates, and wrecked my apartment."

"If you'd only eaten a chocolate, it woulda been a wrap."

"Why did you try to kill me? Why did you kidnap Cedric?"

"Because you're a meddler, Mrs. Woodby. It's a rotten habit. I almost think I'm doing the world a favor by getting rid of you."

I tried to lunge past George to the door, but he made a neat sidestep and blocked my path.

"You killed Arbuckle," I said.

"Bruno had got himself into an awful mess, blackmailing Arbuckle. Anonymously, see. He told me all about it. Needed to get it off his chest, I guess. Then Arbuckle got his hands on the one remaining copy of the film that was at the root of the blackmail shenanigans. Got it from your husband, as a matter of fact."

Alfie. That bastard. Lousing up my life even from beyond the grave.

"Arbuckle was going to figure out, sooner or later, that Bruno had been filming in the warehouse, too, as soon as he got around to watching that film," George said. "That Bruno had seen the bootleg operation. And then Arbuckle would know that Bruno was his blackmailer. I don't know whose idiot idea it was to film that reel at the bootleg warehouse. I guess Arbuckle didn't want any filming at his actual factories. Said it would slow down production. Anyway, I had to protect Bruno. He's gonna be the biggest movie star the world has ever seen, don't you understand? I can't let that go to waste. Even if it means sacrificing myself."

"And Vera Potter?"

"She knew what Bruno was up to. She was going to tattletale. You know that. I had to stop her. And she went and took the film reel out of Arbuckle's safe, the little fool."

Neither Bruno nor George seemed to know that I had found the film reel again, and that it was now with Ralph.

"But how did you know Vera was going to meet me in the dunes?" I asked.

"I overheard her setting up her meeting with you on the telephone. Course, I'd been keeping my eye on her. I knew she was a weak link."

"And you planted Sadie Street's lipstick?"

"Sure. Thought I'd kill two birds with one stone: Get rid of Vera Potter and, by pinning the murder on that wretched little biscuit Sadie, get rid of her, too."

"The police laughed in my face when I told them that was Sadie Street's lipstick."

"Well, you win some, you lose some."

"Did you kill Ruby Simpkin?"

"I would like to, don't get me wrong. She's a loose end. But she took off before I had the chance. I'll find her, though." George's eyes were red. He hunched to cough.

"How come you're such a crack shot?"

"I shoot game on the weekends. Makes me feel happy."

My instincts screamed at me to back away. But I knew that the walkway ended. Dodging around George had failed. I had one

option left, short of shoving the little creep over: Climb over the railing and go around him on the roof, monkey-style, to get to the door.

I hitched up my dress (exposing, alas, my knickers and the
bottom half of my white rubber girdle) and climbed over the railing.

"Hey!" someone yelled far, far below. "Some crazy lady's on the
roof! In her underpants! Hey, lady! Don't you know the house is
burning down?"

I inched along, clinging to the railing. Smoke, gritty and hot,
swirled around me.

"Gee, Mrs. Woodby," George said. "You're making it too easy." He
grabbed my right hand and peeled my fingers away from the railing.

I screamed. My left hand still clung to the railing, but my feet
skittered on the slippery roof tiles.

From down below came cries and shouts.

I gained a foothold by edging the toes of my shoes between the
tiles, but I couldn't quite reach the railing again with my right hand.
All I could do was clench my left fingers tight.

"Everyone down there is watching," I snarled at George. "You'll
go to the electric chair for murder."

"Oh, no." George touched my left hand. "They can't see us too
well through all this smoke. It'll be a terrible accident. I'll say I tried
to save you."

He pried one of my fingers. My knuckle crackled.

I swore at him.

Then, instead of prying off my remaining fingers, George bent
that one finger. The wrong way.

I screamed. I let go. I slid.

It happened slowly. Slowly enough for me to notice the way my
dress and cardigan hiked up to my armpits. Slowly enough to feel
my fingernails split on roof tiles. Slowly enough to hear the cries of
horror down below.

My feet went over the edge. Then my knees. I clawed and scrambled, kicking the air. Over the edge of the roof I went, faster and faster—

And then, I stopped.

My rubber girdle, already torn by the machinery at the warehouse, had snagged on one of the gargoyles along the gutter. I dangled, knickered derriere exposed to the world, half on and half off the roof.

I hooked my arms around the gargoyle's wings and clung like a rayon skirt.

"Don't look down, Lola!" someone shrilled below. It must've been Olive. "The fire brigade is on its way! They've got ladders!"

I looked up. George Zucker was gone.

Off to the side a little, and three or four feet below me, Ralph Oliver thrust his head and shoulders out of a window.

I did a double take, which sent me bouncing, suspended by the girdle.

"Lola," Ralph said in a low, soothing voice. "Don't move a muscle. I'm going to get you."

"Don't you dare touch me!" I coughed. "You—you *stinker*! Why the heck are you even here?"

"I've been a couple steps behind you ever since you stole my motorcar. Had to kinda borrow my landlady's Chevy. But I didn't get to the warehouse on Wharfside till right when you were ripping out of there."

"Tailing me? So you can give my mother a complete report?" I kicked the air. One of my spectator shoes dropped off. The crowd below murmured.

"Stay *still*, for God's sake," Ralph said. "I'm not sure how long that gargoyle can hold."

In the distance, fire engine sirens wailed.

"You know what?" I said. "I'm glad I crashed your motorcar into the ocean. Did you hear that? *Glad.*"

"You crashed my motorcar in the—? Never mind. Tell me later. Listen. I haven't told your mother the truth about anything you were doing, ever since I ran into you that first time at your husband's place. I don't even know why I didn't tell her, either. I just felt like . . . like protecting you, I guess. I kept putting her off, and telling her you were out shopping and having tea with lady friends and going to the hairdresser's."

I shot him a narrow glance.

"You know it's true," Ralph said. "Did your mother ever find where you were hiding out in Longfellow Street?"

"No." I smooshed my eyelids shut. "What about the—uh—?"

"Hanky-panky?" Ralph chuckled. "That, kid, is strictly between you and me and the gatepost."

My eyes flew open. "You were manipulating me!"

"Me? Manipulating *you*? When you kept going around smelling like cookies and blinking those big blue eyes at me?"

"What about your notebook? What about how you'd written 'check' after your note about our kiss in the movie palace?"

"I hadn't finished what I was writing. I was interrupted. I'd meant to write, 'check up on Luciano's past.' A kiss in the picture we were watching reminded me how he's an actor, see, so probably a good liar."

Oh.

The fire engine sirens blared, closer and closer.

"You're so, I dunno, *jaunty*," Ralph said, "and maybe a little crazy, but you've got this sweet, soft side you try to hide, so I—"

"Stop it," I snapped. But my heart was already defrosting.

Out of the corner of my eye, I saw red fire engines surge into the front drive. I dangled for a few more minutes. Then I was draped over the shoulder of one of Hare's Hollow's Bravest and lugged down a ladder to safety.

The fireman set me on my feet. My knees gave out. Another fireman wrapped a blanket around me and held me up.

I glimpsed Ralph climbing down a ladder and then a crowd pushed around me, jabbering in a way I couldn't understand. Hibbers glided through, holding a tray with a glass on it.

I stuck an arm out of the blanket. Hibbers placed a highball in my hand.

37

At the Hare's Hollow Hospital—really a weather-beaten, shingled clinic—the doctor shaved off a strip of my hair and stitched up the gash in my head. He tweezered glass shards from my palms, swabbed iodine on my grass cuts, and assured me that Dune House's gatekeeper, Mr. Strom, was unharmed, and two gangsters matching the description of Mr. Highpants and Frankenstein's Monster had been arrested, according to the ambulance driver. A grim nurse gave me a sponge bath. Then, clean and bandaged and wearing a paper-thin gown, I was escorted to a bed.

"I am told," a disembodied voice said, "that your newfangled rubber girdle saved your life." The striped curtain next to my bed whipped aside.

Berta was propped on a mountain of pillows in the next bed. Her arm was in a sling, and a Frank B. Jones, Jr., novel lay facedown on the blanket. *Trouble in Tokyo.* A vase of pink roses filled her bedside table, alongside a gigantic heart-shaped box of chocolates and the Eastman Kodak Brownie.

"Only a sprain," Berta said, gesturing to her wrist. "Although you will have to cook for me for a few weeks. No chopping or kneading at all, the doctor said."

"Whose birthday?" I gestured to the chocolates and flowers.

Berta flushed. "Oh, well, I—"

"Not Jimmy the Ant!"

"*Don't* call him that. He saved our lives, Mrs. Woodby. He delayed those gangsters at the warehouse long enough to give us a head start."

"How did he send the flowers and chocolates so quickly?"

"He followed us from the warehouse."

Ralph Oliver had been following, too. Quite the circus train.

A nurse bustled in with two glasses of orange juice on a tray. She fussed about Berta and me for a few moments and then went out again.

"Oh, this is lovely," Berta said. "You know, we ought to make the most of this holiday, as it were. We are going to be very busy."

"With what?"

"Why, with our retrieval agency, of course."

"Berta, we're still just as broke as when we started. And now we're laid up, to boot."

"No, no, no." Berta shook her head. She leaned over to her bedside table, extracted a rectangle of paper from the drawer, and passed it over.

It was a picture postcard depicting rolling green mountains. GREETINGS FROM THE CATSKILLS, it said. I flipped it over. A message sloped sideways in a childish hand. It was signed *Ruby*.

"Where did you get this?" I asked.

"From Mrs. Arbuckle. Miss Simpkin, not knowing how else to reach us, mailed it in the overnight post to Dune House. Mrs. Arbuckle gave it to me as I was leaving for the hospital. Go on. Read it."

The message said,

Awful sorry to skip town on you. Things were getting a little too hot in the kitchen if you know what I mean. That short fellow came around to the Frivolities and so I needed to clear out. If you found the reel please destroy it and I will be back in New York next week to pack up my apartment as I got a job here performing here at a resort hotel. Will pay you then no matter what pinky swear. I always make good on my promises. —Ruby

"Short fellow?" I said.

"Mr. Zucker. He must have followed us to the Unicorn Theater at some point and identified Miss Simpkin as one of the actresses on the film."

"Yikes. Then it's a good thing she skipped town, because he might've killed her, too." I paused. "Do you think Lem Fitzpatrick is still dangerous?"

"Of course. But surely he will move his smuggling operation to a new location, after all of this. I would not, however, return to Blue Heaven, Mrs. Woodby."

"Right," I said. "Say, what happened to George? After I fell off the roof, I mean."

"I was not there, of course," Berta said, "as I came here to the hospital soon after we arrived at Dune House. But the nurse told me that Mr. Zucker was captured inside the burning house, and he made some sort of ranting confession of murder to the police."

"He loved Bruno," I said. "He said he did it all for love."

"Oh dear me." Berta touched her locket. "That is not love, Mrs. Woodby. Fascination, perhaps, even obsession. But not love. And it sounds as though he was more obsessed with the idea of Mr. Luciano and his splendid film career, than with Mr. Luciano himself. After all, Mr. Luciano is, despite his good looks, rather a dullard, is he not?"

"I suppose he is." I sipped my orange juice. "One thing I still don't understand is, why didn't Ruby destroy the film when she had the chance, before Alfie ever stole it from her?"

"Perhaps she thought she might save it for a rainy day, and blackmail Arbuckle or Fitzpatrick—or even Bruno Luciano—later."

"What about the money Ruby has promised us? Three thousand dollars is a pile for anyone, and for a chorus girl? That's got to be her life's savings."

"Think of it as *your* money, Mrs. Woodby. I suspect Miss Simpkin procured those funds by selling costly trinkets bestowed on her by, among other men, your own husband."

The door opened, and Mother exploded into the room. "Lola!" she shrieked. "How could you? Oh, how *could* you? Your knickers are to be in the newspapers!"

"No 'glad to see my eldest child is still alive and kicking,' then?" I said.

"Hold the impertinence, *s'il vous plaît*. Gracious. Look at your head. You look like a needlepoint sampler."

"How did you find me?" I asked.

"Daphne St. Aubin telephoned me and said that you and some other lady—" Mother shot Berta a stern look. "—went to her house in disguise." She lowered her voice. "Chisholm thinks that you ought to check into Babbling Brook. Only for a spell, until you're—"

"Check into the booby hatch?" I reeled upright. Orange juice spilled across the blanket.

"Only for a *spell*," Mother said. "Then, when you are quite well, you can come to live at home. I can introduce you to that wonderful Mr. Raymond Hathorne whom I met on the ocean liner—assuming, that is, he's willing to overlook your latest escapades. I am happy to provide a roof over your head, Lola, truly. But you must cease to—"

"Mother," I said. "Why did you hire a private detective to spy on me?"

"Did he tell you? Why, I *knew* that Mr. Oliver was a discount gumshoe. He's so—so *shabby*. And that ginger hair!"

"Why did you hire him?"

"Oh, Lola, can't you see? Your life is a *disaster*. When I heard that Alfie had died, I knew that it would be up to me to find you a new husband, but your ways have grown somewhat . . . dissolute. I needed to find out if there was anything that would embarrass me, and, of course, your sister, when I took it upon myself to find you a new match."

Logical. *Insane*. Hopefully not a hereditary insanity.

"So you didn't suspect I bopped off Alfie?" I asked.

"Admittedly, the thought *did*—"

"Could we talk later, Mother? I've got the most awful headache."

"But I—"

"*Later*," I said.

"I shall be at Amberley."

And *I'd* be anywhere *but* Amberley.

No sooner had Mother left than the door burst open again. In came Miss Ida Shanks, wrapped in her mangy fox fur.

"Burn the photographs you snapped of my underpants," I said.

"Not on your nelly." Ida grinned. "Treasure beyond price."

"What if I told you I've got exclusive evidence of a bootleg operation that implicates not only Lem Fitzpatrick, but also Horace Arbuckle *and* Eloise Wright?"

Ida's grin dropped off. "What sort of evidence?"

"Goodness, Miss Shanks, don't start *drooling*," I said. "Photographs. The film is still inside the camera." I pointed to the Brownie on Berta's table. "Only promise that you'll write up the story, and give Mrs. Lundgren and me full credit for narrowing down the suspects and pressuring the murderer into a full confession."

"Deal."

"Splash our story across the front page, Miss Shanks," Berta said, "and we shall also give you dibs on the story of every new case we crack."

Ida cackled. "Come, now, I don't write for the funny pages. 'Cases'? 'Crack'?"

"Berta and I are setting ourselves up in business," I said. "As detectives. No more murders, or anything like that. Only . . . retrieving things."

"Ah," Ida said. "Two Labrador retrievers, are you? Yes, I can see that. The breed does tend toward pudge and a certain intellectual . . . density."

"Fine." I slumped back into my pillows and folded my arms. "No deal."

"Wait," Ida said.

I lifted my head to look at her.

"Deal," she said.

Berta rifled through her box of chocolates. "As Thad Parker has often commented," she said to me, "welcome to the big time, kid."